# RACHEL LEE

"A highly complex thriller…deft use of dialogue."
—*Publishers Weekly* on *Wildcard*

"*The Crimson Code* is a smart, complex thriller
with enough twists to knot your stomach and keep
your fingers turning the pages."
—*New York Times* bestselling author Alex Kava

"With its smartly paced dialogue and seamless interweaving of
both canine and human viewpoints, this well-rounded story is
sure to be one of Lee's top-selling titles."
—*Publishers Weekly* on *Something Deadly*

"A suspenseful, edge-of-the-seat read."
—*Publishers Weekly* on *Caught*

"Rachel Lee is a master of romantic suspense."
—*Romantic Times BOOKreviews*

# THE HUNTED

## RACHEL LEE

MIRA®

ISBN-13: 978-0-7783-2538-3
ISBN-10:  0-7783-2538-5

THE HUNTED

www.MIRABooks.com

Printed in U.S.A.

To the lost, and the men and women of law enforcement
who try to find them.

# Prologue

*Caracas, Venezuela*

She shuddered as she heard the bolt on the door open. She always did, even after…how many months had it been?

She was sixteen, she thought. Or maybe seventeen. Had it been two years since she'd left home, or three? It was hard to be sure. When she'd been on the streets of Denver, she'd been able to keep track of time. Even though one day had been mostly the same as the next—get high enough to function, then find a john to get money for the next fix—there were cycles. There were the days when the shelters offered free lunches and showers. There were Sundays, when it was more difficult to find johns because they were trying to pretend they were good, churchgoing men. There was the change of seasons.

It was the change of seasons that had done it.

She'd already decided she wasn't going to spend another winter in Denver. Phoenix would be nice, or Los Angeles. Somewhere warm. So she'd forced herself to cut back on the crystal—what a bitch that had been—to save enough money for a bus ticket.

"Anywhere warm," she'd told the woman behind the ticket counter.

"How about home?" the woman had asked.

She'd actually thought about it—for perhaps two seconds. It would have been Thanksgiving soon. The thought of a home-cooked feast, the memory of her mom's homemade stuffing and savory gravy, had almost made her mouth water. She'd almost said, "Yeah, is this enough to get to Virginia?"

But there was her uncle. Living two blocks down. Coming to spend the night drinking with her dad, and then, once Dad went to bed, coming into her room. Again. At least now she got paid for it.

"Nah," she'd told the woman. "How about Phoenix?"

That had been the last decision she'd made. The bus to Phoenix wouldn't leave for an hour, so she'd decided to get some food and crystal money for the trip.

The john had seemed nice enough. Reserved. Not outright leering. She knew the type. In her profession, the world's oldest, you had to learn to spot them. The type who'd settle for a straight half-and-half, a blow job and a fuck, ten minutes each, if that. He didn't even try to bargain. A quick fifty bucks.

Looking back, she realized that should have been the warning sign. Johns always tried to bargain. She was cute and clean, slender, a natural blonde, with high, firm tits and prominent nipples that showed through her T-shirt. So she could get a little more than the older girls who had been doing it for so long they looked and felt like worn-out kitchen sponges.

Even so, fifty had been more than twice the going street rate. He'd just nodded and said, "Fine. I know a place close by. What time does your bus leave?"

And that was when she'd disappeared forever.

Yes, it had been just before Thanksgiving. But what month was it now? She had no idea. When she heard the TV from the next room, it was muffled and in Spanish. There were no windows in her room, and the weather never seemed to change here.

No cycles anymore. One day truly was the same as the next. The food was the same, day in and day out. Even the john was the same. Two, sometimes three times a day. It had been more at first. He'd gotten bored, she guessed.

That's how men were, except for her uncle. If he'd gotten bored, she would probably still be living in the *Better Homes and Gardens* fantasyland of Fairfax County, in the two-story brick front on the eighth-of-an-acre lot, with the perfectly manicured lawn, the three-car garage, the giant-screen TV in the family room always tuned to whatever game was on at the time, listening through the shared wall as her brother whacked off to Internet porn.

But her uncle never had gotten bored, and she couldn't stand him anymore, couldn't stand wondering if her brother whacked off listening to her uncle's grunts and the creak of her mattress springs, wondering if her brother heard or cared when she'd lain in her bed afterward, crying into her pillow and counting the days, the hours, the minutes, until she could get the hell out of that house and never ever come back.

Well, she'd gotten out. And she would never get back.

The door opened, and he stood in the doorway with a bag in his hand. He tossed it onto the bed. "Get dressed. You go home."

He pulled the door closed as he left. He didn't bolt it. First time ever. She pursed her lips, wondering what that meant. His words didn't matter. She'd learned to ignore words. Home. Beautiful. Love. Whatever. But he hadn't locked her door. That mattered.

She opened the bag. Faded jeans and a green T-shirt. No bra or panties, but she hadn't worn them in so long, she didn't care. The jeans and T-shirt still had store tags clipped on. She bit the tags off and felt a tooth chip. It was the diet, the gritty tortillas that wore away at the enamel. But Dad was a dentist. He'd fix it.

New clothes. The door not locked.

She was going home.

She washed up as best she could at the sink. Put on the jeans and the T-shirt. Brushed out her hair with her fingers. It had lost some of its blond luster, but the girl in the mirror still had the big brown eyes everyone had always talked about. Her face wasn't quite as fresh. But with some exercise and makeup and a good diet again… Yeah. She could go home. She could be…

…who?

Candi was the name she'd used in Denver. Her parents had called her Candace. But no one had called her anything since she'd gotten here. Not a name, anyway. Just *puta*. Whore.

Who would she be when she got home? Her uncle's *puta?* Candi? Would she even remember what it meant to be Candace? Or would she take one look at her dad's face, then look at his crotch and wonder how many half-and-halves it'd take to get her tooth fixed?

"Are you ready?" he said, opening the door again. "You look good."

Words. Whatever.

"Sure."

She followed him out of her room and then the front room and then out into the courtyard. She'd only seen it once before, when she'd been brought here. Looking around, she realized she'd been living in the servants' quarters. Well, that fit.

Terra-cotta tiles glistened in the morning sun. It had rained last night, and the air was thick with moisture and the sweet scents of the garish tropical flowers that bloomed in carefully trimmed beds around the courtyard. Not a stone, not a grain of sand out of place. That part was like home, at least.

The black SUV was new, not the same one she'd come here in. The leather was baby smooth under her fingers as she climbed into the backseat. He got in front and pushed a button, and a little screen came down out of the roof. "Movie?"

"Yeah. Sure."

He put a DVD into the dashboard player, and moments later the screen flickered to life. Bugs Bunny, speaking in Spanish. He'd bought the DVD for a child. Maybe a daughter. Maybe she was sitting where this man's daughter usually sat, watching the same cartoons his daughter would laugh at while he drove her…where? To school? To church?

She realized she knew nothing about this man. And that was probably why he was letting her go home. He was just another businessman in a foreign country. She didn't even know what city she was in. She couldn't identify him.

She fought the urge to look around as they drove. Part of her wanted to memorize everything, to pick out some sign, some landmark, that she could recall when she got home and tell…someone. Someone who could come and find this man. Instead, she just watched Bugs Bunny make a fool of Elmer Fudd. In Spanish.

They were climbing into the mountains. The man must have an airstrip up here somewhere. That would make sense. He could hardly put her on a commercial flight. She would probably be sitting atop a pile of cocaine. She wondered if it would be soft.

"We stop here to pee," he said, pulling off onto a side road. "More hours to the airport."

She didn't need to pee, but that was fine. She was used to peeing on command. When Dad had taken the family to Yellowstone, he'd scheduled in every pee stop, a little X in yellow highlighter on his trip planner. She and her brother had giggled because Dad had used yellow for the pee stops. The thought made her smile.

There wasn't a bathroom. That was fine. Living on the streets had taught her the more basic skills of life. She pulled down her jeans, carefully tucking the fabric back between her ankles, turning her hips forward as she squatted, pressing a finger on either side of her urethra and lifting, so she would shoot out rather than straight down, keeping her jeans dry.

She heard the *schlick-schlick* as he worked the slide, and she knew. Part of her thought about trying to run or turning to fight. But her jeans were around her ankles. There wouldn't be time. It wouldn't matter.

Fuck it.

Instead, she looked down at the leaves rippling under her stream, at how they flicked this way and that, and just waited. Her throat caught as she thought about Yellowstone, and she and her brother giggling at a yellow X. Back when she had been someone else. Someone innocent and soft and hopeful.

She heard the crack an instant before the bullet crashed through the base of her skull and exploded every thought, every memory, every sadness, every hope.

The blackness came fast.

She was home.

# 1

Special Agent Jerrod Westlake sat at his desk in the FBI's Austin office, looking out a window at the late-afternoon sky. The ordinarily exquisite February weather was about to give way to one of those window-rattling, tree-toppling thunderstorms for which Texas was known.

He watched the clouds turn blacker by the second over toward Balcones. If it had been raining up in the hill country to the west, floods wouldn't be far behind.

But Jerrod wasn't really thinking about the storm. At thirty-eight, he had a decade under his belt as an agent, and he looked at the building storm with the uneasy sixth sense that life was about to imitate meteorology.

The case file that lay all over his desk, sorted into types and sources of information, screamed things that burned into his brain. Fourteen-year-old runaway female, last seen hawking herself on the streets of Houston. This time, unlike most times, she had been reported missing by another prostitute, an older woman who had tried to take the child under her wing and protect her. It was this woman who had reported the girl's disappearance. Usually they just disappeared into inky silence, without a trace.

Another rumble of thunder, too low to be audible, but strong enough to be felt, passed through the office.

Lately too many of his cases seemed to settle around government contractors. The rush of often poorly overseen privatization of government work, coupled with the spending bonanza of the "global war on terror," had led to a boom in contractor fraud. For a while, it had gone largely unnoticed and unchecked, but then courageous whistle-blowers had begun to come forward. Sadly, despite the whistle-blower protection laws, he knew that those witnesses would probably find themselves out of work and unemployable in the government-contracting sector.

But those cases were not his passion. They were just his job. As another rumble of thunder passed through the room, he looked at the framed photo on his desk. The girl who looked back at him from a face framed by blond curls appeared to be just on the cusp of womanhood, entering the awkward stage of life where her smile was the impish one of childhood mixed with the almost-sensed mysteries of adulthood.

Elena. Resident forever in his heart, an ache that would never end.

He'd known he wanted to be a cop from the time Elena had disappeared. He'd been sixteen then, six years older than she was. Family tragedies hit in a lot of ways. His sister's abduction had sent his mom into an alcoholic spiral and his dad into a withdrawal from which he'd never fully emerged.

After Elena disappeared, all that remained was the silence.

It was his father's sudden, overwhelming sense of powerlessness that had energized Jerrod. He decided he would become a cop. He would step in for fathers whose invulnerability had been irretrievably shattered. He would rescue his father, even if he never found Elena.

That had led him into the army's military police program, the fastest way to get into uniform and on the job, and a way to pay for the college education he would need in order to work for the FBI. His rugged athleticism and quick, keen mind had attracted the attention of recruiters in the special-ops community, shadowy heroic figures who'd told him he was destined for better things than waving cars through the front gate.

Six years later, he'd passed through the revolving door that led from special operations into private military contracting, where the pay was better and the missions even farther from public awareness. The company he'd worked for had specialized in overseas personal security, protecting U.S. businessmen and key employees in parts of the world where a U.S. passport was all too often irresistible bait for rebels who financed their operations with ransom money.

It was there, in that dark, shadowy world, that he'd learned what happened sometimes to those little girls and boys who disappeared. It was the first time he'd learned that there really *was* a white slave trade.

He'd become an expert in finding the missing, sniffing out clues that others might miss, able to project complex networks of informants, sources and dark alliances onto a screen in his mind. He followed links that seemed obvious only in retrospect, guided by intuition, supported by a twenty-hour-a-day work schedule when he was on a case.

And then he'd blown the whistle himself.

Ultimately, the case had gone nowhere. He knew what he knew, but too much of what he knew lay in inferences he had drawn from that screen in his mind. The investigator who had worked the case couldn't verify any of Jerrod's claims, at least not enough for prosecution.

But it had pushed him out of the private sector and into the job he'd always wanted. He'd joined the

FBI. And he'd joined with a résumé and a passion that had quickly turned into a specialty.

He worked all kinds of cases, but Special Agent Jerrod Westlake had quickly emerged as the go-to guy on abductions. A photo album in his desk drawer was filled with the faces of kids he'd found. The bulletin board over his desk was also covered with photographs, those he hadn't yet located.

And on his desk, surrounded by a simple white frame, was a photo of Elena.

He looked at her now, sensing more than hearing the rumble of thunder that reverberated through his window, strong enough to feel in the arms of his chair.

Elena, as sweet as a spring morning, a tiny little elf of a girl who had come into the world one day after his sixth birthday. His mom called her a surprise gift from God. His dad just plain doted.

And it still pained Jerrod not to know. Despite all the resources he could call on, he could find no trace of Elena Westlake. Not even among the hundreds of Jane Does who filtered through morgues and into anonymous plots of ground provided by cities, counties or states.

His reputation now preceded him, and he claimed a network of friends and allies throughout law enforcement who kept him abreast of new cases. When local authorities wanted help, they asked for him by name. And whatever field office he was working from, his special agent in charge would book him on the next flight out.

Twenty-two years ago this week. That was when Elena had disappeared. A ten-year-old girl waiting for her school bus had been yanked into a car by a dark-haired, middle-aged man of medium height and build, driving a late-model blue sedan. The recorded story of Elena Westlake ended on that cold February morning, the description of her last known moments dragged out of the terrified boy who had been awaiting the bus with her.

He knew Elena must be dead. Still, he hadn't given up. One day he would find his sister's body. At least his mom and dad would know what had happened.

The storm rumbled again. Georgie Dickson appeared in the door of Jerrod's cubicle and placed a Starbucks coffee on his desk. Then she sat in the chair beside the desk and sipped her own coffee.

She was a beautiful woman, her café-au-lait skin shining with the good health that came from being physically fit. Georgie had no vices, although the rest of the crew was always trying to find one. It had become a game. Did Georgie ever have a drink? Did she eat meat when she thought no one was looking? Did she really go to church every Sunday?

Georgie knew about it, and Jerrod was sure she enjoyed every moment of being a mystery.

She was also one of his best friends in the office.

As if she'd been reading his mind, she leaned over and picked up Elena's photo. After a moment, she sighed and put it down again. She didn't say anything. She didn't have to.

"Big storm," she remarked.

He nodded, glancing toward the window. There was an ugly swirl to some of those clouds now, the kind of swirl that might portend a tornado. "Has anyone listened to the weather?"

"The usual. Severe storm warning, tornado watch. Were you expecting something else?"

Almost in spite of himself, he chuckled. Georgie was good at dragging him out of his brooding.

"So how did it go, testifying in the Mercator case?"

"Pretty well, I thought. I hung around afterward to listen to some of the other testimony. I got the feeling there might be another whistle-blower, one we never identified."

"Is it worth looking into?"

He shook his head dubiously. "I honestly don't know. This was the stupidest case of fraud I've ever worked. The prosecution won't rest their case until next week, though, so I guess we'll hear about it if they want us to look any further."

Government fraud cases were as varied as the human mind's capacity for dreaming up ways to root a few extra dollars from the public trough.

*Rachel Lee*

Jerrod divided them into three categories: the sinister, the slick and the stupid. The sinister were the most dangerous, occurring at the junction of policy and profit. The slick were the most clever, often using one set of regulations against another, tucking away sometimes obscene piles of money, so close to the legal line that they were often impossible to prosecute.

The Mercator Industries case, on the other hand, was in the category of the stupid, a case where the acts were so obvious and the payoff so small that you had to wonder why they'd even bothered.

"Really dumb," Georgie said, apparently thinking over the facts of the case. She laughed. "I mean, c'mon. Persian rugs and Italian leather executive chairs? What were they thinking?"

"It was a cost-plus contract," Jerrod said, shrugging almost humorously. "They were real costs, right?"

Cost-plus contracting required the contractor to itemize the costs of performing the work. The government paid the costs, plus a profit percentage specified in the contract. Slick contractors looked for creative ways to pad the costs and thus increase the base from which their profit was calculated. This padding often involved layers of subcontracts to companies that were subsidiaries or even mere shells for the principal. Those subcontracts included a profit which was added to the prime contractor's cost, even though that cost was simply money being shifted from one accounting column to another in the corporate books.

When the contractors were slick enough, this padding slipped right through the audits, enabling them to "profit on profit." The Mercator people weren't that slick. Not even by half.

Instead, they'd claimed that the contract had required them to open a temporary office in Houston to oversee the work being done locally. Under the regulations, if the office was temporary—opened solely for that one contract—reasonable office costs were chargeable to that contract.

The key words were *temporary* and *reasonable*. And the office complex in Houston was neither.

Mercator had bought two floors of a downtown high-rise, and its Houston complex housed two dozen executives and their staffs, overseeing no less than ten different contracts throughout Texas and Louisiana. The lavish furnishings might still have slipped through, had Mercator not billed the whole cost of the complex on each of those ten contracts. *Fortune* magazine had broken the story in a three-part whistle-blower saga aptly titled *Deca-Dipping*.

"Y'know what I can't understand?" Jerrod asked, as Georgie thumbed through one of the stacks of paper that had been resting on his desk.

"What's that?"

"Why are they even fighting it? It makes no sense. They have no defense. Christie Jackson said she offered them a quarter-million-dollar fine to plead out. That's spare change for a company like Mercator. Why not just pay the damn fine and move on?"

"They're worried the three-strikes law will actually get passed," Georgie said.

She did have a vice, and Jerrod knew what it was. Georgie was a news junkie. She subscribed to a dozen online newspapers, from the *Times of London* to the *Beijing Evening News,* and a score of newsfeeds. If you wanted to know whether a pilot was missing in Afghanistan or a panda mating in China, all you had to do was ask Georgie.

Which Jerrod did. "What's that?"

"There's a joint contracting reform bill winding its way through committee," she said. "Among other things, it has a three-strikes rule. Get popped for fraud three times and you're out of the government contractor pool."

"Like that will ever pass," he said.

She shrugged. "It might. There's a lot of support for it in the Netroots."

"Huh?"

"The blogosphere," she explained. "More and more, online communities are learning how to lean on government to get things done. When it rose from the traditional media we called it a grassroots movement. When it happens online…"

"I get it," Jerrod said. "But how much influence do those people really wield? Yeah, they can get a story from the outhouse to CNN, but these contractors give huge sums to congressional campaigns. They'll hold a hearing or two and talk about how something has to be done, and then some lobbyist will remind them that they'd shut down a big chunk of the government if they passed a law like that. Hell, we've farmed out so much of what government does, it's not as if we can just turn off the spigot."

"Spoken like a former contractor," Georgie said with a playful grin.

"Hey," he said. "I was just a grunt for hire. Don't go lumping me in with those people."

"Whatever," she said. Lightning flared so bright that it washed out the room, followed by a sky-rending crack. Jerrod looked out the window again, noting that heavy rain appeared to be sweeping closer. Rush hour was going to be a mess.

"So…what? You came in here just to cheer me up?" he asked, swiveling his chair to face her again. "Or did you actually have something in mind?"

"Just to tell you this is probably our one chance," she said. She handed him a printout. "Apparently the good folks there like Houston."

He scanned the page. It was a blurb from one of

her many online newsfeeds. "MMG buys Houston *Examiner.* This matters to me...how?"

"MMG," Georgie said. "Mercator Media Group. Say goodbye to one of the last independently owned newspapers in Texas."

"Interesting," Jerrod said. "But again, how does that matter to me?"

"Erin McKenna broke the Mercator story when she was a freelancer for *Fortune.*"

He nodded. Georgie's other vice was drawing out a story just to the point where he wanted to strangle her. She knew he knew Erin McKenna. They'd never met, but her story in *Fortune* had been so thorough as to be a blueprint for his investigation. "And?"

"She's not a freelancer anymore. The Houston *Examiner* hired her as an investigative reporter."

"And now Mercator owns the *Examiner,*" he said. The pieces came together. He let out a long sigh. "Oh shit."

"Maybe you need to go to Houston," Georgie said. "It would be bad to come this far and lose a key witness."

Jerrod looked at the file on his desk, the paltry window onto a life too short. Or a life that had been turned into a living hell of slavery.

"More than the Mercator case seems to have followed you from Houston. Cold case?" Georgie asked, following his gaze.

"Not quite." He hated to leave it. But he couldn't allow anyone to tamper with witness testimony. Reluctantly, he reached for the phone.

He was going to Houston. Maybe he could nose around on the missing-child case some more while he was there. Two birds with one stone.

Regardless, he needed to find out what was going on with Erin McKenna.

# 2

Erin McKenna climbed the stairs to her third floor apartment, a small box of personal belongings under her arm. As her feet hit each tread, a curse escaped under her breath.

Fired. Just like that. Oh, they called it a staff reduction, but she was too much of a reporter to believe it. Since word of Mercator Media Group's purchase of the paper had begun to filter down, she'd known she was in the crosshairs. She'd expected pressure not to testify in the trial. The pressure had never come, and she'd gone off to Federal Court this morning and testified without one whisper of a suggestion that she reconsider.

Then she had come back to the office to find the news editor and her managing editor standing over her desk, her belongings already in a box, with the happy news that she had just become part of a staff reduction.

Hah!

Something in Bill Maddox's face had communicated the truth. She'd been investigating Mercator again, and only Bill, her news editor, had known. In theory, anyway. And his face said as plain as day that this was no simple staff reduction.

Damn! She slammed her foot down hard on the next riser, so angry that she was grinding her teeth.

Effing giant corporations. Damn money men. Damn the whole corporate plutocracy that America was becoming. They figured money and power meant they were above the law.

She stomped down even harder on the next step. They'd taken all her files, of course, because anything she did on the job belonged to her paper. They'd taken her business laptop from her car and demanded to know if she'd kept any business-related information anywhere else.

To do so would have been a violation of the paper's strict policy. So of course she had lied through her teeth and said she hadn't.

Damned if she was going to tell them about the anonymous online file storage she'd started when she learned about the MMG purchase. She'd even gone so far as to go to a cybercafé to upload the info so there would be no record on any computer she used.

So the bomb was still out there, despite their best

efforts. At the moment, that was the only satisfaction she had, and it was a grim one. She could still nail Mercator to the wall once she finished her research.

Reaching the landing outside her door, she leaned against the wall to hold the box in place while she fished through her vest pocket for her keys. Cell phone, extra pens, package of gum and, as always, way at the bottom, keys.

She pulled them out, sorted through them and then pushed the proper one into the lock. Or tried to. The door swung inward even as she slid the key into the hole.

Her heart froze. Someone had broken into her place. She stepped through the doorway and saw her things tossed about as if a raging tornado had blown through.

She stood stunned, barely able to believe her eyes. At that moment, a man, his face hidden behind a ski mask, burst out of her bedroom. She dropped the box, one part of her mind questioning the utter absurdity of wearing a ski mask in Houston, and charged toward him, ready to head-butt him or knock his legs out or…well, *something*…but before she finished her first step, she knew she'd made a mistake.

She'd exposed her back.

A rustle behind her was all the warning she had. An instant later, stars burst before her eyes; then everything went black.

* * *

She came to slowly, aware first of the excruciating pounding in her head, then, slowly, that she wasn't alone. Hands felt gently around her head. She could feel warm goo on the back of her skull, and somewhere in her befuddled mind, the word *blood* registered.

But in the instant between the dim recognition that she was bleeding and full consciousness, awareness of those hands sparked a surge of fear. Someone was touching her. With her sore nose pressed painfully to a rug that had never offered much of a cushion, she tried to gather her scattered thoughts.

Break-in. Someone had hit her from behind. The fact that she could remember that much was a good sign. The concussion couldn't be too bad.

As she lay frozen, she tried to decide what to do about the person who was with her. If he was the one who had attacked her...

Could she roll over fast enough? She realized she was still gripping her keys in the hand trapped beneath her body. Trying to keep her movements invisible, she slowly worked the keys between her fingers, turning them into a weapon.

In the distance she heard sirens, or so she thought. She couldn't be certain, because she heard ringing bells, too. What difference did it make, anyway? She hadn't called the cops.

Drawing a deep breath as silently as she could, battling the urge to sneeze as she inhaled whatever dust her vacuum had left in the rug, she rolled over swiftly and swung her fist and keys at the man who knelt beside her.

Moving with the speed of a striking snake, he caught her wrist. "It's okay," he said. "FBI. You're safe now."

Still holding her wrist, he reached toward his belt and pulled his badge clip free, holding it up. "Can you see?" he asked.

She swallowed. "Yeah."

"Are you going to try to hit me again?"

"No."

He let go of her wrist. "Don't move," he said. "The paramedics are on the way. I don't know how bad you're hurt. You have a scalp wound, and you were out for a while."

"There were two of them," she said. "I saw one and went after him, but another one got behind me and hit me." Just the memory of it made her mad, and the adrenaline kicked in again. "Damn it!"

Ignoring the painful drumbeat in her head, she started to sit, but he caught her shoulders as she was halfway up. "Which part of 'don't move' did you not understand?"

As the room began to spin around her, she realized he was right. It was worse than being at sea during a storm. Her stomach lurched, and she turned her head, fighting back the urge to vomit.

"Cancel the ambulance," she said, slowly rolling onto her hands and knees, then crawling to her over- turned couch and resting her cheek against the satiny fabric. If she could just make the world stop spin- ning, she would be fine. Really.

"I'm not going to do that," he said.

"Are you going to pay the bill?" she asked, hear- ing herself almost mumble. "I don't have insurance anymore."

"Why not?"

"I got fired today."

She closed her eyes for a few moments, letting the world settle down. When she opened them again, he was still kneeling where he'd been, making no attempt to approach her. Late thirties, she guessed, with a carved, hardened look you didn't often see on FBI agents, who spent most of their lives at desks. This one had spent some time in the elements. His expression was kind, though, his mossy-green eyes concerned.

"Who are you?" she asked. "And what is the FBI doing in my living room?"

"Special Agent Jerrod Westlake. I worked on the Mercator case. You're going to testify on Monday."

Subject. Plus. Verb. Equals. Sentence. Except there was something missing. "That doesn't explain you being here."

"I just heard that Mercator bought your newspaper. I figured it might be wise to make sure no one prevented you from testifying."

She leaned her head back. "Too late. I testified this morning. Then I was fired. Then I was robbed. If you're supposed to be my knight in shining armor, you're a little late. The joust is over, and I got skewered."

He shifted, sitting cross-legged. "So it would seem. Unless there's something I don't know."

Damned if she was going to tell him or anyone else. Right now, lying low and acting dumb seemed the smartest strategy, much as it flew in the face of her nature.

The paramedics arrived, complete with backboard, neck collar and that horrendously big case of stuff they used on people. At least it silenced the FBI guy's questions.

They examined her, questioned her, took her blood pressure and tested her pupil reflexes, all the while asking her what day it was, who was president, and all kinds of other things to make sure her brain was still present and accounted for.

"You need stitches," the female half of the team said to her. "Maybe six or so, and you should get a skull X-ray. Otherwise, you're stable."

They stuck a piece of gauze over the wound and secured it to her head with more gauze wrapping.

"I must look like the mummy," Erin muttered.

The woman laughed. "You're definitely okay."

The police arrived just as the paramedics were leaving. The medics answered questions about Erin's injury, then disappeared down the stairs.

"The whole damn world is lumbering through my life," she remarked, seated against the couch. Nothing had gone according to plan since she'd left court that morning. Not one damn thing.

She might as well have been talking to herself. She couldn't see another victim in the room, but the cops seemed more interested in her FBI rescuer. It took a minute or so, but she realized that they considered Agent Westlake's presence to be an indicator that Erin must be up to her neck in something unsavory. She considered arguing with them, but her head chose that moment to remind her that it wasn't happy. She winced and closed her eyes.

It didn't matter anyway, because Westlake straightened them out.

"Ms. McKenna is a journalist. She's also a witness in a federal criminal case. I received information that she might be in danger, so I came to check on her. I only wish I'd gotten here sooner."

*Go Agent Westlake,* she thought. She was getting sleepy, and she didn't like that, so she forced her eyes open. "The only thing I did wrong," she announced, forcing them all to pay attention to her again, "was investigate fraud on a government contract. I guess that's a mistake I shouldn't make again."

Not that she meant it. Hell, no.

Unfortunately, her bid not to be ignored in the catastrophe of her own life brought the detective over to her with his notebook.

"There were two," she said in answer to his question. "I saw one of them as he came out of my bedroom. The other one hit me from behind, and that's all I know."

"What did he look like?"

"Who? The guy who came out of my bedroom? Average height. Average build. Average ski mask."

Detective Flannery lifted one eyebrow. "Cute," he said.

Erin managed to shrug one shoulder. "I wish I could tell you more, but they came ready for me, I guess. He was wearing gloves. I couldn't pick him out of a lineup."

Flannery almost smirked. Behind him, Jerrod emitted a small laugh.

"Is anything missing?"

"Good question. I have no idea. Might have something to do with being knocked unconscious."

"Do you give everyone a hard time, even when they're trying to help you?"

"Probably. I haven't asked around." She squeezed her eyes closed, then opened them again. "You'll have to help me up if you want to know what's gone. I seem to be on a slow-moving carousel."

Flannery and Westlake obliged, helping her gently to her feet. In one scan she saw the crucial missing items. Or rather, the editor in her brain corrected, she *didn't* see some crucial items. "My computer is gone. All my DVDs and CDs," she said.

"But not the TV," Flannery remarked. "Did you have a stereo?"

"Who, me? With what they paid me, I was lucky to afford that DVD player on sale. And that's still here."

A creeping sense of danger was beginning to run up and down her spine. Discs and computer gone? But not TV and DVD player? "This is weird," she announced.

"Maybe you interrupted them before they could finish."

"Maybe." But she didn't believe it. She looked at Westlake and saw that his eyes were narrowed, as if he wasn't buying that, either.

"She needs to go to the hospital," Jerrod reminded the detective. "I doubt, given the masks and gloves, that you'll ever know who they were."

"Not likely," Flannery agreed, but in a way that suggested he didn't want to cede an inch to the Feds. "Take her to the hospital, then. We'll get the crime unit in, and she can give us a list of missing items later."

"I can't afford the hospital," she reminded Jerrod.

"Sure you can. You're the victim of a crime. The state will reimburse your expenses."

"The hospital won't let me through the door. I did a story on the health-care system recently. You wouldn't believe how many Samaritans aren't good."

"They'll let you in. Under COBRA, you still have insurance, but if it comes to that, I have plastic."

"Witness protection?"

He half smiled. "Whatever it takes."

She didn't argue. She didn't want to stay amidst the ruins of her life. And since thieves had already been through every inch of her apartment, she could hardly feel any more violated by the police following them.

She had to lean heavily on Jerrod to make it down the two flights of stairs. Her knees had begun to wobble as the adrenaline rush wore off. "I hate this," she announced as they reached the street.

"Few people enjoy being robbed and battered."

"I didn't mean that. I hate not being able to take care of myself."

He fell silent as he opened the door of what was apparently his vehicle. Flex Fuel, the dashboard announced with a fancy plate. Under other circumstances she would have asked about it, but right now she lacked the reporter's energy to ask a bazillion questions.

He helped her buckle in, then closed the door. The heavy thud of the black SUV's door was solid, sounding like safety.

He climbed in behind the wheel, and a few seconds later, pulled out into Houston's late-afternoon traffic. He seemed to know his way around.

"How did you get on the Mercator case?" she asked, trying to distract herself from her mega discomfort.

"I was stationed here in Houston when your story came out in *Fortune*. I was part of the investigation."

"Ah." She closed her eyes, since the traffic seemed to want to spin around her. "I was pretty surprised that the FBI paid any attention to that article."

"Why wouldn't we?"

"Mercator is powerful, with powerful friends."

"Thanks a lot."

She tried to look at him, then decided the effort wasn't worth it. "I didn't mean it as a criticism of you."

"Sure you did. The thing is, at my level, politics don't matter. The *law* does."

"I wish there were more of you. But right now I can only see two in the seat beside me."

That got his attention. "You're seeing double?"

"Not really. Well, only once or twice."

"Christ."

"You aren't supposed to use that word around

reporters and other persons not on the inside of your club."

He surprised her with a short laugh. "I know some other words I shouldn't use, too."

"Who doesn't? Well, don't guard your tongue with me. I have a few favorites you might be hearing."

"Curse away."

She sighed and carefully lowered her chin to her chest. "Agent Westlake?"

"Jerrod, please."

"Jerrod. I don't think the break-in was a coincidence."

He looked at her. "Duh. The question is why it happened *after* you testified."

His comment was almost a question, but not quite. She chose to equivocate. "The question indeed."

But she had a pretty damn good idea.

# 3

Four hours and five staples later, Erin was back in the car with Jerrod. In her lap were a bottle of pain meds and standard discharge instructions for wound care and dealing with a concussion. The doctor had wanted to keep her overnight for observation. Jerrod, too, had argued for the stay. Yet here she was, on the way back to her apartment.

"You're stubborn," Jerrod remarked.

"You don't survive in my business if you aren't."

"Same here."

"How cool is that? We have something in common besides Mercator."

He chuckled. "Amazing, isn't it?"

She half smiled. At least her lips were remembering that it was possible.

"But you're not staying at your place."

"No?"

"No. We're going to collect some clothes and things, and then we're going to a hotel."

"Why?"

He looked at her. It was dark now, and flashes of headlights from oncoming traffic chiseled his face even more. "You were attacked at home. Wanna try again?"

She decided he was okay, because he'd asked her instead of telling her. "Honestly? I'm not so sure."

"Me, either. I don't know what's behind this, but my instincts are telling me they're not done with you."

"You have good instincts," she remarked, then wished she hadn't, because he was no idiot and caught the subtext as if it had been a headline.

"What don't I know?"

She hesitated. "Plenty," she said finally. "And I can't talk about it. Reporter privilege." That usually shut people up. Not him.

"We're going to have to talk about it, Erin. Later. When you feel better."

Not likely, she thought, but at least for now he was letting her off the hook. She would take what she could get until she was back in shape.

The stairs were easier this time, and the crime-scene unit was still picking over the bones of her life like carrion birds. As promised, she noted what was missing, which hadn't expanded much from what she had already noticed. Whoever had broken in had been looking for information, of that she had no doubt. Her grandmother's engagement ring, a nice piece of ice, had been totally ignored. Mutely she held it up to Jerrod, and he nodded understanding. Then she slipped it on the ring finger of her right hand to keep it safe.

He helped her pack a suitcase, and she didn't object. Not even when he scooped underwear up off the floor. It wouldn't make any sense to object, since even the thought of bending over left her dizzy and nauseous.

Besides, he seemed as interested in it as if it had been cardboard. He was very…clinical, professional. He avoided her few good dresses and instead packed slacks, jeans, Ts and sweatshirts. Her favorite stuff, to be sure, but it began to seem he had some kind of plan. It was more than she needed for overnight.

Abducted by an FBI agent, she thought. Could the world get any crazier?

When she asked him where they were going, he shook his head and indicated the next room with a movement of his eyes. He didn't trust the local police? Erin began to wonder what *he* knew that *she* didn't.

"Anything else you don't want to leave here?" he asked finally, as he prepared to latch her suitcase.

"All I have that mattered is gone." Except for the ring on her hand.

"Let's move out, then."

Huh, she thought. Military background, or too many movies?

They drove off again in his car, this time headed for Loop 410. "Where are we going?" she asked again. "Or do I need to jump out of a moving vehicle?"

"That would hurt considerably more than being hit on the head. I told you, I'm taking you to a hotel."

"I'm not in the set that can afford hotels."

"I am. And I'm not going to leave you hanging in the breeze. Not at your place. Not even in a hotel under your own name."

She squirmed on her seat and managed to look at him. "You're creeping me out."

"Good. You should have been creeped out before."

"I was, but not like this. What are you thinking?"

"You've pissed someone off enough to commit felony burglary and battery. That's very pissed off. You know something, or they think you do. You're still alive, which can't make them happy. Two plus two equals four."

Gingerly, she reached up and touched the staples on the back of her head. "You have a point. Why didn't you want to say anything in the apartment?"

He glanced her way. "Cops talk. Sometimes idly, and sometimes not."

He was right, she realized. "So I can't trust the cops but I can trust *you?* There's a disconnect there."

He reached in his breast pocket and tossed her a flip-phone. She barely managed to catch it, considering the world was still trying to bob on invisible waves.

"Call information. Get the number for the Austin field office of the FBI. Ask about me. Check my creds. Get my description."

She looked at the phone. Part of her said she didn't need to do that if he was so willing to let her; part of her suspicious reporter's mind suggested that he might be expecting that reaction.

So she flipped open his phone, got the number and made the call. A recording answered her.

"Cool," she said. "A recording can't identify you."

"Keep listening. Toward the end we finally admit that you can reach an agent right now."

"I should hope so. The country could collapse while you guys sleep."

"We never sleep."

"Yeah, right." She pressed eight when the menu promised it would put her directly in touch with an agent. After a couple of rings, a silky woman's voice answered.

"Agent Dickson. May I help you?"

"Uh, yes. I'm with a guy claiming to be Special Agent Jerrod Westlake. Is he for real?"

The woman chuckled. "We often wonder that ourselves. Yes, he's a real agent. Do you want his description?"

"Please."

"Tall, green-eyed, dark and handsome. Well, not really handsome. He looks more like somebody carved his face out of wood. Nice smile, though, when you can get it out of him."

Erin almost laughed. "That sounds like him."

"Put him on the phone for a sec, would you?"

"Sure." Erin passed the phone back to Jerrod.

"Westlake," he said. "Oh, hi, Georgie. Yeah, with what she's been through today, I don't blame her for being suspicious. We're going to ground overnight. I'll get in touch tomorrow. Yeah. You got it."

He flipped the phone closed and tucked it back in the inside pocket of his suit.

"She sounds nice," Erin remarked.

"As long as you don't get on the wrong side of her."

Relieved, Erin let go of the tension. It would come back, she knew, but for now she could allow herself to feel safe. "Isn't your office number programmed on your phone?"

"Of course. But would you have trusted it?"

"Good point." He was outthinking her paranoia. Interesting guy. Then, slowly, she let her eyelids droop closed. It was a relief to go to sleep.

Jerrod almost woke her, remembering the doctor's warnings about sleep, but the hotel was only another twenty minutes away, if that. He figured he could give her that much time safely.

Spunky woman, he thought, wheeling through thinning traffic. Striking. Black hair and bright blue eyes. Arresting. A fair-skinned Irish beauty, with a compact but tempting figure.

But her loveliness wasn't what had struck him most. It was her attitude that had captivated him. Sassy, sardonic, sarcastic—and very, very sharp. Even with a concussion, all of that showed through. She didn't like being told "No," and she didn't care if people knew that.

But she was also a mystery. Jerrod Westlake was no fool, and he knew she was keeping something to herself, something that had put her at greater risk than testifying at that ridiculous fraud trial. He could sense it in the almost slippery way she edged around some things, in the way she chose her words. She didn't believe her apartment had been ransacked because she'd testified, nor did she believe she had been fired because of it.

Nor did he. She was on to something much bigger, and he wanted to know what it was.

But first he had to make her as safe as he could.

The thunderstorm had followed him from Austin. Or maybe this was a new one building. Either way, lightning jumped across the sky, cloud to cloud, a beautiful thing. He waited for the thunder, but if it reached him, it was deadened by the car. Another fork of lightning wrapped the clouds like a spider-web. Still no rain. It wouldn't be long.

He had chosen to go south, the least likely direction for anyone to look for him because it took him farther from Austin. He was pretty sure they didn't have a tail, but he took some side streets to make sure before returning to the highway, and finally picking a hotel. Embassy Suites. Two rooms, which would give her a bedroom and him a front room with a sofa bed if he wanted it. Only one door.

He parked, rather than pulling up under the porte cochere. He would not allow them to be separated, even in public.

Coming around to her side of the car, he woke her gently by calling her name quietly. When her blue eyes flashed open, he saw the momentary confusion. Then he saw the return of awareness. It was almost as if something inside her closed the shutters.

"We're at the hotel," he told her. "I'll get our bags, then we'll go in."

She wasn't ready to talk yet, or even nod. He did catch her wince as she moved her head.

"When we get inside, take one of those pain pills."

"I just might succumb," she admitted.

He pulled their bags—hers newly packed, his always there in case of emergency—out of the trunk, then helped her out of the car.

"You don't seem as wobbly."

"No," she agreed. "I think I'm off the carousel."

"That's good news."

Inside the lobby, he checked them in, using his own credit card. He didn't want Erin's name on anything, at least until he found out what was going on. Check-in was easy and fast, and ten minutes later they were in their suite.

Erin collapsed in an armchair near the door, but despite her apparent physical weakness, those blue eyes of hers suggested she was regaining her full mental faculties, and along with them, a rising curiosity. Reporters weren't much different from FBI agents. Questions were always turning in the backs of their minds. It was just a matter of who broke the ice and asked first.

"There's a bedroom back here," he said, throwing the door open and carrying her suitcase to one of two double beds. "And a bath. It's all yours. I'll stay in the front room."

"Near the door?"

"Near the door. Guard dog on duty." He came back out and shed his suit coat, draping it from a hook in the back of the small closet.

"My white knight," she remarked, sounding a tad sarcastic.

He didn't mind. He wanted her spunky as hell. "That's me," he agreed. Unbuttoning his cuffs, he rolled up the sleeves of his blue oxford shirt. "Hungry?"

"Not yet."

"Stomach?"

"Unsettled."

Her eyes followed him, and for some reason she reminded him of a cat watching a caged bird. On alert again. Returning to the strength and determination that had carried her this far.

He decided to let her watch him, and say nothing for now. He kept his belt holster and gun on, along with his badge, and went to the phone to call room service. "I can get you something later, but I haven't eaten since this morning, and I wouldn't want to become too weak to hold up my lance."

One corner of her mouth curled upward in a smile. "Do they have French onion soup?"

He opened the loose-leaf binder by the phone, flipped to room service and scanned the menu. "One bowl coming up."

"Thanks."

He saw her pull the pill bottle from her vest pocket and went to get her a glass of water from the sink. As he handed it to her, he asked, "Do you always wear those safari vests?"

"Have you ever tried to carry a purse while taking notes on the fly, or even photos?"

"Can't say I have."

"I didn't think so." She downed one pain pill and drained the water glass before setting it on the end table. "A photographer friend gave this to me after

I'd bitched about my purse for the thousandth time.
I never leave home without it."

He brought her another glass of water, then sat on
the couch facing her. "I can see it's handy."

"Oh, yeah. It would be even handier if I kept to
some kind of organization. I tend to drop everything
in one or two pockets, though." She pointed. "Phone,
keys, gum, pens." Another pocket. "Pads, tape re-
corder, wallet."

"And the others?"

"Empty."

"Kleenex?"

"Oh, yeah." She patted a hip pocket. "Tissues are
in there with the notepads. Easy to reach."

"And now pills."

She popped the bottle into a separate pocket.
"They get their own space." Then she touched a zip-
pered pocket on the other side. "I forgot. Makeup.
Lipstick. I don't usually wear it, but sometimes…"
She shrugged. "You do what you gotta do."

Her hand wandered up to her neck, then slowly
slid downward. "I feel naked without my press
credentials."

"I can imagine. About how I'd feel without my
badge and gun."

"We may be on the same wavelength. I can't
allow that to continue."

He lifted a brow. "Why not?"

"'Cuz you're a cop and I'm a reporter, which puts us on opposite sides of a huge divide."

"Not really. I promise not to compromise your professional ethics."

"You already have."

He watched a look of mischief dart across her face. "How so?"

"I'm in a hotel room you paid for, about to eat food you're paying for. That's strictly a no-no. Print press never takes gifts, even if TV reporters do."

"Ah." He narrowed his eyes, trying not to smile. "Well, you're not employed at the moment."

"A saving grace." She closed her eyes briefly, drew a deep breath, then opened them again. "I wish the guy with the jackhammer would clock out soon."

"The pill should help send him on his way."

"I hope. So."

He raised his brows, waiting. That "so" had definitely been a segue.

"What are your bosses going to say about all this?" she asked, indicating the hotel room.

"That I exercised good sense."

"Nice bosses."

"Big expense account."

A chuckle escaped her, causing her to wince. "I can't believe you came all the way to Houston just to make sure I testified. You could have called the field office here and told them to keep an eye on me."

"I knew you were going to be dangerous."

She smiled. "It's my job."

"It's your nature. Okay, I came partly because of you, and partly because there's another case I'm working on."

"I guess I got in the way of that. What's the other case?"

He hesitated, unwilling and, in fact, unable to discuss an active investigation. But there was something she was withholding, something important, and he would never gain her trust if he didn't give her some first.

"A teenage girl disappeared a few months ago."

She cocked her head. "I don't think I heard about it."

"Most people wouldn't. She was a runaway, working the streets. An older street woman had taken an interest in her. Called us when she went missing."

Erin seemed almost to nod, yet barely moved her head. "You're right, that's not the kind of story that gets much coverage. Which is a damn shame."

"I couldn't agree more. Missing persons, especially children, are my specialty."

Her eyes widened a bit. "You're that agent I keep hearing about? The one who works all over the country on these cases?"

He nodded.

"Jeez, wouldn't I love to interview you."

"Maybe after we make sure you're safe. But I can't talk specifics about ongoing investigations."

"I understand that. Still, you've got quite a rep."

"Not enough that you recognized me right off, thank God."

A half smile lit her face. "You haven't quite reached your fifteen minutes of fame yet."

"I hope I never do."

A knock sounded at the door. In one fluid moment, Jerrod rose to his feet, indicated with one hand that she should go to the bedroom, and with the other unsnapped the guard on his belt holster. He was taking no chances.

Over the years, he'd realized something important about his psychology, and possibly the psychology of others: once the unthinkable happened in your life, there was never anything unthinkable again. Forever after, you always expected it.

And something about this situation had him at high alert. He and Erin McKenna needed to have a serious talk very soon.

"Be right there," he called to the door, hand on his pistol butt. As soon as he was sure Erin was concealed in the bedroom, he went to answer the knock.

# 4

Erin kept the bedroom door open a crack so she could watch what happened. Part of her felt that all this was way over the top, utterly ridiculous, but then she remembered her apartment, and the throbbing from the back of her head reminded her that someone was pretty serious about something.

Maybe even serious enough to pursue her.

Still, it was a hard connection to make. She was one of those people who were accustomed to feeling comfortable and safe in almost any situation. Accustomed to believing she could take care of herself. The reporter in her was probably too bold by half.

In fact, she was sure of it. Her past held some episodes that made other people shake their heads and say, "Are you crazy?"

No, she was just a grade-A, dyed-in-the-wool adrenaline junkie. But while adrenaline helped the wise to flee, she had a tendency to walk where only angels dared to tread.

Knowing this about herself did not, of course, make her any more cautious. Nor did she want it to.

The room-service guy appeared to be on the up-and-up. Jerrod pulled the cart into the room without letting the waiter bring it in, and signed the slip. Moments later, the door was locked again.

Erin didn't wait for permission to come out. She walked down the very short wannabe hallway past the kitchenette to the front room. "So what were you expecting? A team of ninjas?"

"I'm working very hard not to roll my eyes at you."

"Don't waste the energy. Roll away. I can take it."

Instead he lifted the covers from the dishes. "Soup." With a flourish, he offered her the bowl on a plate after she resumed her seat in the armchair. A napkin and soup spoon followed it.

She'd expected him to be a meat-and-potatoes kind of guy, but he'd chosen grilled salmon, salad and rice. He put his plates on the coffee table and leaned forward to eat.

"TV?" he asked.

"Why not."

He glanced at her. "I suggested it because you don't seem to want to talk about why someone busted into your apartment and stole anything that might contain information."

"You sure of that?"

Holding his plate and fork, he smiled and leaned back. "You betcha."

She set her soup on the end table. It smelled good, but her stomach rolled over nonetheless. "Maybe the court forgot to tell them I was testifying early. After all, I wasn't supposed to testify until Monday."

"You wouldn't have anything on your computer that wasn't already in the hands of the U.S. Attorney."

"Damn, you're good."

"Don't I know it."

"I wonder if there's any club soda on this planet."

He set his plate down. "Stomach?"

"Awful."

He leaned over and reached for the phone, then told room service to bring up a six-pack of club soda.

"So," he said when he hung up and reached for his plate of salmon, "why don't you tell me what it is about Erin McKenna that's keeping her so calm in a situation that would have most people in hysterics."

"I'm not the hysterical type."

Now he did roll his eyes at her, but the way he did it was humorous. "I'd already gathered that," he said with sarcasm so heavy it was obviously meant as a joke.

"I'm just weird," she said finally. "I've always done things most sane people wouldn't do. I've gone into burning rooms, walked out into forest fires, chased tornados, chatted up gangs for a mega-turd—"

"A *what?*"

"Mega-turd. Newsroom slang for those big in-depth pieces. The official name for them is enterprise stories."

"Ah." He sat back, savoring a mouthful of salmon. "Gangs, huh?"

"Yeah." She shrugged one shoulder. "Once they knew I wasn't a cop and wouldn't rat on them, they were okay."

"And fires? Did you actually walk into a building on fire? This I gotta hear."

At that she had to laugh, despite everything that seemed to be squeezing the joy out of her. "Well, yes. But it was actually a burning room. I suited up and everything."

"What aren't you telling me?"

"That it was one of those practice rooms." She laughed again. "It's like a big trailer. They have gas jets shooting fire, stuff burning, all so guys can get used to the difficulties. Even suited up, it was so damn hot in there I could barely stand it. And the equipment weighed a ton. One of the guys had to help me move."

"And why did you do this?"

"For a story."

"You'll do anything for a story, I take it."

"Well, you know, there were a whole bunch of us media types there. The chief was showing off the room and how they use it. And when he asked if one of us wanted to try it, I was the only volunteer. God, did I have those firefighters laughing. They walk around in that gear as if it's nothing, and I could barely stand up once they got me into it. But it was instructive, too. All that protection and I still felt hot enough to burn, and the smoke made it nearly impossible to see. Believe me, I wasn't in there long before they helped me out."

"That's a rough job."

"You don't know how rough until you've done a training exercise with them." She shook her head. "I had a lot of respect for those guys beforehand, but after that, I'd give them all a medal."

Jerrod laughed again. "You lead an interesting life."

"Sometimes. Like any other job, there's a lot of humdrum."

"But you like it."

"I *love* it." The statement was unequivocal. "And at least I don't have to cover auto accidents and plane crashes anymore. Nothing can prepare you for that smell."

He nodded. "I know what you mean."

She looked at him, studying him. "I guess you do."

"So you've really walked into a forest fire?"

"A TV cameraman and I wanted to see what it was like. So we wandered off down this forest road."

"And?"

"It wasn't what I expected. This loud roar of rushing air being sucked in, and yet it's…cold. I don't know if it was the smoke blocking out the sun or the draft from the fire itself. Maybe both."

"I hope you don't plan to do that again."

"You sound like my mother."

"Still…"

"We came back fast, and we didn't go that far."

He seemed to study her for a long moment. "What part aren't you telling me?"

"You mean, the part where we were walking back and the fire jumped across the road?"

"No!"

She nodded. "Yeah. For a few seconds all I could see was fire. Everywhere. But it was arching through the branches overhead. Not down to ground level yet. We ran like hell, and the next thing you know it was behind us. It was way cool."

"Cool? You *are* an adrenaline junkie."

She rose from the chair and began pacing, unable to hold still despite the jackhammer in her head. "Y'know where the real adrenaline rush is?"

"Tell me."

"Writing the piece up under deadline. Racing the clock to get the front page done when the people down in production are screaming for the layout and everyone around you is yelling at someone because they need some little tidbit to finish what they're working on. TV blaring so if the world comes unglued we'll know it, plus so we know what the Barbie-and-Ken world are saying about the story. It's barely controlled chaos, a dozen blindfolded foxes chasing chickens around the same yard, knowing Farmer Time is just around the corner with a shotgun and that's why they call it a *dead*line. That's the *real* rush."

She realized she'd been talking a blue streak, and sat down and went silent for a moment. He was eating his salmon, yet she knew he'd taken in every word. Finally he looked up. "I knew guys like you in special ops. The crazier it got, the more they felt at home."

"But not you?" she asked.

His eyes took on a faraway, haunted look. "Nah. I couldn't feel at home when I was holding an artery closed, trying to keep a buddy alive until the evac team got there. All that training and discipline and focus, and y'know what I was thinking at that moment?"

"No," she said, and forced herself to down a spoonful of soup.

"That he and I wouldn't be shooting hoops anymore. That's what we'd done, last thing at night, every night. There was a basketball net in the hangar back at base, and every night, we'd wind down from the shit by playing three-on-three or H-O-R-S-E or just whacking the damn ball off of the backboard until the world no longer seemed so...loud. No way we were ever going to do that again, not with his leg hanging by a tendon and me pinching the femoral artery so he wouldn't bleed out. That's when I knew I wasn't like you, that I couldn't shut everything out and learn to love the chaos. That's when I knew I had to get out."

Her soup had lost its appeal. She pushed the bowl aside and looked at him. "I know. Kind of. Some stories still give me nightmares. Ever since a plane crash I covered, I still can't eat spaghetti. A county commission meeting may be boring, but at least I know that after the deadline rush passes, I'll sleep."

He nodded, but offered nothing else in return. She fell silent, then got up and began once again pacing the room, hating this caged feeling, hating the notion that her movements were limited because someone was after her. They really wouldn't go far enough to kill her—would they? It was like a bad movie. Reporters didn't get killed for doing their jobs.

But this story... Something inside her seemed to freeze. Maybe some stories were worth killing over. Maybe this was one of them. It was certainly worth dying for.

"What are they after, Erin?" Jerrod asked quietly behind her.

She paused, then wrapped her arms around herself. She realized that someone else *had* to know. In case… This was too important. If something happened to her, someone else had to be able to pursue this, and who better than an FBI agent? She decided to take the leap of faith.

"I think Mercator's in the white slave trade."

Seconds ticked by in silence. Then he said, "You think, or you *know?*"

"I knew most of it. I needed confirmation."

"Jesus." He was quiet for a little longer. "And they took everything you had."

She faced him. "I'm not a bimbo. When I work on a story this big, I keep backups."

"So they didn't get it all?"

She almost forgot and shook her head, but caught herself just in time. "I send everything I get to an anonymous e-mail account."

"Could they trace it from your computer?"

"Not unless they've been following me. I used cybercafés all over town. I guess at some level I was already paranoid."

"Not paranoid," he said. "Careful. There's a big difference. So…what do you know?"

"I had a source. Inside Mercator, I think, but I'm not positive."

"Then he's in their crosshairs, too," Jerrod said.

She shook her head. "Maybe not. I *hope* not. After our first contact, I never dealt with him on my work or home machines."

"Why did he contact you to begin with?"

"He saw the story in *Fortune*. He said I'd caught the jaywalkers and missed the killers."

"He said that?"

"Word for word," she said. "He said it was one of the perks Mercator offered for some customers. Buy Mercator's stuff and they'll get you a girl."

His face seemed to freeze. "Shit."

"That's what I said."

"Can you prove it?"

"That's what I was working on."

He nodded. "And your boss knew about it?"

She faced him. "Yeah."

He sighed and rubbed his face, as if he were tired. "You really *do* need protection."

"They don't know I have anything. With luck they think they took it all."

His cheeks were taut, the muscles in front of his ears flexing as he drew a slow breath through his nose, as if trying to hold back some part of him that she found almost…frightening.

"They want the whistle-blower. They think you

know who he is. Or she. That means they need you, Erin. And you don't want to even think about what they have in mind once they have you. You don't know these people."

"And you do?"

"Yeah," he said. "I do. I was one of them."

# 5

"Okay, who are you really?" Erin asked.

It was a good question, Jerrod thought. He wasn't sure it had a good answer. "I'm not who I was."

"So who *were* you? You said special ops before. But that's not what you meant just now."

He nodded. "Once I got out, I did what a lot of special ops guys do. I went to work for a PMC."

"Private Military Corporation," Erin said. "So you were a mercenary."

He'd always hated that word, but he couldn't deny it. "Yeah. I was a mercenary. Private executive security at first. Then K R-and-R work. Kidnap, Rescue and Recovery. There are a whole lot of fringe groups whose main source of income comes from kidnapping foreign executives or their families. The execs usually have insurance for it, if the companies they're working for want to spring for it. Some of them buy it for themselves. The company I worked for had a K-R-and-R team that contracted out to the insurance companies. We'd handle the ransom negotiations, cover the exchange, and generally keep stressed-out people from making stupid mistakes."

"And rescues?" she asked. "You'd try to find the victims and get them out without having to pay?"

He stifled a bitter laugh. "I wish I could say yes. That's what I'd hoped I'd be doing."

"But you didn't?"

"Almost never. It was a straight business deal. Negotiate the ransom down to a reasonable amount. The insurance companies had actuaries who actually had tables of this stuff. A site manager for a Fortune 500 company is worth X. Chief engineer is worth Y. Everything according to the ransoms that were customarily paid. The kidnappers knew it, and we knew they knew it. So they'd give their demands, we'd go through the motions, and they'd eventually come down to the standard asking price. We'd show up at one side of a bridge with a big bag of cash. They'd be at the other with our client. Sometimes the guys even shook hands at the exchange, like they'd bought a house or a car."

"Sounds…cold," Erin said.

"It was." He chewed his lip for a moment. "It was like a big play. GloboCorp wants to build a pipeline in some dust- or mud-covered corner of the world. The locals have two legal choices—go to work for

GloboCorp and help tear up their ancestral homeland or be out of work. So they pick door number three. They get together and give themselves some fancy name…the People's Liberation Army of Revolution or some such. They write a big manifesto against GloboCorp. GloboCorp buys K-R-and-R insurance and sends in a supply of easy-to-abduct workers, guys who want the hazard pay or whatever.

"The People's Liberation Army abducts a few of them a month, not enough to really upset GloboCorp's pipeline project, because then the gringos would come down in force and stomp the 'movement' into so much jungle jelly. So long as the kidnappers don't get too greedy, the insurance geeks dutifully pay up. GloboCorp builds its pipeline. The locals make some money in the process, plus they feel as if they stood up to big, bad GloboCorp, fought the good fight, even if they lost."

He shook his head. "Truth is, they were all just going through the motions. The K-R-and-R insurance and our fees and the rest of it was budgeted from the start, assessed within two or three percent by some math whiz wearing Coke-bottle glasses sitting in a Manhattan office and crunching numbers. It was all just the cost of doing business."

"Pretty pragmatic," Erin said.

"Hell, yes," Jerrod agreed. "A few years later, the locals find a way to live with the pipeline and the guys who were running around the jungle kidnapping people are running for office, talking about how they fought for the people, and how they're going to reform the government and end corruption. But by then, they've made so much money from the Globo-Corps of the world that they're as corrupt as the rest."

He paused. "And if they weren't, if they were really serious about protecting their native land and culture...well, then they've gotta go. We send in one of my former colleagues to plant a car bomb or, even better, to set it up so the local cops or army can do it. Some lieutenant in the godforsaken army gets a medal, and good ol' GloboCorp keeps racking up the profits. The Dow Jones Index goes up, and all is right with the world."

In the silence that followed, Jerrod realized he'd said way too much. He tried not to let himself think about those days. And this was why.

"And I thought *I* was a cynic," Erin said. Her eyes were neither approving nor judgmental. There was something else there, something he couldn't quite read. "So what really happened, Special Agent Westlake?"

He shook his head. "Another time. Or...not."

He expected her to fire back another question. But this time she did seem to take "No" for an answer. He turned on the TV to a low volume, some program about global warming. He stared at the scenes of disappearing glaciers, while Erin dozed off. Meltwater running down through moulins, cutting loose the Ross Ice Shelf. The world coming apart.

But the scenes of dying glaciers merely provided a backdrop to his thoughts. *White slavery.* It existed. Law enforcement knew that without a doubt. But it was rare to find anyone involved who wasn't beyond reach. Or to be able to prove the case once they were caught. The Dutch, a few years ago, had managed to crush some powerful white slavers who were bringing women out of Russia, promising them good jobs and then throwing them into brothels, where threats of violence against their families held them silent.

But there was another, even dirtier, side to that kind of operation. A much more clandestine one. The kind where individual children were snatched off the streets, young girls and boys, and sold to the twisted wealthy and powerful in other countries.

Those were the ones almost impossible to trace. The scumbags law enforcement found too slippery to grab. Somehow when Erin said that Mercator, a huge defense contractor, was involved in white slavery, he didn't think she meant the kind of rings the Dutch had broken. There would be no advantage to Mercator in such a thing.

He closed his eyes against the doom portended by

rapidly calving and melting glaciers, and turned inward to dark places he had to visit too often in his job. Places where innocent children were nothing but things to be used by someone with sick desires. Places where Elena lurked even yet.

If those were the kinds of things Erin was uncovering, then he wasn't going to tell another soul. Not if Mercator was involved. That company had too much power and too much influence, and all too often he had seen where that could lead. They might take a hit on a penny-ante corruption case, but on something like this, they would be covered nine ways to Sunday.

The Mercators of the world didn't get caught for things like white slavery.

Emotions he didn't allow himself to have any longer tried to wedge their way up to his heart and mind like those moulins melting their way through the glaciers. They would have their day, but their day would be destructive. He forced them down again, and instead focused on the cool anger and determination that had proved his best friends for many years.

No heat. No passion to interfere with reason. He might be propelled by passion, but he steered by cold reason. Passion must be kept in the background, simmering and providing energy, but never dined on. Never indulged.

He opened his eyes again to discover that the very

place he was sitting would probably be underwater in a hundred years. He supposed the global scale of the impending climate crisis might cast his obsession with the missing into obscurity, at least to some, but he felt differently.

That was why he climbed out of bed every morning.

Erin stirred, murmuring something in her sleep, and he took that as a good sign. She hadn't sunk into a sleep so deep it meant the concussion was creating a problem.

He needed more information from her. Much more. Then he could decide a course of action. Although if she was right about what she claimed, then only one course lay ahead of him.

On the television, the narrator's focus had shifted from glacial flooding to mega hurricanes. Erin spoke without opening her eyes. "Rita was a rush."

"What?"

"Hurricane Rita. I covered it. Can't say it was a happy rush." Her eyes opened, as blue as gas flames. "It hit us hard. It kind of got lost in the wake of Katrina. It wasn't as bad because there were no levees left to break." She stretched and yawned, then winced a little. "My neck is getting stiff."

"Not surprising. You took a pretty hard blow."

She stretched again, more cautiously, and curled up in the other direction. The TV commentator was now talking about desertification. Erin indicated the TV with a slight wave of her hand. "You listen to too much of that, you might get depressed."

"It's background noise. I already know about it."

"Yeah? Do you do anything about it?"

He tilted his head a little to one side. "Do you?"

"Parry," she said, with a smile that barely creased the corners of her eyes. "You're as good as I am at dodging questions. Ever consider becoming a politician?"

"I'd have to sell my soul. And you didn't answer my question."

"That's a two-way street. But yes, I try to do my part. I walk or take public transportation. I've re-placed all my incandescent bulbs with those compact fluorescent ones. I don't turn on my heat unless my fingers turn blue, and I do without air-conditioning unless it's night and I can't sleep. I also try not to buy anything that had to come from far away. You can't always tell, but 'grown in Chile' or 'made in China' are good indicators."

"You're doing better than I am, then."

"Aha."

But the reaction lacked spirit. They were walking around the edges of a peril that could destroy them both, trying to reach for some level of normalcy and banter.

He knew all about that, and he suspected she did,

too, from the way she was behaving. Sometimes you just had to ignore the elephant in the room, especially when you couldn't deal with it right that instant. The other elephant, the one unfolding before them on TV, seemed more like a parable than a science program.

Finally Erin spoke. "I guess I'm going to have to trust you."

He looked at her. "That's another two-way street."

"Is it?" She appeared dubious.

"Yes. I could get fired, too. I could get killed, too."

"Then why?"

He returned his gaze to the TV, knowing he had to offer an answer, but unwilling to get too personal.

Finally he found a way. "I've spent my entire career in the Bureau trying to nail white slavers. I spend my personal time on it. It's an obsession."

She fell silent in thought. "But you do other stuff?"

"Of course. It's part of my job. But finding the missing is my specialty. It's what I do best. And my life doesn't matter a hill of beans if I can put one white slaver into prison or save the life of one kid."

He turned to her again and found her eyes had darkened, as if someone had turned down the gas flame and replaced it with blue ink.

"I believe you," she said. "It's like that for me,

too. I don't have a personal score to settle or anything, but the idea of those little kids…" She trailed off, frowning. "I make my living with words, but I deal in facts, so it's hard for me to explain what I'm feeling. I just knew, when my source tipped me off to this, that it wasn't a story I was going to let go."

"Then we're on the same page."

"Maybe." She stared at him hard, as if trying to see into him. He stared right back. He wasn't one to blink.

"Okay," she said finally. "Where do I start?"

"How about telling me just how much about this you shared with your editors? Then I'll have some idea what the bad guys know."

"I didn't tell them much."

"Apparently it was enough."

She sighed and touched the side of her head. "Where are those pain pills?"

"In your upper left vest pocket." He went to the kitchenette to retrieve a club soda out of the fridge and then poured it into a glass for her. Then he returned to the couch, crossed his legs loosely and waited while she swallowed the medicine.

"You don't trust easily, do you?" he asked.

"Apparently this time I trusted too much."

One corner of his mouth lifted. "That's how we learn, Erin."

"Yeah, right. By being whacked on the head." But

he saw her gaze drift to the badge clipped to his belt. "I usually have an adversarial relationship with cops."

"What do you mean?"

"Oh, I jolly around with them and build relationships, but I'm always trying to learn things they don't want me to know. Things they've done wrong. Things they haven't done that they should have. They see my role as being their mouthpiece. I see my role as being the public's eyes and ears. The two are not the same."

"Of course not."

She raised her gaze to meet his. "It's going to be weird being on the same team."

He uncrossed his legs and leaned forward, resting his elbows on his knees and clasping his hands. "Here's how I see it. You're not going to walk away from this story, no matter what they've done. Firing you. Taking your work. Breaking into your place. Putting you in the hospital. You're not giving up, right?"

"No way!"

"If I can see that, having known you only a few hours, then they know it, too. So now you're the best source I have on an international crime ring, and the bad guys know you're not quitting. I wouldn't walk away from the crime regardless. I'm also not walking away and leaving you in their crosshairs. Since we're stuck with each other, we may as well work together."

She seemed to consider it for a moment before

replying. "You have access to resources that I can't get to on my own. So sure, we can work together. Just don't try to shut down my story once this is over. You can put these people in jail, but I can put them on the nightly news. Which do you think will cost them more?"

He nodded. "You can write it once we've got the case. I won't gag you. But look at it this way, Erin. Right now, right this very instant, while you're hesitating about what to share, they're still trying to find you. Because you can lead them to their leak. Quit wasting time. They sure as hell aren't."

She lowered her head briefly. "It's easier to walk into a forest fire," she said quietly. "At least you can see where the danger is."

"The problem is, you're already *in* the fire. Now we have to walk through it."

"Yeah. Okay. Nobody knows how much I know. Nobody knows who my source is, not even me. My editor knows only that I have one, and that he's feeding me information to check on. And that so far I've been able to verify most of what he's shared."

"How much is that?"

She shrugged. "Not enough. This guy is scared to death. He's handing out information as if it were nuggets of gold. A little here, a little there. Then he seems to panic and shut down. After a while, he comes back."

"So you think he works for the company?"

"I don't know how else he would get flight information."

"Flight information?"

"Yeah. He's told me that some shipments out of Colorado Springs are listed as going to one country but actually go to another. But the manifests don't add up."

"How so?"

"Equipment that's supposedly being shipped isn't leaving their factory. They list it as being shipped by cargo carriers, but they're not cargo carriers. They're private jets. Too small for the equipment that's on the manifest, and not going to the country that's supposedly getting the equipment."

"So he got curious?"

"Yeah. And then one night he worked late and overheard a conversation about how the cargo had to be sedated."

"And that made him think it was white slavery?"

"It made him curious. Curious enough to go out to the corporate airport and try to check on the cargo, thinking maybe he'd miscounted the inventory back at the warehouse, because his first count showed no product in transit. So he started looking around, and that's when he saw two kids being carried aboard a jet, both of them asleep."

"Some executives' kids being flown back home,

maybe?" Jerrod asked, almost wishing it could be that innocent.

"Home to Venezuela?" Erin replied. "Somehow I don't think so."

"He knows the flight went to Venezuela?"

She nodded. "Flight plan was for Brazil, but the aircraft never went there."

"How would he know that?"

She shrugged. "That part I'm not sure about yet. But his e-mail sounded pretty sure, and everything he's told me before has checked out."

"Does he have any idea why Mercator would be doing this?"

Erin shook her head. "Not yet. I mean, would Mercator be trafficking in kids just to get contracts?"

He glanced her way. "Every foreign-arms sale has to be approved through the government. Which basically means armaments are going only where our policy wonks want them to go, never mind that we may live to regret it two or three years later. Which means there's a certain amount of quid pro quo going on between government and contractors."

Her eyes widened. "You mean, the government might…know about this?"

"Maybe. Maybe not. But I've found it's always dangerous to underestimate your enemy."

# 6

Jerrod and Erin left the hotel before the eastern sky began to brighten. At a gas station, Jerrod bought them large coffees in metal travel mugs and breakfast tacos he'd heated in a microwave.

"Sorry it's not a better meal," he said as they pulled away. "We'll get something farther down the road."

"It's amazing what we'll accept as food," Erin said with a sleepy laugh. "I wonder if there's anything organic in these things?"

"Probably not," he said, chuckling. "But at least they're calories."

She nodded as she chewed and swallowed. "And they aren't the most horrible thing I've ever tasted."

He laughed as he ate. "No. If I close my eyes and let myself imagine, I can almost believe they're fit for human consumption."

She laughed with him, trying to cling to the

humor of the moment, knowing it couldn't last. It didn't.

"I'm going to keep to the back roads for a while," Jerrod said. "I'll make sure we don't have a tail."

Erin's neck prickled. "What if we do?"

"I'll drive off that bridge when we get to it."

It was an odd kind of confidence, she thought. They had only the barest notion of a plan and no real idea what might happen, yet he seemed comfortable with that, as if the uncertainty itself were a security blanket. Then again, given what he'd told her—and what he hadn't—he likely had a lot of skills that she didn't necessarily want to think about.

Some of the prettiest countryside in Texas slid by, invisible in the predawn darkness. There were no headlights to be seen, and rarely a streetlight. They could have been driving through grass-scented ink, with only the thrum of the tires and the occasional chuckhole to pull them back to reality.

They rode silently, sipping coffee. Just as trees were beginning to emerge from the darkness, Jerrod spoke.

"I'll have to stop by my office and do some things, but I'm going to leave you somewhere while I do."

"Why?"

"Because it's in the Houston police reports that I found you. And someone may also have reported that I took you away from the apartment. Point is, it's no secret we met. So I don't want anyone to know you're still with me."

"You think they'd be watching that closely?"

He glanced over at her before returning his attention to the road. "What do you think?"

"I don't know what to think. I'm not used to being paranoid."

"Like I said, you're the only link they have to your source. They want to know who you're talking to. Then they want you both dead."

"Thanks for the message of cheer," she said. "So they think I'm going to lead them to this guy?"

"That's what they're hoping. They're hoping we'll do exactly what we're going to do. Find the source. So we have to do that without them knowing we've done it."

"And if we can't?"

He looked at her. "Then we'll be taken out of the equation, and a whole lot more girls will go into it."

"The equation?"

He nodded. "Ever ask yourself what it means when a corporation changes the name of its 'personnel' department to 'human resources'? We're not people to Mercator. We're variables on a balance sheet. Until you tumbled onto this story, the paper had you in the assets column. But once you got onto this…"

"I became a liability."

He sipped his coffee. "It's as easy as that, when your personnel are just human resources. Move them from column A to column B. Eliminate as necessary."

She shivered. "I don't like the world you've lived in, Jerrod Westlake."

"Neither do I."

"Are you going to tell your office about this?"

"No." Unequivocal and flat.

"I guess the FBI has human resources, too." She settled back and sipped her coffee again. "So we can't trust anyone. Hell, for all I know, you were sent here to gain my trust so I'd lead you right to my source. For all I know, you're on cleanup detail."

He laughed quietly. "Now you're thinking like me."

"I'm not so sure that's a good thing."

"Actually, it is. You'll live longer."

No clouds marred the sky of Austin when they arrived. The heavens shone a breathtaking blue, and the air invigorated her with just a touch of winter's chill. Erin could have wallowed in the lack of humidity.

Jerrod surprised her. She'd half expected him to put her into another hotel, but instead he left her on the St. Edward's University campus in South Austin.

"It's busy, and it's public. Nobody will bother you here. And their library will have Internet access." He glanced at his watch. "I'll be back in two hours. Will you be okay?"

"Sure."

When he glanced into his rearview mirror, he saw her disappear into the library. Then he sped north to the Federal Building, already planning his story.

Inside the library, Erin found quite a few students working busily. Near the elevators, she found a pair of public computers that required no log-in, linked into the library database and the world beyond. While she couldn't connect to her anonymous account, she could look up "white slavery" on Google and see what was out in the public domain.

While some dismissed it as myth and others as women knowingly entering the sex trade for its economic opportunities, the statistics were staggering. Whether abducted, enticed, purchased from their parents or simply drawn by the lure of leaving home and gaining some measure of social and psychological independence, women and teens entered the international sex market on a horrific scale. Most knew they—or the daughters they were selling—would soon be working as "bar girls," "comfort women," "escorts" or "house girls." What they too often did not know was the degrading, violent and often deadly conditions under which that work was done.

Although the U.N. and many countries had funded countless studies and passed legislation to eliminate white slavery, the trade went on. In some societies it was accepted as a matter of course. Girls were imported, often as young as eleven or twelve years of age, and then schooled in the skills of their new profession. By their midteens they were ready for resale, often convinced that they were graduating into the adult world, a world where their bodies were fungible assets.

Waves of revulsion rolled through Erin as she read. Most repulsive of all was a question that slowly grew and began to gnaw at the back of her consciousness: what if these girls were not brainwashed, not victims, but self-motivated entrepreneurs who had chosen what they saw as their most accessible path to economic independence?

Some of the girls interviewed in the studies almost seemed to have been put forward as poster girls for prostitution, with gilded stories of having paid for college and opened doors that would otherwise have been forever barred by using their earnings. If she let herself see their perspective, it was almost as if prostitution was the female equivalent of military service: trading one's youthful body for the rights and opportunities of adult citizenship.

But for every one of those stories, there was a story of another kind, of beatings, of rape, of feeling one's heart and soul hollowed out, twenty minutes and as many dollars at a time, trying to pay off the "loan" that had brought the girl from Russia or

Thailand, Burma or Brazil, until she realized that she could work the rest of her life and never be free of the debt…or the memories.

The more Erin read, the more convinced she became that the human species could rationalize away the most abhorrent evils imaginable. If this was the best humanity could do, she thought, perhaps a radical global climate change would not be a disaster at all.

Perhaps it would simply be Mother Earth washing herself in disgust.

Alton Castle was probably the least important accountant at Mercator Arms, and that was fine with him. He handled shipping invoices on classified projects. Like everything at Mercator, his job was compartmentalized, so that none of the junior employees would have a full picture of what they were doing on any contract. It was standard security doctrine, and Alton liked it that way.

In fact, he would have vastly preferred not to have learned what he knew.

When he'd joined Mercator seven years ago, he'd had ambitions. He'd seen his job as a stepping-stone to greater things. He'd poured heart and soul into his work, aware that accuracy was crucial on government contracts, aware that inspectors didn't always give warning before they arrived. He'd wanted to ensure that Mercator was doing everything by the book, so Pentagon Inspector General teams would never have reason to challenge the company on anything he'd been involved in.

But he also had a daughter. Like many employees, he kept a picture of his wife and their child on his desk, a reminder that his job was a means and not an end in itself. First-time visitors to his office often commented on how beautiful both were, and his chest swelled with pride each time. They were beautiful. Stunningly, amazingly so.

He might be a mere "bean counter," as other parts of the company referred to the huge staff of accountants and lawyers, but bean counting was essential to the company's life. Absolutely essential, he often thought, for if the government noted any discrepancy in the billings, they might be audited, and while the audit continued, the government could refuse to pay the company's bills on suspect contracts. He might be a cog in the wheel, but he was an important cog.

He sat in his small cubicle, matching bills of lading with contracts and invoices. He also maintained completion tallies, so he could report on the accounting status of each of the contracts he managed.

But he had been *too* diligent. He'd tumbled into a snake pit, one his conscience would not let him ignore. Every time he looked at the face of his daughter, he felt the jolt of his discovery anew.

"Alton?" One of the women in his group appeared

at his doorway with an armful of papers. "These bills of lading are all verified as to contract. The preliminary invoices are clipped to them."

"Thanks, Cecile. Just put them in my in-box." He had to check over all the prelims, then make any necessary adjustments.

She did as asked, gave him a flirtatious smile and sashayed out of the cubicle.

He returned to the file he was pretending to examine and tried to calm himself. The increased security at the plant, begun only a few days ago, had unnerved him. As yet the changes were minimal, but given what he knew, and that he had shared it outside the company, he was sure that every new edict was aimed directly at him. He felt as if he were wearing a neon sign.

His computer dinged at him, and he turned to check his mail. His heart stopped.

We have reason to believe there has been a security violation at our Colorado Springs facility. All briefcases and purses are subject to search, and all telephone calls will be randomly monitored. Other measures may be instituted as deemed necessary.

Thank you for your cooperation.

Neils Ingram, Facility Security Officer

"Jesus," he whispered, then looked swiftly around to ensure no one had heard. He skipped to the next e-mail, something less likely to give him a heart attack, and pretended to read it.

His heart slammed so hard and so loud he was certain someone else in the office must have heard it. But outside his cubicle, nothing seemed to change. Phones still rang, voices could be heard talking quietly, the copier *thunked* away in the nearby copy room.

The e-mail could be about something else. Of course it could. He hadn't taken anything out of the facility. He hadn't made a single phone call from the office or home about this. He hadn't even used his own computer here or at home to send information.

If they had tumbled to the leak, there was no way they could trace it to *him*. No way. Besides, who would think that kind of a leak could issue from some cog in the accounting department?

Gradually calming, he forced himself to begin looking through the invoices on his desk, as if he were working industriously. He was safe. He had ensured that with his caution. Even his nosing around in inventory was so far in the past now that the computer audit trails had probably been erased. They would be investigating persons closer to the activity than a mere accountant.

A half hour later, he was almost back to normal. But he had decided he wasn't going to do another thing to help that reporter. She had enough information now. Let her do her own work. He'd done his by tipping her off.

When Jerrod returned to pick up Erin, he found her sitting outside the library with a visible bubble of empty space around her. That was hardly surprising, given the angry scowl on her face. The students milling around had obviously seen it, too, and had instinctively kept her at a safe distance. He didn't have that option.

"Come on," he said. He figured she would tell him what had ticked her off if she wanted to.

When they reached the parking lot, she looked around. "Where's your car?"

He pointed. "It's the white one. I couldn't take a Bureau vehicle for this. Especially since it has a LoJack and we could be tracked."

"And yours?"

"Nothing trackable. Just your basic four-wheel-drive Suburban."

This one was smaller, with a gray cloth interior, much better suited to the hot Texas sun. Not to mention that it was fully equipped with his collection of Willie Nelson CDs.

"What did you tell them?" she asked, as they pulled out of the campus lot and started north on Congress Avenue. Here Austin still reflected its small-town roots, from the days before zoning. Houses and businesses met and mingled, and the trees were old and grand.

"Who? You mean, my bosses?"

Her hands clenched into fists on her lap. "Who else would I mean? Did you tell them about me?"

"No. I'm not telling anyone anything they don't absolutely need to know."

"Then how can you get away?"

"I have a certain amount of leeway when I'm investigating something." He braked at a stoplight and looked at her. "What has you so upset?"

"I was reading about white slavery."

"And?"

She looked at him, and her blue eyes seemed to burn. "I've never seen anything so twisted in my life."

"What do you mean?"

The light changed, and he touched the accelerator.

"Do you have any idea of the scale of this kind of thing?"

His face tightened. "Some."

"I couldn't believe it!" she continued, oblivious. "I've been so busy, I haven't taken time to do the background research, but this kind of stuff is a major business."

"In some places."

"Parents actually sell their daughters. Not just a handful of parents, but *lots* of parents. I mean, I knew it happened sometimes. I'm not totally stupid. But I had no idea of the *scale!* Some of the girls go on their own, trying to escape poverty, but they really have no idea what they're getting into. And then there are the five- and six-year-olds who actually get sent to schools to learn how to be prostitutes."

"I know."

His tone appeared to arrest her flood tide of anger, and he felt her eyes on him as he navigated the traffic. As he passed Oltorf, he caught sight of a car in his rearview mirror. Something about it bothered him, so he turned left onto Live Oak, figuring they could take the First Street Bridge into the downtown area—if they weren't being followed. To his relief, the car didn't turn with them.

"Sorry," she said after a moment. "You probably know all this."

"Some of it. I get as angry as you, when I let myself think about it. But I can't do anything about what's going on in Asia and other places around the world."

From the corner of his eye, he saw her hands relax.

"You're right," she said. "We have to concentrate on the things we *can* do something about. Like what my source told me."

"Exactly. I agree that it's horrifying, ugly and debasing, and I can't begin to understand why women are treated as subhumans in so many places and by so many people. Even here. But I learned that I can only go after the things that are within my power to change. We need to save our energy for that, Erin."

She sighed. "I know. Part of me is a crusader. I guess that's why I got into journalism. I want to right wrongs, change the world. That's hard enough to do on your own block, let alone on a global basis."

"Actually," he said kindly, "one good story from you might motivate a greater change than any arrest I make."

She snorted. "You think so? I never let myself forget that I'm writing birdcage liner. The best birdcage liner I can write, but still…"

"What do you mean?"

"That what I write on Wednesday sees print on Thursday, is forgotten on Friday, and by Saturday is being pooped on in the bottom of some canary's cage."

He laughed, turning right onto First Street and heading toward the bridge. "That's lowering."

"It never pays to let your ego get too big."

He felt a strong spark of liking for her. She kept amazing him and delighting him. "Yet you got Mercator for fraud."

"That's true. But it's actually no big deal."

"Why not?"

"Because they'll just find another way to get more taxpayer dollars than they should. It won't change Mercator one whit."

"Maybe not the fraud thing. But this could."

Her fists clenched again. "Yes," she said. "Yes, it could. Why is it so hard to stop this stuff?"

"Well, partly because it's done so secretly. And then there's the problem of gathering evidence that will hold up. In Holland, where brothels were legal, none of the women would admit they were being held against their will, even though some authorities suspected it. But the women had been told their families would be killed if they talked. So anytime the Dutch tried to investigate, they'd meet a stone wall of silence."

"What finally happened?"

"Some of the women finally came forward after their colleagues had died from maltreatment and the lack of basic health care. Sex workers are invisible to society, so they often don't have access to things you and I take for granted, not without putting themselves at risk. These women took that risk, and Interpol broke up the ring." He shook his head. "And it's probably growing back right now, if it hasn't already."

All of a sudden he hit the brakes and wrenched the wheel to the left, centrifugal force hurling them across the car as tires squealed. His seat belt locked from the sudden acceleration, and they were jolted again as he stamped on the accelerator and the SUV shot down a side street.

"What the hell are you doing?" she demanded as they cleared the intersection. "My God, are you nuts?"

"No. But I think we're being followed."

# 7

Jerrod nearly mounted the curb as he dodged a slow-moving subcompact, one eye on the road and the other on the rearview mirror. The afternoon rush hour hadn't begun, but traffic was already thickening. Interstate-35 was only a few blocks away, but he knew better than to go there. It was far too easy to track a vehicle on a limited-access highway. He stuck to the city streets instead.

"My fault," he said, as he steered them through another sharp turn.

"I hope you're watching for city cops. And how did they find us, anyway?"

"I had to go to the office and my apartment. Obvious places to tag me."

"What if we can't lose them?"

"Then we'll go to the Federal Building. I defy them to follow us in there."

"Great. Then how do we get *out?*"

"I realize that right now I don't look very bright," he said as the car lurched into an alley, "but I do have a few brain cells functioning. Getting out of the Federal Building will be the least of our problems."

"If you say so." But she sounded dubious. "I didn't realize you doubled as Houdini."

"I'm still working on the water-barrel trick, but I've got the rest figured out."

"Sure." As they started to spin into another turn, she reached up and grabbed the handgrip over the window. "I'm almost wishing the cops would arrest us."

"No, you're not." He maneuvered them through a turn that threatened to roll the car, correcting just in time to land all four wheels on the pavement as he shot down an alley. "No one is safe in a cell."

"Oh, man, and this from a cop. Are you sure that badge is real?"

"Last time I checked."

"Maybe you should check again. Maybe it's like Cinderella's pumpkin and we just passed midnight."

"How many people do you know who walk around with a gun holstered on their belts?"

"In Texas? Only a few tens of thousands."

He shook his head and zigzagged them ahead of slower traffic. "We're going to Colorado Springs, right?"

"Are we? I think that's where the guy is, but until I get to my stuff online, I can't say for sure."

"The probability will do. Time to head south."

"South?"

He pulled a U-turn just before they reached the bridge. More burning rubber and squealing tires, greeted by honking horns and angry gestures. The State Capitol disappeared from view, replaced rapidly by the sprawling Civic Center, then the south view of First Street. Trees on the right, and small buildings, and on the left a school.

"Maybe I should hide on the floor," Erin said. "This is embarrassing."

"Does anyone in town know you?"

"I've only been here once, briefly." She looked out the back window. "Which one is following us?"

"The black Mercedes. See it?"

"Yes. I guess Mercator can afford high-class goons with fancy cars."

"So it seems."

She turned around and hung on. "Are we going to San Antonio?"

"Right now we're going insane."

"Ah." She grabbed on tighter. "I had that feeling."

"Since you haven't spent a lot of time here," he said, zipping past a delivery van, "allow me to tell you some of the more interesting local lore."

"Be my guest."

"Our State Capitol, the building I was hoping to drive toward until I noticed our tail, was built in

1888 with a limestone foundation, and faced with sunset-red granite, quarried only fifty miles from here."

"I'm wowed."

"I knew you would be." Another turn caused them both to lurch a bit. "Are you aware that there's a federal law barring state capitol buildings from being taller than the U.S. Capitol?"

"I had no idea. What an ego trip."

Another lurch to the left, to avoid rear-ending a rental truck driven by an apparently confused driver.

"Well, the Texas State Capitol is fifteen feet higher."

"So they ignored the law?"

"They circumvented it."

Acceleration pushed her back in her seat. "How'd they do that?"

"Lady Liberty, the statue on top, is fifteen feet tall."

"Brilliant." She tightened her grip as she saw a knot of slow traffic ahead. She had no idea how they were going to avoid crashing into it.

"I thought so," he said, wrenching the wheel. "But Lady Liberty has an even more interesting story."

"That's pretty good for a statue." Her teeth snapped together.

"Ladies lead interesting lives."

"So what's the story?"

"She was removed from the dome during renovations and underwent a little face-lift of her own. It was a big day when they brought her back to enthrone her again."

"I can imagine."

"Only, they couldn't get her back on the pole that supported her."

"A case of coitus interruptus?"

He snorted. "Something like that. Finally Texas, proud Texas, had to beg the Louisiana National Guard for help."

"That must've hurt."

"Excruciatingly. But the Louisiana guard possessed something conspicuously missing from the Texas armory."

Another hard turn, and almost before she knew what was happening, they were back on South Congress. "Are we going in circles?"

"Not exactly. Ah, there's what I want."

Having no idea what he meant, she prodded him to continue the story. "So what did Louisiana have that Texas didn't?"

"A Skycrane. Louisiana made it look like a slam dunk, and Lady Liberty was enthroned once again. Galling, but worthy of celebration."

"Absolutely."

Another screeching turn onto a narrow street and they were westbound, running through an old, gracious neighborhood of towering live oaks and small houses. Another turn and they were heading north on Lamar.

"He's gone," Jerrod announced.

Erin squirmed around on her seat and looked. No black Mercedes. "Are you sure?"

"Absolutely. He missed the last two turns. Though I can't take credit for it, really. One of Austin's finest didn't like being cut off."

"A cop? I didn't see a cop."

"Unmarked car. Just what I was looking for."

Erin turned around, facing forward again. "That's cheating."

"We're not out of the woods yet."

"How so?"

"They have my license number and vehicle ID."

"Oh, great." She sighed. "Look, why don't we just go to your office and tell them everything?"

"Because," he said quietly, "as I told you before, defense contractors have major pull. For all we know, this trafficking is going on with someone's approval."

"I'd like to feel shocked by that idea." In fact, she was appalled that she wasn't.

"So would I."

"I need to get to my e-mail," she reminded him. "How else am I going to figure out what we need to do?"

"First things first."

He pulled off Lamar into the entrance of an apartment community. Once they'd reached a parking area out of sight of the street, he pulled into an empty spot, turned off the ignition and climbed out.

"What are we doing?"

He shook his head. "Just trust me."

Trust wasn't a natural condition for her, so she climbed out. Unfortunately, that meant watching him commit a crime.

He removed his license plate with a ratchet wrench, and exchanged it for a plate he had in the back of his car. "Don't ask," he said.

She didn't. Even a reporter sometimes recognized that ignorance was the better part of valor. Ten minutes later, they were back on the road.

"Computer," she said again.

"Not here. Not in this town. I'll get you to one. Are you getting hungry?"

"I'm famished, frankly." It had already been a long day, and since what had passed for breakfast tacos before dawn, they hadn't eaten anything.

"Pick your poison. I'll find a drive-through."

"Just make it easy," she said. "Easy and fast. I don't want another drive like the one we just took. I'd spill my fries, and that makes a mess."

He picked a small business, a privately owned sandwich shop where they were able to order loaded subs and salads. The unusual part came when he pulled up beside the Dumpster and passed her his cell phone. "Toss our phones in there."

"Why? Are you crazy? We might need them!"

"Toss them. They can be triangulated. I picked up a couple of pay-as-you-go phones before I came to get you."

"What if we just turn them off?"

He shook his head. "Not good enough."

"Big Brother is watching all the time, huh?"

"He is. Toss them."

She turned them both off and did as he said, wincing a little because she'd paid a tidy sum for that damn flip-phone. They disappeared into the mounds of trash in silence. Then he passed her a new one. A cheapie.

"Yours," he said. "It's programmed with my number."

She slipped the ugly thing into her jacket pocket without turning it on. "I suppose," she said, "that I should be thrilled by all this cloak-and-dagger. My adrenaline should be rushing madly."

"It isn't?"

"Not one bit."

"You're tired," he suggested. "Plus you had that bang on the head."

"Whatever. I am not a happy camper."

"Who is?"

She glanced at him and noticed for the first time

that he looked tired, too. Tired and determined. His jaw was set as he pulled back out into traffic.

"Sorry," she said finally. "I shouldn't whine."

"Be my guest. You can whine for us both."

"How about we eat instead?"

"It might help."

She unwrapped half of his sandwich just enough that he could start eating it, and opened a bottle of water and placed it in the cup holder on the console between them. "I don't know where all this is taking us," she said after a moment. "But I guess it's a journey we have to make."

"My feeling exactly. And if I find out any Feds are involved with this trafficking, I'm going to take huge pleasure in nailing their hides to the wall."

That brightened Erin a bit. "Yeah," she said. "I'll load the nail gun."

Georgie Dickson sat in her cubicle, tracing the tendrils snaking outward from a civil-rights violation by some local cops. The pair of cops who had initially appeared to be the sole problem now seemed to be part of something larger that lingered elusively just beyond her reach.

Which, of course, was the reason for her involvement. Otherwise the suspension meted out by the Austin PD internal-affairs department would have ended the matter.

Absorbed in her thoughts, she started at the rap on the side of her cubicle. Looking up, she saw Derek Monfort, the assistant special agent in charge, or ASAC.

"How's it going?" he asked.

This was the first time he'd expressed any interest in the case, so her radar started beeping, just a distant early warning, the kind that said something unexpected might be flying into her airspace.

"I'm still trying to catch the ectoplasm that's holding whatever this is together."

He laughed. "It seems that way sometimes, doesn't it?"

"In the early stages anyway. You need something?"

"Did I see Jerrod in here earlier?"

Her radar began beeping faster. "Yes. He was here for a few minutes."

"Did he say where he was going?"

Georgie shook her head. "Is something wrong?"

"He's not answering his cell, and I needed to ask him something about the Webly case."

"Can't help you there, Derek. All he told me was he was exhausted and taking some personal time. He's probably at home, sleeping."

"Maybe so. Thanks, Georgie."

Derek walked away, and Georgie forced herself to look down at the papers on her desk as if nothing were out of the ordinary. But the truth was, her shoulders and neck felt as tight as coiled springs, and the invading aircraft was now dead center on her mental screen.

She knew Jerrod well enough to be sure he was on to something big, and she knew Derek well enough to be equally certain he hadn't come to ask her about Jerrod for something so simple.

In fact, she was almost **certain** the visit had been precipitated by the e-mail Jerrod had written during the ten minutes he spent in the office:

Urgent personal matters require me to take leave at this time. I can't say for certain how long I'll be gone. Will keep you posted.

Not the usual way an agent requested leave. Far from it. So far from it that Georgie knew something else was going on, and probably so did Derek.

She tried to assure herself that Derek's curiosity had been aroused by the e-mail. Nothing more. But she still wished she could pick up the phone and warn Jerrod.

Because Jerrod had told her something she hadn't shared with Derek.

"I'm going to be undercover for a while, Georgie. Don't tell anyone. You won't be able to call me."

She'd wanted to protest at the irregularity, but she knew it was hopeless. If Jerrod considered something important enough to trash his career, he would trash it, and no argument in the world would stop him.

So she stared blindly at the papers that only a few minutes before had intrigued her so much, and wished she could warn Jerrod that Derek was asking about him.

Because if the FBI started looking for him, they were going to find him. Like the Mounties, they always got their man. Eventually.

She rotated her shoulders, trying to loosen them. Trying to shake the awful feeling that Derek's question hadn't been pure curiosity.

What the hell was Jerrod into?

# 8

Alton Castle didn't get hit on the briefcase check until two days later. By then he'd begun to relax, certain that if it were *his* leak they were tracing, they hadn't followed it back to him.

Nor was there any reason they should have. He reminded himself of all the precautions he'd taken. Over and over. It was like a stuck record playing in his head in response to the anxiety he couldn't quite shed.

And, of course, there was nothing in his briefcase to cause him any trouble, although he did feel a little insulted that they checked it for a false bottom. When he caught the glance of a woman behind him in the line at the checkpoint, he saw his own irritation magnified. Well, if he felt annoyed by having his briefcase checked, he could only imagine how a woman felt about her purse. He knew what his wife kept in hers, and having some strange man pawing around in those intimacies would have sent her through the roof.

It was different for an airport check-in. Screeners there usually relied on X-rays. These guys were looking for things that wouldn't show up on X-rays, so they went through everything by hand.

His own briefcase contained nothing but the remains of his lunch, his favorite pens, a blank tablet for note-taking and a thin stack of employee evaluation forms he needed to work on. In one short minute, they were done with him and he was out of the building, crossing the huge parking lot to the distant corner where his car waited.

Stepping out of the building, he suddenly realized, no longer meant simply stepping out into the twilight of a cold Colorado evening. The chilly breath he drew tonight tasted more like freedom.

In the car, seized by impulse, he pulled his cell phone from the glove box. Cell phones weren't allowed inside the building for a variety of reasons, all of which he agreed with. As he waited for his car to warm a bit, he called his wife.

"Let's go out for dinner tonight."

There was a pause, then, "But, Alton! I've already thawed a chicken."

"Is it in the oven?"

"No…"

"Then stick it in the refrigerator."

"But why?"

"Because," he said, "I feel like celebrating the fact that I'm in love with you."

And he did. He had tasted fear, and he was safe—for one more night, anyway. And somehow that seemed to narrow things down to what was genuinely important.

"All right," she said. He could hear the smile in her voice, the girlish excitement. "Shall I call Tammy?"

He took a moment to remember that Tammy was their usual babysitter. "If you can get her. If not, don't worry about it. A family night is good, too."

She laughed. "I love you, Alton."

"I love you, too, sweetheart."

The smile on his lips reached all the way to his heart as he closed the phone and slipped it into his coat pocket.

Crossing Raton Pass in Northern New Mexico took Erin and Jerrod into the full snow and ice of winter. Even with the heater on full blast and her light jacket wrapped snugly around her, Erin could still feel the cold through the window beside her.

"It'll be warmer once we get down lower," Jerrod assured her as she shivered.

"I know. But I still think maybe I should find something warmer to wear. It may be spring in Houston, but it's still only February."

"We'll take care of it," he promised.

Overhead, the sky was the color of flat, burnished aluminum, and was growing even darker now that night approached. Snow fell steadily in small flakes. The road followed frequent switchbacks to ease the descent, but snow limited visibility. Worse, the fresh fall was beginning to cling to the road.

"I hope we get down before dark."

"We should," he said bracingly.

"And then you'll find me a computer, right?"

"Nag, nag." But his tone teased her. "As soon as we get to Pueblo."

"Good. I'd sure hate to find out we've come all this way for nothing."

"But you said your source's initial call came from Colorado Springs. And Mercator is headquartered there."

"Very true. But that doesn't mean the source lives there."

"Save the headaches for later, okay? It's not as if e-mails will give you his address."

"But what if he doesn't live there?"

He glanced at her, then returned his attention to the treacherous road. "You need to eat."

"What makes you say that?"

"Your moods follow your food intake like clockwork."

She flushed. "No they don't."

"Yes, they do. It's not all that unusual, you know. The first place I can, I'll get you something. Then life will look more positive. I should probably carry candy bars in the car."

Before she could retort, the car skidded a little, and he quickly took his foot off the accelerator.

"I'm not a mountain driver."

They were already in four-wheel-drive, so the car came out of the skid quickly and the tires grabbed the road through the snow again. Nevertheless, he downshifted into second and let engine drag slow the car down.

"I wanna go back to Houston," she said. "Where the worst thing on the roads is flooding and debris."

He laughed. "Snow isn't that bad if you treat it with respect."

"*Lots* of respect."

"Tons of it."

A snowplow came around the curve ahead of them, chugging its way to the top of the pass, scraping the pavement as it went.

"I guess they're expecting more of this stuff," Erin remarked.

"Or they had a lot of it already. Either way, we're heading for the sun belt."

She gaped at him. "We're heading the wrong way!"

"In Colorado, Pueblo is considered to be practically tropical."

"No way."

"Not for real, of course. But they don't get a whole lot of snow compared to other parts of the state, and it's pretty sunny."

"Hmm. Coming from Houston, I may have trouble noticing those important things."

"You're just blinded by the snow."

"Ha ha." But then she giggled. "I'm being a sourpuss."

"Like I said, you need to eat."

She wasn't really keen on having her moods diagnosed this way, but neither could she really argue about it. She'd known all her life that she wasn't one who could skip meals safely. Not that she would get sick or anything, but she certainly grew crabby.

"Quit reminding me I'm like my mother," she finally said.

"What's wrong with your mother?"

"Not a thing. Except that Dad always said the only way he could travel with her was to feed her six times a day."

"I'll keep that in mind. What about your family? Where do they live?"

"The end of the world."

"What's that mean?"

"They got a wild hair a few years ago and moved to New Zealand. My brother went with them."

He eased them through a tight curve. "Why didn't you go?"

"Because I was just starting to make a name for myself here. Seems pointless now. And frankly, sheep ranching in New Zealand is sounding pretty good at this juncture."

"I imagine so. But once this story breaks, you'll go where you want in your career."

"I hope so." She shivered again. "But it's not just my career, Jerrod. This whole thing makes me so sick I want to throw up. I've been facing this for months, but there's a part of me that just shies away from the enormity of it. I don't want to believe it's true."

"Nobody does," he said quietly. "Nobody."

"So how many missing persons have you found?"

"Quite a few. I don't keep a tally." Which wasn't true. He kept a tally, all right, but only for the kids.

"It must be satisfying."

"When I find them alive, very. Not quite so much when they're dead. But still satisfying even then. It's an interesting thing about humans. We *need* to know what happened to our loved ones. If possible, we need to bury them and know where they rest. If not, we still have to know what happened. Otherwise we can't get over it in some essential way."

She sighed. "That's so sad."

"Not being able to get over it?"

"Not knowing. Thank God I can only imagine it. But I did learn one thing when my aunt died."

"Which was?"

Another shiver ripped through her. "She didn't want a funeral or a memorial. In fact, in her will she stipulated that. I don't know if we were bound by it, but we honored her wishes. To this day, I feel as if something is unfinished about that. I realize it's not the same as not knowing what happened, but I guess there's a need for family and friends to get together and mark the passing. Isn't that why rites are so common in all human societies?"

"I don't know much about it."

"Then take my word for it. Rites of passage exist in every society. Rites involving birth, reaching adulthood, marriage and death. Every time the status of a human being changes, it's marked by the society around them in some way."

The snow had thickened even more, and he allowed the car to slow down further. "That's interesting. I haven't thought of it that way. I wonder why that is."

"I don't know, but it seems to be extremely important to us. So not following the death rituals has to be disturbing at some very basic level."

"And families who don't know what happened to their loved ones can't do that."

"Well, if they did, they'd be admitting the person

is dead. And few people are willing to do that without some kind of evidence."

He nodded. "That would be my assumption."

"From my experience, I'd guess people could go a whole lifetime and not be able to admit someone was dead without proof."

"So would I," he said, almost too quietly to be heard over the straining engine.

Erin looked at him, but something in his expression kept her from asking the question. He wasn't the subject of a story, and even reporters could be tactful. Even stupid, determined, crazy reporters who went off to uncover a white slavery ring, risking their lives in the process.

Far from lightening as they descended, the snow seemed to be increasing to blizzard intensity. "Was this on last night's weather?" Erin asked. They'd stayed in some fleabag motel in the Texas Panhandle, where he could pay with cash. Erin had been afraid to take her clothes off, and had slept on top of the covers of the twin bed. Jerrod seemed impervious to the substandard conditions, although he didn't take off his socks or slacks.

"I don't know. See if you can find anything on the radio."

What she discovered was a lot of static. It was weird in this day and age to find herself cut off electronically, but there were evidently still places in the world where radio and cell phones couldn't reach. They seemed to have found one of them.

Finally she switched off the radio. "I'll try later."

"I guess a weather report wouldn't be much help right now. Predicted or not, we're in it."

"Damn, that sounds like a description of *life*."

Mercator's public reach included private security, weapons, even intelligence satellites. But its fingers delved further, into supersecret, so-called "black" contracts. While still government contracts, the money came from budgets that not even Congress itself could look into, because they were considered so highly classified. And most of them endured almost no oversight from the government agencies that issued them.

Some of those contracts issued from the military. A surprising number issued from the Department of Homeland Security and bore innocuous titles such as "Restructure of Emergency Response Vehicles."

The titles, of course, had nothing to do with the actual contracts but were a facade to fool those outside the actual black work itself.

Black budgeting served a useful security purpose. No one would argue that it didn't. Development of stealth technology had, for years, been under the umbrella of the black budget, and so were any number of technologies still successfully hidden from curious eyes.

But by its very nature, black budgeting created opportunities for other actions. Actions that could never become public, and if they did, would be disavowed by everyone who could muster a claim of ignorance. The persons who carried out these actions always had their sights set on a different purpose.

Kendall Warrick, the chief operations officer of the Mercator Industries Weapons and Security Group, was one of a small handful in management who knew about the black work. Someone had to commit the company to these projects and ensure that they were carried out, and he was the man.

*The man.* The words floated through his mind as he stood at the windows of the tenth-floor conference room and looked out over a darkened Colorado Springs. Snow obscured Pikes Peak, but he could still see the hulking foothills to the west of town, like the wall of a fortress. He loved this city, and he loved his country and he loved his work. There wasn't an inkling of a doubt in his mind that he achieved more on a daily basis than any government functionary, or any soldier on the ground, for the well-being of the United States.

And he achieved that in part because he knew how to sweeten pots. Only one other person knew the extent of that under-the-table business, and he meant to keep it that way. Certainly nobody else in the company knew…or should have known. He was too smart to allow that. As long as he kept making the big foreign sales deals, his future was gold.

Right now he was awaiting a visit from one of his most important contacts. The guy was in the government but did a little work on the side. Useful work that was of value to Kendall Warrick and hence to Mercator. As everyone slipped away from Mercator for the evening, the real business could begin.

He heard a chair creak behind him and turned to look at one of his top security specialists, a man who was a field operative in the action arm of their subsidiary, RoughRider Protection, Inc. Chuck Besom had changed to corporate coloration for this meeting, a blue suit and red tie, but Kendall had seen him in his other uniform, the one he wore on assignments. A modern-day ninja. A useful man, one well-prepared by his former life in special operations to take orders without question.

"He's late," Chuck remarked.

"He usually is. You should understand *that*."

Chuck nodded, his fair hair glinting in the dim lighting. "Never follow a schedule."

"So it seems. You're sure you lost them?"

Chuck nodded, his face as hard as granite. "I don't know how, but we sure as hell did. I'm going to nail some balls to the wall over this."

"Well, it's not as if you're up against someone who hasn't walked in *your* shoes."

"No excuse. The tail was sloppy and tipped them off. The idiot should have backed off the instant he knew he was spotted."

"You're sure they're not still in Austin?"

"They could be, but I'd be surprised, given the intel we have, what we know she knows. And Westlake has a rep as a bulldog. He's not going to let this one go." Chuck rapped his fingers on the table. "Of all the damn agents to meet up with her... We could control anyone else."

"We can still discredit the reporter."

"I'm working on it."

"And still no idea where the leak came from?"

"Nope."

Kendall turned back to the window. The snow seemed to be whirling faster now. "I don't like this. Our security should make these leaks impossible without detection."

"That's the idea of all security measures," Chuck Besom agreed. The kind who hated to be still, he rose and began pacing.

Kendall was used to it, so he didn't bother to look. "They'll come here," he said.

"Yes, they will."

"We're moving the operation?"

"As soon as we can. Right now I advise against any kind of change in routine that could raise questions."

At that Kendall faced him. "Why?"

"The leak spotted something. Something so subtle we didn't know it was there to be seen. Moving the op in the dead of night would be like hanging a billboard on it."

"We could put a clamp on it."

Chuck laughed sarcastically. "The thing is, Kendall, people aren't stupid. They know more than we think they know, more than they know themselves, until something happens and things click into place."

"You think everyone's as suspicious as you are."

Chuck nodded. "That's my job. Nothing changes until we get a handle on either the leak or the reporter and Westlake. Until then, the contract goes silent."

Kendall returned his attention to the storm outside. He didn't bother mentioning the delivery delays Chuck was insisting on. After all, that was why they were waiting to meet with the man whose other job was with the NSA.

# 9

Erin and Jerrod stayed at a better motel in Pueblo. Not the height of luxury, but the sheets smelled fresh, and the room boasted a high-speed Internet hookup.

"No good without a computer," Erin pointed out. "I guess I'll have to buy one."

"My advice is to stay off the grid. Besides, you don't need to buy one."

"Oh, I suppose if I beep and buzz just right, I can talk directly to the server over the phone?"

He laughed, a laugh that shook his shoulders. "Do you have any idea how much fun you are?"

Erin blinked, astonished. "Um, you're a minority of one in that opinion."

"Smart mouth, smart brain. I like it." Then he passed through the door into the whirl of a blizzard that wasn't supposed to happen. Erin went to the window and watched as he got their bags from the car. She did, however, turn away when she saw him start to remove the license plate from a vehicle similar to theirs. Definitely breaking the law. She didn't want to know.

When he returned, he was covered with snow and carrying both their suitcases, plus a laptop bag.

Her eyes immediately latched on to the bag. "Is that what I think it is?"

"You bet." He laid all the bags down on the bed and watched as she hurried to check out the computer. "It's my personal machine. I haven't used it in a year, so you're going to think it dates from the Stone Age. And you need to wipe any cookies or other identifiers before you plug it into the Net."

She straightened. "Do I look like a computer geek?"

"That's the last thing I'd compare you to, although I know lots of great geeks." His eyes were twinkling a bit. He enjoyed getting her goat. "The thing is, we want to be as anonymous as possible. There's no real privacy online, but we have to try."

She sat on the bed and looked at him. "Then maybe we should just find a cybercafé. That's as anonymous as you can get."

"Ordinarily I'd agree, except that when you're the subject of a manhunt, people will remember having seen you there. You're not exactly forgettable."

"Damn."

He reached into the laptop bag and pulled out an operating system disk. "Try this. It'll wipe the whole machine and start it like it's a brand-new baby. It'll kill my porn collection, but what the hell."

She busted out in laughter. "You're joking, right?"

He nodded, his face not entirely transparent. "Of course. Mostly. Maybe."

"Well, say goodbye to Miss Big Boobs 2004. Time to wipe your hard drive."

"Then make up a generic name for yourself and get on some Internet provider that doesn't require a credit card or bank account for a thirty-day free trial."

"You think of everything."

"No, I've just investigated enough fraud cases to know some tricks."

She looked at him from the corner of her eye and wiggled her eyebrows. "You walk a fine line, eh?"

"The line between legal and illegal can sometimes be almost invisible. I'll go scrounge up a meal."

A fine line indeed, Erin thought as she set up the laptop on the small desk. Like switching license plates.

Formatting and reloading the operating system was a slow process, but she hovered over it anyway, ensuring that when it wanted to fill in blanks, it didn't use previously stored information. Apparently not everything got wiped, despite the warnings. She considered searching for his porn collection but convinced herself that had been only a joke. He didn't seem the type.

Jerrod returned with a blast of icy air, blowing snow that reached all the way across the room, and a large paper bag full of Chinese food.

"I figure, from the look of things, we might not want to go out in the morning, so I got enough for an army."

"No complaint from me." She glanced toward the whirring computer. "It wants to remember you."

"I hope you're telling it to forget."

"As best I can." She sat at the desk, one leg tucked under her, and accepted a plastic container. "Wonton soup!"

"Or egg drop, if you prefer."

"No, I love wonton."

"Good, because I love egg drop. And hot and sour." That container was a full quart size.

"I hope you're planning to share."

"Everything."

The soup was wonderful. Erin cupped her hands around the container and drank, rather than fussing with the small plastic spoon. The warmth hit her stomach, then began to spread throughout her body.

"How is it possible to feel so content right now?" she remarked.

"Something about good, hot food."

"And being inside during a blizzard."

"That, too, I'm sure."

She smiled at him. "You're an okay guy, you know."

"Why do I get the feeling that surprises you?"

Her smile broadened. "Because I'm a reporter. Like I said, my relationship with cops is usually not the friendly kind."

"Except when you need us."

"Same here," she answered tartly. "You guys use the press all the time."

"Ah, but only for the noblest of ends." He sat on the edge of the nearest bed, sipping his soup and regarding her with amusement.

"I'm not always sure of that."

"Probably wise not to be." Then he set aside his bowl and leaned forward earnestly. "Erin, I'm not using you in this. I want to get these bastards."

"I want to get them, too."

"So we're a team. And I really can be a nice guy, at least until we've achieved our mission."

She wondered how to take that. "Aren't you always a nice guy?"

"No. Not always." He reached for his soup again, and something in his face closed down.

Erin felt a trickle of uneasiness, then realized something she'd never considered before: sometimes you didn't want to be partnered with a nice guy.

And this was undoubtedly one of those times.

\* \* \*

Dawn Jettis, two weeks from her fourteenth birthday, lay naked and facedown on a bare mattress supported by a creaky iron bed frame. She kept her eyes closed, pretending to be asleep, but she couldn't stop the shaking that racked her body from head to toe. She wasn't cold. The sterile, windowless room was, in fact, warm.

But she *was* terrified.

Her head throbbed as if someone were pounding on it with a hammer. She knew she must have been drugged, and her memory since the moment when the guy had waved her over to his car was less than sketchy. He'd asked directions. The next thing she remembered was being stripped and thrown onto this bed. That and voices speaking a language she had never heard before.

Even if she could have gotten out the locked door, she suspected she wouldn't have anywhere to go, because she felt she must be in another country. Why else wouldn't they speak English to her?

She tried not to cry, but tears squeezed beneath her lids anyway. She attempted to pray, but she couldn't seem to form a whole thought beyond, Please God, please God, please God…

Her mind kept filling with images culled from movies and stories from newspapers about what happened when girls like her were kidnapped.

It was all her fault for having that stupid fight with

her mother and running away. All her fault. If only she'd stayed in her room instead of deciding to teach her mother a lesson by disappearing for a day or two. If only...

The door opened, and a woman wearing a long, straight black dress came in carrying a plastic bowl. Dawn watched her from eyes she barely opened, not wanting the woman to guess she was awake.

Apparently it didn't matter. The woman simply put the bowl down on the floor near the bed. It smelled good, reminding Dawn that she hadn't eaten in a long time. Her stomach rumbled, but the woman seemed not to hear it. Dawn held perfectly still.

There was a clatter, and then the horrifying feeling of metal around her ankle. The woman held Dawn's leg for a moment, and the metal band tightened.

Filled with the urge to scream and strike out, Dawn remained frozen. Some part of her knew what had just happened. Like a deer, she simply couldn't move, though now she desperately wanted to.

The worst was about to begin.

God and all his angels couldn't help her now.

The man who entered the conference room was known to Kendall as Bill Tatum, although Kendall had long wondered if that was his real name. But why change it? Black contracts by their nature created plausible deniability.

Tatum sat at the polished table, facing Chuck Besom, while Kendall remained with his back to the window.

"Somebody," said Tatum without preamble, "must have seen one of the outbound flights."

Kendall started to object. "We have strict security around—"

Tatum cut him off. "Telescopes. Binoculars. There isn't an airfield in the world that isn't watched by those damn plane-spotters." The worldwide group of hobbyists who routinely watched airports, recording the tail numbers, make and model of incoming and outgoing planes, then logging them, had long been the bane of Intelligence's existence. "I ought to know. The agency's most secret planes are on those damn logs, and those bastards know they belong to us. We keep reregistering our aircraft, and they still figure it out."

Chuck nodded. "I know about them. But we've taken measures to—"

"Either the measures aren't good enough, or somebody on your crew is talking. Those are the options, gentlemen."

Kendall hated it when this guy stated the obvious. "We've already figured that out."

"Well, congratulations," Tatum said sarcastically.

"You know," Kendall said, "I told you in the beginning that using planes was dangerous." So *there.*

The childish moment of satisfaction at once pleased and shocked him.

But Tatum surprised him by agreeing. "I know you did. But no other method of transport was feasible."

"So you said," Kendall agreed, keeping his tone neutral.

"We're suspending the contract indefinitely," Tatum continued. "Until we get rid of the leak, the reporter and Jerrod Westlake."

Chuck picked up on something in the man's tone. "You know Westlake?"

"He's dangerous," Tatum said. "More dangerous than you can imagine."

"Then maybe you should tell us what we're up against. I know he's a bulldog."

"It's more than that." Tatum threw a personnel file onto the desk. "He has—what should I say?—a talent for finding missing…persons. He has contacts on four continents, including some he made when he worked for us."

"He's one of ours?" Besom asked, thinking that surely he would have known if Westlake had ever worked for RoughRider.

"Not directly. He was a subcontractor, hired through another firm. Probably didn't even know he worked for us. But the man's diligent, and he's dangerous. He took a team in on the Henninger gig, in

Malaysia. East Timor Liberation Army or some such. The op went to shit. Agency working both sides of it against the middle. The team walked into an ambush. But Westlake came out with the kid."

Tatum rose. "Bury the contract until you deal with this guy. Until then, I don't know you."

With that, he walked out the door.

Kendall and Chuck looked at one another. Finally Kendall slapped his hand hard on the table. "Great," he said. "Just great."

"We'll deal with it."

He glared at Chuck. "Oh, you'd better. Because if Mercator is left swinging in the breeze on this, you're going to need somebody to sew your balls back on."

"Fucking Jerrod Westlake," Besom said. But already his brain was buzzing in overdrive. There was something about Westlake he didn't know, something he *needed* to know, because Tatum had acted as if Westlake were an extraordinary threat.

Kendall Warrick spoke. "*You* are in charge of security. *You* said you could do this hush-hush. *You* said we wouldn't have any problems."

"I'll take care of them."

"See that you do." He turned his back on Chuck and looked out at the snowy night once more. "I want you to remember something."

"What's that?"

Kendall faced him. "I'm not going to hang on this one. I'd never have agreed to this shit if you hadn't personally guaranteed to oversee it. I trusted you to do it right, Chuck. Don't disappoint me."

By midnight, Erin had logged into a free service with fictitious personal information. She reached out across the winding web of Internet servers to an anonymous server in Finland. From there she bounced to another anonymous server with yet a different name.

"I thought you weren't a geek," Jerrod said. He was leaning over her shoulder, watching. His breath made the side of her neck tingle with warmth and awakened something deeper that she didn't want to think about right now.

"I'm not. I just learned a few tricks. Okay, I'm getting my files now."

She initiated the transfer, and the hard drive indicator light on the laptop began to flash faster.

Jerrod spoke. "I hope they're encrypted."

"They are. A friend of mine, who *is* a geek, gave me encryption software guaranteed to withstand the NSA for a few weeks."

"How lovely."

She glanced at him. His face was close. "You disapprove."

"Actually, no. Are you going to be able to decrypt them again?"

"Of course." The drive stopped spinning, the file access closing automatically. "There. Should I start decrypting now?"

"No." He straightened. "Get your stuff together. We're leaving."

She gaped at him. "I thought you said we weren't going anywhere until the blizzard let up."

"I changed my mind."

"But why?"

"Like you said, we snoop through everything. Call me paranoid, but we just poked our noses into the big bad world. I don't want to still be here when the snoops figure that out."

# 10

Georgie Dickson felt a tingle down the back of her neck, like the whisper of a breeze lifting her hair. Six years with the Bureau had taught her not to ignore that feeling, and she instinctively reached toward her purse and the Glock-9 she'd never used apart from on the target range.

She never got close to it.

Her fingers had just touched the clasp of her purse when the blow came, low on the left side of her back, both dull and sharp at once. Part of her tried to diagnose what weapon had been used, even as the blinding pain exploded into dizzying showers of white light, her kidney sending the most primitive and effective of alert signals to her brain: *pain-danger-pain-danger.*

Sucking in breath seemed almost beyond her, even as she knew that she couldn't continue without it. Part of her brain told her to turn to face her attacker, left foot back and stamping down, hoping to catch an instep or an ankle as she pivoted through her left side and stepped into him with the right foot, closing the range and thus evading the next blow.

Had she done that, she might have gained a critical second to assess the threat, to form the barest bones of a strategy and begin to reclaim control of the situation.

But no sooner had she stamped back with and shifted her weight onto her left foot than the second blow came, on the outside of her left knee, heavy, carrying through the point of impact, caving her knee inward, shredding ligament and cartilage. Her brain reacted to the new injury at a level far beneath conscious control, telling the muscles of her left leg to go limp, offering no further resistance to compound the injury, and she collapsed onto her left side.

Animal instinct took over then, as she curled into the fetal position, arms wrapped around her head, right knee tucked up, even if the left leg would not yet answer her body's attempt to protect the most vital organs, to somehow steal a precious moment or two in which to find a life-saving response to sudden, brutal violence.

Instead of a third blow, hands grasped her wrists and yanked them down and back, flipping her onto her stomach. She lifted her head to look, but blackness immediately swept over her face, drawing tight at her throat as she felt the bite of plastic at her wrists, tight enough to distend tendons and curl her fingers into unnatural, fast-numbing claws.

*Two of them,* she thought, still trying to fight the fog of pain and shock. One person could not have simultaneously flex-cuffed her wrists and hooded her. There had to be two attackers. At least.

Within seconds, the air inside the hood was warm and stale and reeking of sweat and fear. The scream she let out as she was hefted by her bound wrists and ankles sounded beyond human, rising to a thought-splitting crescendo as her body was tossed onto something hard.

Mercifully, her brain chose the least traumatic of the remaining options. Darkness fell through her thoughts like a gentle rain, putting out the fires of agony as she lapsed into a world where the last ten seconds had not happened.

Jerrod had spent the last hour in silence. Erin was asleep in the passenger seat, the seat back reclined to give her some comfort as she hugged the laptop case to her chest. Her face was turned toward him, and several times he'd been tempted to wake her, lest her neck get stiff from the unusual position. But she needed the sleep, and he would rather see her face than the back of her head when he glanced over.

In sleep, her features softened dramatically. Gone

were the taut, inquisitive lines of the career journalist, replaced by the placid curves of a strikingly beautiful woman in repose. Hers was, he thought, a face he could all too easily get used to watching as she slept and waking to in the morning. Whether animated by her razor-sharp mind when she was awake or relaxed into the peace of Morpheus, hers was a beauty he'd rarely seen before.

The road was climbing steadily, the temperature dropping in counterpoint to it, as they headed west on Highway 50. His plan was to head for Cañon City, a town of roughly sixteen thousand. He knew it was easier to disappear into a larger population center, but Cañon City was a place where strangers could pass unnoticed. With nine state and four federal prisons in its immediate environs, visitors were common and commonly ignored. It also provided a selection of modest motels where they could hole up until they figured out their next steps.

The night seemed to wrap itself around him like a blanket. His mind's eye painted images of broken, rugged terrain that he could not see, because the swirling snow cut visibility to only a few yards. It was only thirty-nine miles from Pueblo to Cañon City, but conditions forced him to creep along at less than twenty miles an hour. No sane person would be out on the road in this. Which made it the safest, sanest time for them to move.

So long as he kept it slow, they were fine. His four-wheel drive vehicle could easily handle the fluffy powder on the road, and it had been cold enough for long enough that the falling snow was not thawing and refreezing into the icy glaze that would have made travel impossible. The roadside reflectors kept him oriented to the pavement, and the near invisibility of the outside world left him time to think.

Jerrod didn't like the creeping sense of paranoia that had overcome him in the past twenty-four hours. His life was one of peeking under other people's rocks, and he much preferred that to the knowledge that, even now, people were peeking under his. Somewhere, right this instant, someone was wondering where he and Erin were, how to find them, and probably how to dispose of them without thickening the vile stew they'd begun to stir.

It was a disquieting thought.

He'd been marked before. When *they* marked you, your life got ugly, unpredictable and usually short. He had come out of it before only because he'd been willing to do things he would rather forget. Things he now faced having to do again.

The prospect of his own death did not frighten him. He'd been at that doorway before, close enough to taste what lay beyond. He could easily have let himself fall through it into the emptiness where rage and guilt and cold calculation would no longer have driven his body and mind. He hadn't stepped back from that doorway for himself. He had stepped back for Claire Henninger, an eleven-year-old girl whose only crime was being the daughter of an American businessman in a country and at a time where that single fact made her a target.

In the world's largest Islamic country, Indonesia, her fate had not been set by religious fanaticism but by the lingering stains and scars of the Age of Empires. With a wealth of oil sought by Japan, China and the U.S. alike, and straddling the Southwest Pacific sea-lanes, Indonesia was a fault line of conflicting aspirations and shattered dreams. Chinese immigrants, Japanese cartels, the CIA and U.S. oil interests threatened to swamp whatever flames of independence and self-determination had flickered in the wake of the Second World War, and wave upon wave of unrest and violence had rolled across the rugged islands.

Claire Henninger had been a drop in that ocean, an opportunity seized by four factions. For East Timor rebels, she was a pitifully frail lever with which to force out an American industry. For Jakarta, she was a reason—no, an excuse—to set loose the CIA-trained "special forces" battalions whose specialty was torture, terror and murder. For the Chinese supporting East Timor, she was an economic window, a chance to extend the reach of Chinese investments and influence in Indonesia. For the CIA, she represented a festering sore to be dealt with as quickly as possible, so the United States could go back to business as usual, business dominated by Wall Street and Washington.

But to Kenneth and Elizabeth Henninger, she was the girl who bounced out of bed giggling on weekends, if not on school days. She was the girl whose taste in music tended to indecipherable hip-hop, whose eyes were always as bright as her shins were bruised from her daily practices at the local soccer club. She was a kiss of heaven, a sparkle of God-ness in a world too often fraught with adult conceits and deceits. She was a reason to hope there was something bigger than the next deal, the next year's bonus.

It was that last image of Claire Henninger that had motivated Jerrod. He cared not one whit whether East Timor gained independence, Jakarta retained control, the Chinese found another way to invest billions of carefully hoarded U.S. dollars, or the U.S. firm employing Ken Henninger had a big quarter. They were relevant only insofar as they were tools to be used or obstacles to be overcome. What mattered was that bright-eyed, bruised-shinned sparkle of God-ness.

It was for her that he'd pulled back from that dark doorway where eternity had beckoned. It was for her that he'd cinched an improvised tourniquet around his elbow to staunch the crimson fountains that had billowed from the ragged hole in his forearm, lowered his head, retched until some sense of clarity returned to his thoughts and reached for the Heckler & Koch MP-5 that lay between his legs. For a moment, the gun had seemed to get farther away, his mind still reeling close to the point of surrender.

Then Claire Henninger's tiny hands had picked it up and placed it on his stomach. The thought of her handling the weapon, of her world defiled by what those bright, shining, innocent eyes saw around them, had propelled him back into action.

It hadn't been his own courage that brought him out of that steamy night where rivulets of blood were washed away by rivers of tropical rain. It had been hers.

Her darting eyes and flaring nostrils had guided his pain-numbed senses from threat to threat, her tiny finger pointing in the same instant that his tightened on the trigger and the clattering pop of automatic fire sprayed death into human flesh. She had led him out of that night, out of that darkness.

Hours later, as he lay on a cot with an IV in his arm and narcotics dulling the pain, her parents had tugged her away as her head lay on his chest, her hand still clutched in his. His last memory of that night was of two tiny fingertips touched to her lips before she was returned to the warmth of her parents' embrace.

Four of his colleagues had died to make that embrace possible. A dozen other young men—sons, brothers and colleagues—had died to prevent it. So much blood spilled, so many dreams stilled forever, so that she could fight away the nightmares she doubtless endured, and try to reclaim something of the innocence and wonder that had once filled her world.

"Are you okay?"

Jerrod glanced over to see Erin studying him, almost as if from sleep, for she still had not moved.

"Yeah."

"You're rubbing your arm."

"Old injury," he said. "The cold makes it ache."

"I can drive for a while if you want."

"Nah. We're almost there."

Her brow furrowed, and that alone made his heart ache, the graceful, languorous curves of sleep replaced by the creases of thought again. "Where were you, Jerrod?"

"I've been right here. Driving."

"No, you weren't here. You were somewhere else."

"Long time ago."

"Want to talk about it?" she asked.

"No."

"I'd never judge you."

He nodded. "You wouldn't have to."

"I don't know if this matters," she began, "but I'll

say it anyway. Whoever you were, whatever you did…I like the man you are now."

He nodded again. Did it matter? Not enough. But it was what he had left. "Thanks, Erin."

She turned and looked out the window. "Looks as if there's a prison out there."

"There is," Jerrod said. "There are lots of them."

The cheap motel was easy to find and, even at this ungodly hour, easy to check into with cash. No questions asked about credit cards or license plates. Some of the people who came here to visit didn't want to be tracked.

Once inside the room, Erin watched through the window as Jerrod changed the license plate again. He hadn't used the one he'd swiped in Pueblo yet, he'd explained, because its owner was too near. He replaced the plate on a nearby car with the one he had swiped in Pueblo, further muddying the trail.

Every little bit helped.

Erin had just opened a carton of chicken lo mein when Jerrod came back in.

"How long will it take you to read everything?" he asked her.

"Do we need to get moving?"

"Not till morning."

"Then sleep," she suggested. "Decrypting is going to take longer than the download."

"You'll wake me?"

"As soon as I have everything ready to look at."

He seemed to take her at her word and, after shedding his jacket, fell fully clothed onto the bedspread and closed his eyes. He fell asleep in seconds, something she'd seen before while covering firefighters combating forest fires. She supposed he'd learned the skill in the military. When danger stalked all waking minutes, sleep was a precious resource to be seized at every opportunity.

The decryption software was grinding away at the e-mails. Her favorite geek, Yance, hadn't been able to leave well enough alone, however. Instead of a progress bar across her screen, she was watching an animated Mr. Potato Head change appearance, piece by piece, while a thermometer on the side of the screen indicated that the potato was baking nicely at four hundred degrees. Explosion of the potato would indicate that the program had finished its chore.

That was Yance. She sighed and drummed her fingers quietly, wondering why he couldn't have chosen something more pleasant, or more interesting. Then it struck her that he wasn't so stupid. Anyone who tried to run his program without knowing its purpose would probably dismiss it as a college student joke video. *Genius, Yance,* she thought with a smile. *Sheer genius.*

Still, it seemed odd to be waiting impatiently for

a head to explode, even an animated cartoon potato head. In the real world…

In that instant, she put down the box of lo mein, no longer able to so much as look at it. It had been years since she'd covered the plane crash, a small private plane that had gone down in the hills near the first newspaper she'd worked for. What had been left of the pilot was a sight that had taken months to erase from her retina, months in which she'd been unable to eat any kind of noodles, nor even think about cooking raw meat.

That was, she thought, how life happened. One by one, experience by experience, life ripped away something you'd seen one way and left you with a soiled, nauseating image of what it really was. Then you spent weeks or months or years trying to wipe away the imprinted ruin and regain what had once been there, thinking you were gaining ground, making progress, until some stupid animated potato ripped open the scars again.

Regaining innocence was, she supposed, a fool's errand. She would never again live in a world where human beings could not become human refuse in a single, life-shattering impact. She would never again live in a world where young girls weren't treated as pleasure toys. She would never again live in a world where cops could automatically be trusted, where an editor might not tell the boss what you were working on, leading him to send someone to have you killed. She would never again live in a world where a story was just a story, just interesting fodder to sell ads on tomorrow's birdcage liner.

The answer wasn't trying to return to those pristine worlds. The answer, she thought, must lie in recognizing that she'd never lived in those worlds at all and deciding how she was going to live in the world she now knew.

She could get cynical. She could get outraged. She could get resigned.

Or she could get busy.

Mr. Potato Head exploded. She forced herself to take another mouthful of lo mein.

Time to get busy.

# 11

Chuck Besom left Mercator's executive building as soon as he could, images from two personnel files burned into his retinas. He'd read both files before leaving, but they were thin, and he would need to call in some favors to get more information tonight.

Something in the way Bill Tatum had talked about Jerrod Westlake had set off alarm bells. Tatum and Westlake knew each other, and the history was bad. That could prove to be a useful lever at some point.

The storm continued to thicken as he drove back to his apartment. The trip gobbled up time, but it was useful for thinking. Bill Tatum was former special ops. Besom had known that, of course. That kind of experience was a given for the job Tatum did with Mercator. But he was more than that. He was former CIA—or would have been, if the phrase "former CIA" were not an oxymoron. In Chuck Besom's experience, that was not a snake pit one ever really left.

Chuck smiled into the teeth of the storm, and his hands tightened on the steering wheel. His Hummer plowed through the snow and ice like a behemoth forging through grass. There was very little traffic on the roads, giving him plenty of space to move faster.

Kendall's insults hadn't bothered him. Kendall lacked the language or imagination to arouse any true emotion in Chuck. Nor was Kendall a real threat. He could bluster, but the man had no street chops. He could be controlled, if necessary. Kendall had a family, after all, and family made a man vulnerable.

Tatum was a different story. Whatever conscience birth had given him had long since withered in a world where ends justified any means, including sacrificing your own assets when you thought the sacrifice gave you something better. Tatum's loyalty to Mercator, and to Besom himself, went only as far as Tatum's next chance to look out for himself and what he wanted. If Tatum thought sacrificing Chuck would give him a leg up, he would be dead before he knew he was in danger.

Chuck knew that meant he needed to know more about what made Bill Tatum tick, especially vis-à-vis Jerrod Westlake. If he was going to run into trouble from his own side, he wanted to know it before the shooting started. And Tatum's file, the redacted version Besom had seen, was a résumé with gaping holes that screamed Trouble-with-a-Capital-T.

Worse, he was starting to get the feeling that there was something about this entire operation that he didn't know, despite his role as security chief. Feeling that way, he couldn't let even the most minuscule thing slide now.

But if Tatum and Westlake had scores to settle, Besom intended to know what they were…and how he could use that knowledge to his advantage. Because something warned him that he would need every advantage he could get.

Erin didn't wake Jerrod the moment Mr. Potato Head exploded. Instead, she scanned the files by herself, a combination of a handful of e-mails and her notes about the situation. She needed to reassure herself that she hadn't made a mountain out of a molehill. That this really was the unspeakable evil she suspected.

Perhaps, she thought, that was how unspeakable evil survived. Even when faced with the evidence, people questioned whether something so horrific could be possible, whether *Homo sapiens* could be so perverted, so twisted, so empty of moral judgment. The more comfortable choice being denial, she thought, people looked the other way and allowed the evil to continue. As if in illustration of that fact, she found herself picking over each scrap of data her source had sent, not wanting to believe that the clues could indeed point to what he suggested, what she feared.

The source had given her a series of tail numbers for planes belonging to Mercator, and links to plane-spotting Web sites that had tracked the flights of those aircraft. He'd copied shipping manifests that listed those flights as carrying specific cargoes—item numbers whose meanings she could only guess at, descriptions blacked out for security reasons—and inventory records showing that the specified cargo had never left the warehouse.

The e-mails explained that he'd been concerned about fraud. New congressional crackdowns after the early chaos of questionable contracting practices during the Iraq War were probing more deeply into whether defense contractors were, in fact, supplying what they'd sold in the quantities and at the costs specified in their contracts. Anxious to protect his company against the possibility that someone in the shipping department was billing the government while selling the goods on the black market, but unwilling to do so publicly lest he draw law enforcement attention, he'd decided to investigate on his own. He'd found a scheduled flight that fit the

profile—small aircraft leaving in the wee hours—
and had gone out to see what, if anything, was being
loaded.

To his amazement, he watched as two young
women—girls, really, though he couldn't guess their
exact ages—were carried aboard the small executive
jet, both of them limp, as if drugged.

He hadn't believed what he'd seen. He'd searched
his mind for reasons. Perhaps the girls were the
daughters of a Mercator executive, being flown
home after visiting their father's office. But why,
then, the false shipping manifests? Why the middle-
of-the-night departures, after the control tower had
closed? And why were the flights going overseas?

He'd checked two more flights in the next month,
and again found false manifests for overseas flights
carrying young girls, two on the first flight, three on
the second. All the girls seemed to be in their young
teens, right on the cusp between childhood and
womanhood. And all were apparently unconscious
as they were carried aboard.

Erin had confirmed as much of the information
as she could, tracing the tail numbers through her
own search of plane-spotting Web sites. The flights
checked out; those aircraft had indeed made the
listed departures and landings.

She couldn't verify the shipping manifests and inventory records, though—not without confronting

Mercator directly—but overseas contracts often wended their way into the news, and she had researched online news databases. Mercator did have contracts with the buyers referenced in the manifests, although those buyers did not always match up with the countries where the flights had landed. Nor could she dismiss those landings as mere refueling stops, because the aircraft often did not continue on to the country where the buyer was theoretically located.

That in itself was not proof, of course. Cargo could have been switched from one aircraft to another, or from aircraft onto trains, ships or trucks. Planespotters did not track cargoes but only the aircraft themselves. And trying to cross-reference all the shipments leaving a given airport was an impossible task without a level of access Erin did not have. It would mean prying into the shipping manifests of every company receiving and/or shipping cargo from each of the three airports in question on each of those three occasions, including the possibility that the cargo had been stored at an airport warehouse for a day or a week or a month before being shipped on to the destination.

This would be a daunting prospect, even for ordinary cargo. But overseas arms sales, by their nature, were even more surreptitious. The bookkeeping was kept purposefully labyrinthine. The putative ownership of cargoes shifted from producer to holding company to shipper to holding company, with the merchandise being flown to one city, trucked to another, loaded on a conveyor ship to a third, then trucked to the ultimate purchaser, with manifest details changing at each stop.

Even for a government agency, running down shipments was like trying to diagram a bowl of spaghetti. It was far beyond Erin's investigative means, so she'd e-mailed back to her source, asking for more documentation that she could verify in the public record.

Then he had fallen suspiciously silent. Which left her hanging in a very cold breeze, left to find what she needed on her own.

She finally woke Jerrod, who moved from deep sleep to full wakefulness instantaneously. She watched him scan what she had, nodding as if it helped him absorb what he was reading.

"You see," she said as he finished, "I can't really prove anything. If these manifests and inventories are accurate, obviously someone's defrauding someone. But if I go to Mercator to challenge them, you know they'll produce documents that seem to resolve the inconsistencies. I have no information on who these girls were, where they came from, why they were flown to these cities. I can't even prove they were on the flights. I've only got my source's word on that. I'm really not a threat to Mercator at all."

He leaned back in the chair and looked at her. "But you are. First of all, they don't know how much evidence you actually have. Second, they know you're talking with the FBI now. Third, they think you know who the leak is. They need to cover their asses, tie up loose ends. And quickly. Before anyone gets solid proof."

He looked back at the computer. "I'm really concerned that your source hasn't gotten back to you. Did you tell your editor you had a source inside Mercator?"

"I said I had a source. I didn't say where, or what specific kinds of information the source had given me."

He sighed and rubbed the back of his neck. "The CIA hates those plane-spotters, you know."

"Oh? Why?"

One corner of Jerrod's mouth lifted. "The CIA is constantly having to change the names of its so-called secret airlines and reregister their aircraft with different tail numbers, selling them from one executive transport company to another, all because of those guys. They also have to constantly sell and buy aircraft to try to stay ahead. They've leaned on airports to disrupt plane-spotting, make it as inconvenient as they can, even going so far as to run them off the airport grounds."

"I didn't know that."

"Yeah. Some people have put it under the umbrella of national security since 9/11. But people can still buy binoculars, and airports can't put big tarps over the runways, so…"

"The plane-spotters find ways."

"Yes, they do. And together they create a log for the entire life of an aircraft. That helps buyers to double-check when they're looking at a plane. They can tell whether it's flown as many hours as the seller claims, or more."

"That sounds useful."

"It is, unless you're trying to move people and things around secretly."

"So what do you think?" she asked. "Have I gone out on a limb over nothing? I mean, could this really be…?"

His expression darkened. "If I'd had any doubts, what happened in Houston and Austin erased them. C'mon, Erin. They broke into your place, whacked you on the head, then tailed us through Austin. They're serious about whatever it is. Serious enough to risk committing crimes."

"So you could start an official investigation."

He nodded. "Yes, in theory. But that creates its own problems. Mercator has a lot of pull on Capitol Hill, and that flows downhill to Justice and the Bureau. Agents can be 'reassigned.' U.S. attorneys are political appointees who can be replaced, not always for legitimate reasons. A system is only as reliable as the people who run it, and like any system, ours has its share of political operators who will bend events to their own agendas."

Erin felt anger rise in her belly. "Great. So why are we bothering? Even if we find out exactly what's going on, if we could connect the names of missing children with the kids who were shipped on those flights... If Mercator has as much clout as you say, they'll just lean on whoever they need to, and your investigation goes away."

He shook his head. "You can put it all over the front page of any major newspaper. You're that good, Erin. I've read some of your work. If we can nail down your sources and verify the information, you can write a story that any newspaper will snap up like cops on doughnuts. Once it's all over the news, no one can sweep it under the rug."

Her burst of anger fled on a sigh, and her shoulders slumped. "Sorry. Of course that's the point."

He leaned toward her and lifted her chin with his index finger so he could look right into her eyes. "I know it's maddening. This kind of investigation shouldn't be about money and politics. But you know it is. Lord Acton wasn't an idiot when he said power corrupts."

She stared back steadily. "No, I know. I'm not

naive. But something like this…there ought to be *some* boundaries people won't cross just to make a buck."

"There should be. But there aren't."

Like her source, Erin had tried to imagine legitimate reasons for transporting the girls. Like her source, she'd come up empty. What was it that Conan Doyle had written into the mouth of Holmes? When you have eliminated the possible, then what remains, however impossible, must be the answer? As horrifying as it was, she couldn't find a less horrifying explanation for the evidence.

"We've got to stop this," she said, looking at him. "No matter what."

Jerrod nodded, a flash of something cold in his eyes that made her shiver. "Yes. We will."

# *12*

*P*ain.

A single word summarized Georgie Dickson's existence. Again and again she fought to distinguish, diagnose and decide. Again and again she lost the battle, her entire consciousness reduced to a single word.

*Pain.*

They were certainly professionals. That was obvious from the precisely tied cords that pinioned her elbows together behind her back, her wrists bound with her palms facing out, the rotation only adding to the strain in her shoulders. There was no question of escape. Both her thumbs and pinkie fingers had been bound tightly together with what felt like kitchen twine, holding the backs of her hands together, rendering her other fingers useless, even if she had still been able to feel them.

But sensation in her fingers was only a memory.

They had progressed from cold to tingling to, it seemed, absent.

She was hanging by her bound wrists, arms cruelly hefted behind her back in what she remembered having read was an ancient torture known as strappado. Its inventor, whoever that was, had known his art. The shrieking pain in her shoulders never let up, not for an instant. Every breath, every movement, spiked it, as connective tissue was stretched almost to the breaking point and nerves screamed futile warnings to her brain.

But these men were not satisfied. She had been stripped naked—a common tactic for torture, she knew, to break down the victim's sense of self—her legs splayed obscenely wide, tight ropes at her ankles playing over pipes off to either side and then knotted to the handles of large plastic buckets that were slowly filling with water.

*Think,* she told herself. If she could keep thinking, she could retain some small measure of control. A gallon of water weighed about eight pounds. The plastic buckets were of the sort painters used. Five gallons? When full, forty pounds. Or was it more? Would forty pounds tear through the thick bands of cartilage and tendon that held her hips together? Would she, as the men had told her, be torn apart if she refused to talk?

*No.* Something told her she could hold out.

Maybe it was wrong. But it was all she had. Because she would not betray Jerrod. Period.

"Fuck you," she said, spitting out the words as if she'd bitten into rotten lettuce.

"Oh, we'll get to that soon enough," the man said. "But business before pleasure. What does Jerrod Westlake know? We know you've talked with him. We know you know what he knows. You're going to tell us. It's simply a matter of how much pain and damage we'll need to apply. Everyone talks, Georgia Maria Lopez Dickson. Everyone."

So they knew her complete name. If that was intended to intimidate her, it failed. They had searched her purse. It didn't mean they knew anything special about her. This, too, was a common interrogation tactic. The idea was to make her think her questioner knew more about her than she did about herself, that he was already inside her head, that her thoughts, as well as her fate were in his hands. That he could twist and distort her sense of self as much as he was twisting and distorting her body.

"I'm sure men look at you a lot, Georgia Maria Lopez Dickson," the man said. He was wearing a balaclava, hiding his features. "Or they used to."

His arm swung with a casual one-two, his hand clutching a gardener's claw, deftly turning the tines away at the last minute so only the smooth metal backs smacked across her right breast and then her left, the pain hardly having time to register before two more blows fell, one across each cheek.

"All I have to do is turn this over," he said, holding the claw in front of her face, "and no one would mistake you for beautiful ever again. Just imagine the damage it would do. Cheeks shredded. Chunks of those pretty breasts ripped out. You might take pride in holding out right now, but a year from now, or five, when no man will touch what's left of you, when everyone you meet recoils in revulsion when they look at you... what then, Georgia Maria Lopez Dickson? Then you'll think you were a fool. Why waste what God gave you?"

Georgie was not vain. But neither was she inhuman. At some level, she knew her attractiveness made life just a tiny bit easier. People smiled when she smiled. Laughed when she laughed. Knew when she was deathly serious, and wanted to see her smile and laugh again. Like anyone, she used that to her advantage as an FBI agent. It was one more reason for someone to talk to her and one less reason to stonewall.

She told herself it was this, and not personal concern for her beauty, that began to gnaw at her resolve.

She heard water dripping onto stone and looked over. The buckets were full. And she had not been torn in two, no matter how horrific the tearing pain in her pelvis and hips. He'd lied about that. He was lying about the rest.

"Fuck you," she said again.

He simply nodded and turned away, returning the claw to the table, now picking up a straight razor, his eyes fixed between her legs.

For the next ten minutes he did not say a word. They were, she thought, the worst ten minutes of her life. When he was finished denuding her, he dunked a towel in one of the water buckets, then almost gently washed away the stubble. She found herself wishing he'd used the claw instead. She would have found mutilation less horrific than the humiliation that now washed over her.

"If I didn't know better, I'd think you liked this," he said. "That's fine for later, but first we have to finish our work. Where is Jerrod Westlake? What does he know?"

*Stimulus-response,* she told herself. It was purely physiological. He was lying now, every bit as much as he'd been lying about the buckets, and the claw. She could not believe a word he said. His promises—of pain, of mercy, of freedom, of life itself—meant nothing at all.

*He* meant nothing at all. Not even as he began to probe, first with two fingers, then with three, finally grinding his entire fist into her. The punch to her cervix carried up through her body into a spray of vomit that left her gagging and spitting.

"I can do this for hours, Georgia Maria Lopez

Dickson. If I get tired, my associates will take over. We will rest, but you will not. What we would leave behind would make a coroner vomit. So much beauty reduced to so much mutilated meat. Why do that to yourself? Where is Jerrod Westlake? What does he know?"

"Fuck you," she said, spitting vomit in his face. "Fuck you all."

Hours later, Dawn heard the woman retching and sobbing in the cage beside hers. Thick wool blankets covered the cages, and even if they hadn't, Dawn could not have seen through the cotton balls taped over her eyes. Leather straps held her arms behind her as she lay on her side in the cage.

It was a dog kennel, she realized. That was what they'd kept her in since they'd last moved her. Locked, even though there was no way she could have worked the latch. Not that she minded. So long as it was locked, *they* stayed outside. It was a cage, but at least inside the cage she was alone, except for the sounds of the woman next to her.

At least here the people spoke English.

"Are…you okay?" Dawn whispered.

She knew the answer, even before the woman groaned in response. They'd made her watch. This was what happened to girls who disobeyed, they'd said. The horrific images were burned into her brain forever.

"You should have just told them," Dawn whispered.

"No," the woman replied.

"They're going to kill you if you don't."

"Yes," the woman said.

Something in the woman's voice both broke Dawn's heart and left her in awe. The woman knew she was going to die. She'd given up any hope of release, any hope of salvation. But she was not going to give up on her friend and tell the men what they wanted to know.

"I'm Dawn. Dawn Jettis. I'm from Denver. I'm fourteen years old."

The woman gasped and sobbed. "I'm sorry, Dawn Jettis from Denver. I'm so sorry."

"It's not your fault."

The woman paused for a moment. "Have they hurt you?"

"Not like they did to you. You're Georgia?"

"Georgie."

"You're pretty."

"Dawn…"

"I wish I could hold your hand, Georgie."

"Dawn…"

"You wouldn't hurt me."

There was a long pause.

"No, Dawn, I wouldn't hurt you."

"Don't let them kill you, Georgie. I need you."

She heard the woman draw a long, shuddering breath, the sound broken by hisses of pain. The men had hurt her bad. Real bad.

"Promise me you won't let them kill you, Georgie."

Silence.

"Please, Georgie?"

"Yes, Dawn. I promise. We'll get out of here."

Dawn nestled against that side of her cage and imagined that she could feel the woman's warmth through the blankets that separated them, imagined that she could hold the woman's delicate hands in hers.

"Thank you, Georgie."

A rustle against her back. It wasn't Dawn's imagination. The woman had crawled next to her, only steel bars and wool blankets separating them. Dawn pressed a finger into the woman's back.

"I'm here, Georgie."

The woman wept. "Thank you, Dawn."

Jerrod's promise revived Erin's sense of resolve. Whatever they ran into, they would run into it together. Chase down together. For the first time since she'd begun to work on this story, she did not feel alone.

"We need to tear up our credit cards," Jerrod said, opening his wallet.

"I know we can't use them, but why ditch them?"

"Radio transponders," he said.

Her jaw dropped. "You're joking."

"No, I'm not. Supposedly the range is only ten feet, but that's just what they're saying publicly. Now you can just tap your card on the terminal and the transaction is done. It's supposed to save time and make using the card easier and safer, because it never leaves your hand. Except for the radio signal, of course."

"Why does that give me chills?"

"Because it's a helluva quick way to track someone."

"My God, this is *1984!*"

"Orwell just had the year wrong."

She shook her head. "I can't believe this."

He leaned toward her again, lowering his voice as if to add to the gravity of what he said. "Erin, a lot of the things that make life more convenient can also be used in other ways. It's like fire. Sure we learned to cook our food so we could digest it better. So it tasted better. But we can also burn ourselves with it. It's been the same old story since the beginning of mankind. The transponders in credit cards make them quicker and easier to use. We like that convenience."

She nodded, her head and neck feeling like lead.

"Convenience always has a downside. It's a risk. I'm not saying they *can* track us with credit-card transponders. But it's a risk I don't want to take."

She reached for her purse and pulled out her wallet. "ATM card, too?"

"Better to be safe," he said.

"Okay." She handed him her two credit cards and her ATM card. "Do whatever you need to do."

He put them with his and went to work with a pair of scissors from the hotel sewing kit. "We'll leave the bits in different trash cans on our way out."

"This seems so extreme," Erin said.

His eyes were cold. "Mercator has the kind of access we can't risk. We have to go off the grid. Totally."

"I don't know—"

"I do," he said. "The irony is, they taught me. And you're going to have to trust me."

She studied him. Hour by hour, minute by minute, his face was changing. His eyes were harder, darker. His lips smiled less, and with less sincerity. He was becoming someone he knew how to be, someone he'd been trained to be. But that person wasn't the Jerrod Westlake she'd met.

She'd only just begun to trust that Jerrod Westlake. Now she had to find a way to trust this one.

"What do we do now?" she asked.

"Get a few hours sleep," Jerrod said. "Then we start hunting."

"Hunting," she repeated.

His eyes fixed on hers. "That's what it is, Erin. In

this world, you're either predator or prey. I'd rather be the predator."

They'd been prey, she realized. She didn't want to go back to that. She nodded. "Okay. Teach me how to hunt."

# *13*

"That ridge at two o'clock," Erin said, pointing.

Jerrod glanced over from the highway, needing only an instant to both identify and verify the scraggly, wooded mound of rock ahead and to the right. "Distance? Don't think. Just say."

"Half a mile."

"Dead ground?" His eyes flicked over at the back of her head as she scanned the terrain beside the road. "Too much time, Erin."

"That low hill out in front?"

"Is that an answer or a question?"

"It's an answer. I think."

He shook his head. "Not good enough."

"Yes, behind that low hill."

"Distance to the ridge?"

"Maybe a quarter mile?" She caught herself even as the sounds came out. "A quarter mile or a little under."

"Good," he said.

He had maybe two weeks to give Erin a crash course in special operations. If things went the way he expected, they were going to have some close work to do. He couldn't afford to leave Erin alone and defenseless behind him, and he couldn't drag her along as deadweight. She would have to be able to pull her own. The intensive physical training would start tonight, once they reached Pete Thomassen's place outside Colorado Springs. But the drive itself need not be wasted time.

"Damn, it's pretty out here," Erin said.

"Why?"

She looked at him. "Why what? Why is it pretty?"

"Don't look at me. Look at the terrain. What's out there? What are you responding to?"

"Yes, sir," she snapped.

"And don't call me 'sir.' I work for a living."

"Fine."

Her face was set as if in stone, and she sat silent for a moment, pupils unfocused. She wasn't scanning, he knew. She was sulking.

He understood the reaction. The last two hours had been a whirlwind of activity. When they'd awakened in the hotel in Cañon City, he'd led her through seventy-five jumping jacks and forty sit-ups. For him, it had been a light workout, but he knew her hips, thighs and abdomen would be burning in ways she was not accustomed to. Then had come breakfast in the hotel lobby, a boiled egg apiece, along with two slices of toast, a glass of juice and a mug of black coffee. It was Spartan, but that was what he had to teach her to be. A Spartan.

The novelty of the experience had worn off by the time they'd packed their bags in the back of the car and gotten on the highway. The mountain roads were still impassable from the blizzard, so they'd headed back toward Pueblo, where they picked up the interstate for Colorado Springs. The plows and sanders had made the road passable, if still icy and dicey on bridges and overpasses.

Along the way, he'd begun to drill her in a military sense of terrain. Commanding ground, features that allowed someone to see for miles around. Constricting ground, bridges and gorges and defiles that channeled movement. Swept ground, open land that could be observed from the commanding heights. Dead ground, subtle rolls and valleys that blocked line of sight, where enemies could stalk you, or you them. The concepts were simple enough. Recognizing them in the jumbled terrain around you was not. Getting it wrong usually meant getting killed.

"So why is it pretty?" he asked again. He understood why she wanted to sulk. He also knew they didn't have time for it. "What do you see? In detail."

"You can see forever," Erin said finally. "Or at least it seems that way. Your eyes can get lost in the distance."

"What's that?" he pressed.

"Umm, swept ground?"

"Is that an answer or a question?"

He heard the groan even as he began the sentence, a groan he'd heard at least two dozen times in the past hour. But hesitancy, like misreading the terrain, got you killed. Much as he wanted to give her a break, he knew a single skipped lesson could end in her death. He felt relieved when she snapped back at him.

"No, damn it. It's swept ground. From the heights up ahead, you could see for miles." She paused, and he watched the implications finally settle. "If Mercator had someone watching this road, they'd know we were coming long before we could see them."

"Bingo."

"So why are we on the interstate? The back roads might be clear by now."

He nodded. "They might be. Then again, we might end up stuck in an unplowed snowbank, and we don't have the time for that. Anyway, I doubt Mercator would waste manpower by having someone sit on a hill watching a stretch of highway. If they were certain we were coming this way, this morning, and wanted to ambush us, maybe. But I don't think they can be that certain."

"I hope you're right," Erin said. She pointed to a small bridge a mile ahead. "Constricting ground."

"Is it? Is it really?"

She gave him a glare. "It is unless we're going to get out and wade across that damn creek in ice-cold water. So, yeah, it is."

"Good answer."

"Thank you."

They rode on in a chilly silence, chilly both from the tension between them and because he'd turned the car heater to its lowest setting. It was another subtle discomfort, like the ones she would have to learn to cope with over the coming days. Learning to ignore discomfort was part of the training, and his had been far more brutal than what he would subject her to.

"So is this the way you see the world all the time?" Erin asked. "Always looking for sources of danger, avenues of approach? Don't you ever get to just watch a brilliant sunrise or sunset, or admire the wispy clouds halfway up the mountains?"

"You don't like seeing the world this way," he said.

"No, I don't."

"Neither do I, Erin. But when you do what I've done, what we're going to be doing, it's what keeps you alive. Thinking ahead, knowing how you're going to respond before it happens, so you can react immediately, is crucial."

"Like learning to drive," she said. "When you

learn to drive, you have to learn to read the road. You look under parked cars, in case there's a shadow or the feet of some kid about to dash out. You watch the faces and movements of other drivers."

"Exactly," Jerrod said, nodding. "And you have to know whether you're going to brake or swerve if that car ahead on your right suddenly decides he wants to be in your lane. Your responses have to become as automatic as breathing."

Erin nodded. "We watched training movies in driver's education."

"Those are...graphic."

"No," she said, shaking her head. "Not those. I mean, we watched those, too. The scare-the-shit-out-of-you movies of what happened to people in accidents. But no, I meant the I-P-D-E films."

"Hmm?"

"Identify, Predict, Decide, Execute," Erin said. "My driver's ed teacher had a series of films shot from the perspective of a driver. Identify the situation. Predict the hazards. Decide how to respond. Execute the response. We had colored cards to hold up for the various answers, and he barked questions at us as we watched."

She paused to smile. "Kind of like you've been doing all morning."

"That's exactly what I've been doing," Jerrod agreed.

"I hated that teacher, you know. He was also the head football coach. He'd have us sit on the end of a desk, and if we got an answer wrong, he'd kick the back end of the desk one way or the other, like we were going into a skid. We had to turn our hands to steer the right way, into the skid, or he'd tip the desk over and dump us on the floor."

Jerrod chuckled. "That'd probably get him arrested today."

"Yeah," she said. "It probably would. But I knew how to steer into a skid before I'd ever actually sat behind a steering wheel. He made damn sure of that."

"So he was a good instructor," Jerrod said.

"I guess so. But I still hated him. I hated being barked at like that. I hated not having time to *think* and make up my mind before I gave an answer."

"When you find a way to make the cars around you freeze in space while you think, let me know."

To his amazement, she threw an elbow into his arm. Not to his amazement, she immediately withdrew and crossed her arms over her belly. "Oh shit, that hurt."

"It's the sit-ups," he said.

"I know what it is. It still hurts. And I'm getting stiff from the cold. Can't you turn the damn heat up?"

Jerrod looked at her. "I'll make a point of telling the Mercator people to make sure the weather is sunny and warm when we meet up with them."

Her face darkened for a moment. "You can be a real asshole, Jerrod Westlake."

He nodded and answered without a sliver of pride. "You don't know the half of it yet."

Chuck Besom had spent most of the night scanning databases to which he should not have had access but did, thanks to twenty years of networking in the defense and intelligence communities. What he'd found was both very revealing and very disturbing.

Bill Tatum had been right. Jerrod Westlake was no ordinary FBI agent. It wasn't simply that he'd been in special operations before joining the Bureau. It was what he'd done, how he'd done it and who he'd done it with.

The "what" was simple. Staff Sergeant Westlake had been a sneak-snatch-and-scram specialist. He'd kidnapped people for the United States government, and he'd been damn good at it. So good that he'd almost always been the mission leader, even if other operators on the team outranked him. That was common in special ops, Besom knew. The role of mission leader went to the operator most capable of directing the task in question. When it came to kidnapping a terrorist leader, or snatching an informant out of harm's way before the bad guys slit his throat, no one was more capable than Westlake.

The "how" was less simple but no less impressive. Precise intelligence, meticulous planning and rehearsal, and bold, unhesitating action. One after-action report, written by the senior operator, read like a Hollywood screenplay. They'd narrowed the target to a specific room in a specific apartment in Islamabad, accessible from an interior corridor with exits at each end. The corridor would allow them cover in which to organize themselves before the final burst through the door; the multiple exits made it easier to spirit away the principal after the snatch.

Westlake had not only obtained a detailed floor plan; his team had built a mock-up in a remote camp north of the city, where they'd drilled until each man could perform his role blindfolded. Only when Westlake was sure he could enter the city, complete the operation and get back out before anyone—including the police and the Pakistani army—could respond, was he ready to act.

Even then, the young captain on the team had noted, they had paused while a fish-eye video camera was snaked under the door, allowing Westlake to confirm exactly where the principal and his three bodyguards were sitting. By the time the echo of the shattering door frame and the flashbang grenade faded, the bodyguards were all slumping to the floor, three neat holes stitched in each man's chest, and Westlake was already kneeling on the principal's back as he whisked a hood over the man's face.

Only the young boy emerging from across the corridor, drawn by the crash of the door and crack of the grenade, had marred an otherwise flawless operation. The captain, waiting outside the door as corridor security, had clamped his hand over the boy's face and slit his throat from ear to ear.

The investigation that followed had exonerated both the captain, for the boy's death, and Westlake himself, who, once they'd spirited the principal out of the city and were waiting for the helicopter, had taken out his ceramic combat knife and sliced through the captain's hamstring. The other men on the team said Westlake had done it as coldly, as devoid of visible anger, as if he were butchering a hog.

Westlake's reaction to the boy's death had been, he'd said, simple mission economics. A dead boy in a corridor, with blood spattered all over the walls, meant that they'd most likely left physical evidence behind. Boot prints in the blood. Microscopic bits of ceramic in the boy's throat. Evidence that, if the Pakistani police had the technology and expertise to process it, might have implicated the U.S. in ways that could not be denied, given that officially the two countries cooperated with each other, while their mission could be interpreted only as an act of war.

The captain had fucked up the op, and Westlake had fucked up the captain. It was as simple as that.

They'd both been reassigned, although the special-ops community was small enough that they were bound to cross paths again. Eventually it had been discreetly suggested that Staff Sergeant Jerrod Westlake opt out of reenlistment and go into private work instead. Better to make sure neither he nor the captain chose the middle of a delicate operation as the time to settle an old grievance.

Captain William Tatum was not the type to forget. And that was the "who."

Chuck Besom knew Bill Tatum hadn't forgotten. That left Besom in a delicate quandary, like a snake charmer working with two cobras at the same time. Tatum, he now knew, was a man who would not shrink from confrontation. He was, by training, temperament and experience, a very skilled, very cold-blooded killer. Men like that had to be watched. Watched closely.

As for Jerrod Westlake, Besom did not for a moment believe the "mission economics" explanation for what he had done that night in the Pakistani desert. Whatever his stated reasons, Westlake had quite simply objected to the killing of an innocent child. His record before and since was that of an idealist. His detailed, meticulous methods were designed to minimize violence, to avoid contact with bystanders, to secure the principal and the principal only, making the target disappear as if he had evaporated into the ether. That had been Westlake's modus operandi in every mission he'd planned, both in the military and later on in private kidnap, rescue and recovery work.

On the one hand, that idealism seemed to paint Jerrod Westlake as a lesser danger. Unlike Tatum, he was not the type to kill without remorse. But, Besom thought, only a fool would misjudge Westlake that way. When he'd had to, he'd struck, swift and silent. Including a single stroke with a combat knife into the back of Bill Tatum's thigh, what Westlake had known could have been—should have been, and indeed was meant to be—a permanent, crippling wound.

Two cobras, reared and with hoods spread, cold eyes following the end of the charmer's flute, tongues flicking out, trying to sense the precise moment of opportunity.

Okay, Besom thought. He just had to make sure the cobras struck one another.

And not him.

# 14

"Jerrod!"

Pete Thomassen was, Erin thought, one of those human fireplugs that are so often mentioned and so rarely met. He was barely five foot four, barrel-chested, broad-shouldered, short-necked, with arms and legs that looked like coiled strands of harbor line. His slab-angled face held deeply inquisitive brown eyes beneath a more-salt-than-pepper crew cut. Erin could tell that, even in his midsixties, he was in prime physical condition.

Pete greeted Jerrod with the hearty, bone-crunching handshake-into-hug she had often seen among male colleagues in the police, military and fire services, a physical intimacy that was both warm and purposefully overpowering, lest it be mistaken for something more than friendship.

"How the hell are you?" the older man asked.

"I've been worse, Pete," Jerrod said. "And I've been better."

Pete's smile dissolved. "Well, c'mon in. Get out of the cold, at least."

They followed Pete into a neatly kept living room, the back wall of which was dominated by sliding-glass doors that offered a magnificent view of the distant cone of Pikes Peak. At this altitude, just over eight thousand feet, the air was so clear that it seemed to Erin as if she could reach through the glass and touch the heart of the earth itself.

"This is Erin," Jerrod said as Pete took their coats. "We're working together."

The handshake Pete offered her was nothing like what he'd shared with Jerrod. As she grasped his hand, she could feel that his index finger bent side-ways at the middle knuckle, as if it had broken and healed poorly. Still, his stubby fingers were surprisingly gentle. "Pleased to meet you, Erin."

"Jerrod's told me a lot about you."

Pete winked. "Only the bad stuff was true."

The truth was that Jerrod had said very little, apart from the fact that Pete was an old FBI colleague who had retired two years ago. The rest—that they had more in common than simply crossing paths in the FBI—had become apparent in the first moments of that greeting. A quick glance at the walls of Pete's living room, devoid of family photos, splashed with the vibrant colors of Leroy Neiman lithographs, suggested that Pete was a man of action rather than reflection, the kind of man Jerrod would instinctively have been drawn to as a mentor.

"So what's going on, amigo?" Pete asked. "Can I get y'all a cup of coffee?"

"Black, please," Jerrod said, taking a seat at one end of the sectional sofa that surrounded a flagstone hearth. "What do you know about Mercator Industries?"

Erin noted that Pete didn't ask her how she wanted her coffee. Some subliminal conversation had already happened between the two of them. As she sat at the opposite end of the sofa, she suspected her coffee would be just as devoid of cream as Jerrod's.

"What do I know about snow?" Pete called from the kitchen. "More than I want. Less than I wish." He returned with two navy-blue mugs with FBI logos. Both held black coffee. "And least of all, where it's going to land next and how deep it's going to get."

"What are you saying?" Jerrod asked, taking his mug.

"Let me put it this way," Pete said. "Remember what the Mouse was like when we were in Orlando?"

"Of course," Jerrod said.

"Mercator is the Mouse of this town."

"I'm lost," Erin said. "What does that mean?"

Jerrod turned to her. "Disney basically runs the city of Orlando. While Pete and I were there, the people of Florida passed an amendment to the state constitution, demanding high-speed rail service throughout the state. The project bogged down because Disney insisted that it would not allow a rail stop at Disney World unless there were no other stops between Disney World and downtown."

"Needless to say," Pete said, "that was unacceptable to Sea World, Universal Studios and the other theme parks around the city."

"And equally needless to say," Jerrod added, "it made no sense whatever to have high-speed rail service through Orlando if there wasn't going to be a stop at Disney World. It's a huge tourist draw, after all. Orlando is Florida's most centrally located city. It was going to be the hub of the high-speed rail network. So…"

"Disney basically vetoed the plan for the entire state?" Erin asked.

Jerrod nodded. "In a nutshell."

"But the voters had put that in the constitution," Erin objected. "That's the highest law in the state. It should've trumped those objections."

"It should have, maybe," Pete said. "But the provision in the constitution simply said that a high-speed rail network should be built. It didn't appropriate any money, and it didn't specify a deadline. So as long as the negotiations were dragging along, the state legislature was fulfilling the letter of its constitutional mandate."

"A couple of elections later," Jerrod continued, "there was a repeal amendment on the ballot. It was billed as a budgetary issue—you could have high-speed rail *or* better schools, but not both, unless you wanted higher taxes—so the people repealed the high-speed rail."

"Point is," Pete said, "Disney has a lot of clout in Orlando, and in Florida as a whole. The company brings in a ton of tourists who spend a ton of money, not just at Disney World but at other parks and hotels in the area. Plus Disney keeps a lot of people employed, funneling their tourist-earned dollars into the local economy, as well. Disney doesn't have to approve everything that happens, but if it comes out and works against something…"

"Then that something doesn't happen," Erin said.

"Bingo," Pete said. "And Mercator's like that here. Instead of tourist dollars, it's federal contracting money. A whole lot of it. Enough to keep over ten thousand people employed. And those employees spend their money here in town and…"

Erin nodded. "I get the picture. It's almost like the old company towns."

"Not quite," Pete said. "This is also an air force

town. Cheyenne Mountain. The Air Force Academy. There are two other air force bases, plus the army's Fort Carson. And don't forget that we're also the American Vatican."

Both Jerrod and Erin gave him uncomprehending looks.

"American Vatican?" she asked.

Pete chuckled. "A couple of the largest and most influential evangelical ministries have their head-quarters here. They're a powerful influence, too. So no, Mercator isn't all-powerful, like the old company towns. But they do have a lot of pull, and, just like Disney in Orlando, if Mercator works *against* some-thing, it's probably not going to happen. And they're growing all the time. Too much money in defense contracting not to, I guess."

"That's going to make things…more awkward," Erin said cautiously.

Pete's smile shut down in an instant. "So what are the two of you into? I know Mercator's up on a cor-porate fraud case." He looked at Erin. "You're *that* reporter, aren't you?"

She nodded.

"There's a lot of folks here in town that wouldn't be happy to meet you," Pete said with a wry smile.

"I'm not surprised," she replied. "Considering they broke into my apartment and put me in the hospital…and that was *after* I testified."

"After? That doesn't make sense, unless this is more than corporate fraud."

Jerrod nodded. "It is. Way more."

"What do you need?" Pete asked. "How bad is this going to get?"

"That depends on them," Jerrod said. "This isn't one I—" he looked over at Erin "—*we*...are going to let go. It involves kids, Pete."

"Shit," Pete said, shaking his head. "I should have known, you being involved, but...ahh, shit. Okay, tell me what you know, or think you know."

They spent the next half hour laying out the evidence they had, including showing Pete the e-mails and documents from Erin's laptop. The older man's broad face seemed to darken with each passing moment.

"You don't have enough," he said when they'd finished. "You don't have enough by half."

"We know that," Erin said. "That's why we're here."

"I thought you might know some people in Mercator," Jerrod said. "Small town, big company."

"Well, sure," Pete replied. "Hard to live here and not know someone who works there, or someone who knows someone. But it's not as if I have inside access to their executive-level files. And that's what you're going to need."

"That would be ideal, yes," Jerrod said. "But you and I both know we're not going to get it. So we'll have to find someone to squeeze. Someone in a position to verify this stuff."

"And my source," Erin said.

"Easier to find the former than the latter," Pete said to her. "A big company like this always has its share of people who aren't totally thrilled with the boss. But to find that one guy—the guy who's been talking to you—that's going to be a challenge."

"We could probably get by without him if we could verify his info otherwise," Jerrod said. "But it'd be a lot stronger if I could show the origins of the case."

"I'm not going to ask why you're not working with the local field office on this," Pete said. "You're out on a limb, aren't you?"

Jerrod nodded. "Georgie knows what I'm working on. Nobody else. This isn't the kind of case I wanted wafting around the corridors and getting bollixed before we could get it nailed down."

"I can see that," Pete said. "But it's yet another complication. Any more roadblocks you want to throw up for me to sort through?"

"Yeah," Jerrod said. "Mercator knows we know. So we've gone off the grid."

Pete burst out in a laugh. "Well, ain't that just the topper of all toppers?"

"And Erin has zero training if things get ugly, so we'll need to get her ready," Jerrod added.

Pete continued to laugh, shaking his head. "Okay, okay. So you want miracles, and I'm guessing you want them fast. Yesterday, if possible."

"That's about the size of it," Erin said.

"Perfect," Pete said. "Just perfect."

In the wake of the blizzard, the night turned cold and crystalline. A gibbous moon cast blue light on the snow atop Pikes Peak, giving it a brilliant glow. From Pete's deck, where Erin stood wrapped in one of Pete's parkas, the night shone with beauty and magic.

As long as she could avoid thinking about why she was standing there, the night remained untarnished.

Behind her, the sliding-glass door opened and shut. Footsteps crunched on snow over wood; then Jerrod stood beside her at the rail.

"It's beautiful," he said.

"Are you wearing your other eyes tonight?" The question came out more sarcastically than she'd intended, but she didn't try to smooth it over. He'd been giving her hell all day. It was her turn now.

A half minute passed before he answered. "It took me a long time to get to the point where I could see the beauty again. I'm not trying to take that away from you."

Instantly, she felt like a bitch. "Sorry."

"No, that was justified. I've been riding you all

day. And I'm going to be riding you again come morning. But you know why."

"Yeah." She *did,* and she really disliked her reaction to the training she knew was necessary. "I haven't been very good about it."

"You've been good enough. Look—" he turned sideways so he could face her "—you didn't volunteer for this. You were simply going to research and write a story. You didn't decide to involve yourself in clandestine operations."

"That's not true," she answered honestly. "Sure, it would have been nice if I could have done this like most stories I write. But I was the one who decided I wouldn't let go even if it became dangerous. If what this guy told me is true, there's too much at stake. Little girls at stake."

He nodded, folded his arms and leaned against the railing. "You've got guts."

"Which is another word for stupidity, but there it is. So I'll try harder."

"You're trying hard already. And I don't want to take tonight's beauty away from you by discussing this right now. Morning is soon enough. So, your family moved to New Zealand? Any particular reason?"

She rested her elbows on the rail. "We took a vacation there when I was a kid. They never stopped wanting to go back."

"But not you?"

"By the time they left, I was invested here. Maybe someday. It's a beautiful country. Less of a military-industrial complex."

A quiet chuckle escaped him. "I don't know quite how to answer that."

She shrugged. "Depends on your politics. Moving to New Zealand would, unfortunately, make it harder for me to do exposés."

"Very practical point of view."

"Yeah. I somehow don't think they have as much scandal in New Zealand. Fewer people. Smaller government."

"That's a point."

She looked at him. "I miss them like hell."

"I know."

"What about *your* family?"

"My folks are still in Ohio. Schoolteachers."

"Good for them." She sensed that wasn't the full picture but feared pressing him. Sometimes he could look as forbidding as a rocky cliff. With a sigh, she turned back to the view of Pikes Peak. "That's a million-dollar view."

"Yeah. Pete was smart and bought this land years ago. Otherwise, I doubt he could afford to live here."

"These days, yeah. There don't seem to be enough beautiful places for all the people. Not that it matters. People come, and it becomes less beautiful anyway."

She felt him glance at her. "Environmentalist?"

"Common-sense-alist," she retorted. "If we could just build a cabin in the woods, that would be one thing. Unfortunately, we need to bring the mall with us."

Another chuckle escaped him. "Very true."

"It's so nice here," she said after a moment. "The air smells like pine, cold and fresh. And the view is stunning."

"Yeah, it is."

"It would be nice," she said wistfully, "if the whole world could be just like this all the time."

He didn't answer, but he seemed to move a bit closer. She took that as agreement and was grateful for the way his body blocked the breeze, allowing her to warm up.

She wanted to stay here forever. Just like this.

And then she remembered little girls being carried aboard planes to fates she could barely stand to think about.

The respite, so brief, had ended.

# 15

The reporter's e-mail seemed to wrap a noose around Alton's neck. He sat in the cybercafé, in a dark and quiet corner usually occupied by gamers, and stared at the words gleaming on the screen.

Need more information. Must meet.

Yeah, as if. He'd taken serious risks in compiling and sending the information he'd already given her. Now Mercator was tightening its security even more. There was no way he could get the files she needed without leaving tracks…tracks that a corporate Big Brother was already on alert for and sniffing after. *She* was supposed to dig up the rest of the story, not him. He'd given her enough, right?

Right.

He deleted the message, determined to ignore it, and called up a game for cover. Time to bash some monsters. Here he was, thirty-two, and he still loved to play these stupid games.

Maybe because life was simple here. Here he could see who the monsters were. He could take that as a given and hack away without wondering whether he'd crossed ethical lines or kicked over any rotting logs. If it was ugly, scaly, furry, drooly, fiery or otherwise monstrous, he could draw his twice-blessed battle-ax and wade into the fray with his virtue unchallenged, secure in the knowledge that even death itself was only a temporary setback—so long as he paid his monthly dues to the game server.

It was an online game, one he played with people from all over the world. It was, in truth, a world all its own. He had friends here, and a few enemies. While he wasn't the type to seek star status in anything, he'd founded a guild, a virtual space where he and his friends could meet to set off on group adventures. Because this particular online world was a pseudomedieval, largely agrarian culture, and because he was not as devoid of humor as most people assumed accountants were, he'd named his guild the Bean Counters. Their crest—which his wife had designed on a lark, but everyone in the guild had loved—was a green shield with three neat rows of ten kidney beans.

He was proud of that crest. It was a way of carrying her into his online world. She didn't like to play, but she didn't mind his playing, so long as he kept it to two nights a week. And while he could as easily have played from his computer at home, they'd both felt it would be harder for him to stay away from the game if it were right there in his den. Going out to the cybercafé increased the transactional cost of playing the game, requiring as it did that he stay dressed, drive a few miles, wait for an open slot at the café and pay their nominal online fees, but it also kept him from spending too much time in a virtual world, and thus failing as a husband and father.

*Father.* The word struck him like a lightning bolt, diverting him from his game. He closed his eyes, wishing away the images of unconscious young girls being carried aboard a plane. He never should have looked. Never.

But he had. His own virtue—his need to be sure no one in the company was committing fraud—had pushed him into this mess. He ought to have passed his suspicions up the chain and let the company's own fraud squad handle it. But he'd wanted to be a hero in the real world. Now Mercator was tightening a security vise that, Alton knew, would sooner or later squeeze the life out of him.

He'd tried to tell himself that the new security measures might not be about him. They could be about something else entirely, a leak of information about some classified contract, some problem he knew nothing about and had played no part in.

But he didn't believe it. He couldn't let himself believe it. At the very least, he had violated DOD rules for handling classified information by sharing that information with a reporter. He'd redacted it, yes, to remove any national security information, but that wasn't the point. He lacked the authority to release it, even in redacted form. That wasn't his job.

Worse, he'd uncovered a crime. It had to be a crime. Otherwise, there would be no reason to conceal it.

And not just some ordinary crime. No, he couldn't have simply stumbled over another routine fraud, like the case in Houston. He'd come upon something so horrific, so monstrous, that it still left him aghast. Selling young girls as sex slaves, just to sweeten an arms deal? Who could be so morally empty?

Mercator, apparently. The company he worked for. The company whose interests he'd been out to protect when he'd started on this sordid adventure. He wasn't protecting helpless, innocent virtual villagers from a marauding band of evil orcs. He was part of the evil orc band himself.

Even as he chatted with his guild colleagues about their next quest, he couldn't yank his mind away from the reporter's e-mail.

Need more information. Must meet.

He couldn't risk meeting her. And he couldn't risk *not* meeting her. He'd chosen her, after all, and not only because she'd been the reporter to break open the Houston fraud case. He'd done his research. She had built a solid reputation, and so far as he could tell, she had never once burned a source. If she said she needed more information, if she said they needed to meet, she had good reasons.

He switched out of the game back into his e-mail box. He'd marked the message for deletion, but it wouldn't actually be purged until he logged off. Clicking it open again, he hit the reply button.

Meet me here.

He attached a single *jpeg* file, the image of a green shield with three neat rows of ten kidney beans. He couldn't risk meeting her in the real world. But if she found him in a virtual world...

Yes, he thought. He would meet her in his second world, in a world where he knew he was one of the heroes. It was time to pay his dues. To the game server, to his wife and daughter and to himself.

Across town, Chuck Besom sat at his personal computer in an apartment darkened except for stray moonlight and his desk lamp. He preferred the dark, always had. At least since he'd begun his military training. The preference remained like a brand on his soul.

Although he wasn't supposed to be able to do this, Chuck Besom was a man of many resources. So, in a very quiet way, he had arranged for a back door to the Mercator computer systems. He had originally planned it as a way to protect the company against information leaks, a way to detect unwarranted activity that might harm Mercator.

Tonight he was after something else. He knew that Tatum and Kendall Warrick were taking homeless persons off the street and using them to train interrogators. How could he not know, when he was security chief for RoughRider, Inc.? The private military arm of Mercator received calls for a lot more than mercenaries and truck drivers with nerves of steel. They received orders from all over the world from governments that needed interrogators on a moment's notice, or that wanted someone to train theirs.

Hence the use of homeless people as subjects. It wasn't pretty, but it was safe. When they could, they handed the subjects a little cash and returned them to the streets, where no one believed their wild tales of being abducted and tortured. When they couldn't return them, no one missed them.

Chuck had no problem with that. Those people

were invariably the dregs of humanity, chosen because they'd sunk to the gutter through use of
alcohol or drugs, not through simple misfortune. He
liked to think of it as cleaning up the streets.

But something wasn't right. He smelled it. There
was something going on between Tatum and Warrick that had put him on the outside. Something that
seemed to worry them far more than the fear that
someone would reveal that they were hijacking
homeless people. Lack of knowledge could be a
deadly thing, and Chuck Besom was ready to fill in
a few blanks.

Sitting at his computer, he looked for the secrets,
looked for the leak. He didn't really expect to find
the secrets. He was certain that absolutely no record
of the homeless people they picked up could be
found on this system. It would be too dangerous.

But there was something else. Something Kendall
referred to as "pot sweetening." Something that was
getting the company an awful lot of orders from
certain quarters.

And somewhere in here, among all the records of
shipments loaded and sent, he was going to find
whatever had tipped off the leak.

Or so he hoped.

In the wee hours of the morning he moved from
the shifting of funds to shipments of goods. It was
there that he noted something that woke him up from

his near stupor. As the sun's rays began to poke through the windows, he called up his own private audit software, software that didn't erase data every few months, unlike the company's own audit trail, and discovered who had been there before him.

Goddamn, he thought, all urge to sleep forgotten. His heart thudded loudly in his hears. *Goddamn!*

He peered at the screen again, but there was no escaping it. Executive jets leaving not only Colorado Springs but the training camp, as well. Those jets couldn't possibly carry the equipment on the bills of lading. No way.

In fact, all they were good for was shipping *people. Pot sweeteners.*

Jerrod turned away as Erin vomited. He knew it was embarrassing enough for her—God only knew how many times he'd done it in Ranger school— without his watching. He waited until she'd finished clearing her mouth before squatting beside her to offer her his canteen.

"Feel better?" he asked.

"No," she said, still on her hands and knees, head hanging low. "I don't."

"Take a minute, Erin. Then rinse your mouth out."

She looked up at him with skin as pale as porcelain. "How about I take an hour? I'm not in shape like you are."

"We don't have an hour," Jerrod said. He gave the canteen an encouraging shake. "And you'll never get in shape on all fours with your breakfast on the ground in front of you."

She sat back on her heels, snatching the canteen from his hand and taking a mouthful of water, then spitting it out. "You really are a bastard, Jerrod."

"I know it feels like that now," he said with an impassive shrug, deliberately concealing his concern. "But needs must when the devil drives."

"What's that, a Ranger saying?"

He shook his head. "British, I think. I heard it from a former SAS guy I was with on an op."

She took another mouthful of water and nodded as she swished it around in her mouth, then spat again. "Yeah, well, what if *you're* the devil driving?"

"I'd say I'm sorry, but I'd be lying. Would you rather I were an honest bastard or a supportive liar?"

She laughed. "Well, I'd rather you were a supportive friend, but since that's not on the menu…"

"Then on your feet, Erin. It's two miles back to Pete's place, and that's where lunch is."

With a resigned nod, she struggled to her feet and fell in beside him as he broke into a jog. The truth was, after only ten days, her body was already adapting to the altitude and the increasing pressure of her training. She didn't realize it yet, of course, but he could see it.

He saw it in a host of tiny details, like the way she held her head a bit taller, looking up and out as they ran rather than staring at the ground in front of her. That meant her core abdominal muscles were gaining strength, holding her posture more erect. It also meant her calf and thigh muscles were firming up, developing the springy flexibility that allowed her to trust her feet to find and maintain her balance.

That combination of stronger core muscles and firmer thighs and calves, keeping her posture more erect and her head up, meant she was giving her lungs more room to work inside her rib cage. There hadn't yet been time for her to gain much in the way of aerobic fitness, but simply running taller, giving herself more room to breathe, had already added measurably to her stamina. Three days ago, she'd only been able to sustain a brisk jog for five minutes before needing to rest. Today, he was pushing her toward ten, and for the past two hours she'd been walking through the rest breaks rather than standing still, bent over with her hands on her knees, gasping.

Until this last break, that is, when she'd hit the proverbial wall. The combination of lactic acid buildup in her muscles and oxygen deprivation in the high mountain air had taken its inevitable toll. At eight thousand feet, she wasn't likely to get severe mountain sickness, but he didn't want to risk it.

"Why on earth do runners want to train up here?"

she asked as they jogged along the forest path. "There's no *air* in the air!"

Woodland Park, where Pete lived, was two thousand feet above Colorado Springs. While it was well within the range of human tolerance, the air was indeed thinner. She would need another few days to get past the nagging headaches and near-constant thirst. He passed her the canteen again. By now she knew better than to refuse it, taking sips in time with her strides and breathing. Hydration was essential in order to adapt to higher altitudes. The dry air sapped away fluids, and the increased hemoglobin could turn blood into thick, viscous sludge if they weren't careful.

"The theory," he explained, "is that your body creates more red blood cells at higher altitude, so you can extract more oxygen from the air. When you get down to sea level, you'll still have that extra oxygenation capacity, at least for a few weeks."

"I don't like the way you said that word *theory*," she said, looking over at him.

He gave her an amused shrug. "In truth, it doesn't seem to work all that well. Those extra red blood cells also raise your blood pressure at sea level. It seems you need to train at about the same altitude you expect to compete at and acclimate your body for that."

"So you think whatever we do may end up being in the mountains?" Erin asked.

"It seems likely. Plus, we don't have a wealth of choices for training areas. We need to be somewhere safe, and somewhere with access to Mercator. That's here."

"So you have me running up and down mountains."

He smiled. "Exactly."

She winked. "So maybe you're not a totally heartless bastard after all."

Something in the way she winked made his heart jump. Beneath all her grumbling, she was actually enjoying this. That part didn't really surprise him. She'd said she was an adrenaline junkie, and the things she'd done as a reporter seemed to prove that. He could understand that she would get a charge out of physical training with a former special-ops guy.

But there was something else in that wink. He was sure of it. She was not only enjoying the training, she was enjoying his company.

And, he had to admit, he was enjoying hers.

"Shh," he said. "You'll ruin my reputation."

She laughed. That she could laugh at all, now eight minutes into a brisk jog uphill over uneven ground, was yet more evidence that her body was responding to the hard training.

"I thought your reputation was the knight errant on a white horse, riding to the rescue of lost kids."

"Well..." he began.

"So how am I going to ruin that by noting that you're not a totally heartless bastard?"

"I'm your drill instructor right now," he said. "Drill instructors are supposed to be heartless bastards. It's in the job description, right below constantly screaming and just above impossible to please."

She shook her head. "Sorry. You're failing."

"Story of my life," he said with a chuckle.

"Somehow I don't think you've failed *all* that often," Erin said. "You're not the type."

"Not all that often, no."

But the times he had, beginning with his inability to find his sister and leading to the other kids he hadn't been able to find in time…

"No," she said. "Don't go there."

"Sorry."

"Or at least, if you're going to go there, take me with you. Tell me what happened, Jerrod."

"It's not a place you want to see, Erin."

"Let me decide that. You *are* a knight errant on a white charger. That doesn't happen by accident. No one sets out to tilt at windmills."

"No, I guess not."

"So?" she asked.

He glanced at his watch. It had been ten minutes. Time for a rest break. But he couldn't rest. Not and tell this story. Instead, he quickened the pace. To his surprise, she stayed with him stride for stride.

"It started with my sister," he said. "Elena. One day she was a happy, giggling, routinely dysfunctional ten-year-old. Then she went over to some guy in a car, next to her school playground. And vanished forever."

"Shit," Erin said, her breath starting to grow raspy with the faster pace. "They never found her?"

"No. Neither have I."

"It wasn't your fault, Jerrod."

He shrugged. "Of course not."

"It wasn't."

His eyes met hers. "I know that, okay? But one day I have a kid sister who, when she isn't annoying me all to hell, is making me laugh myself silly. The next day...I don't. She's just...gone. And the longer she stays gone, the more it starts to feel as if maybe she was never there at all. Like I'd dreamed her. What starts to hurt is that it *doesn't* hurt anymore. What really tears you apart is that you know you could forget her altogether."

"You'd never do that," Erin said.

"But I have," Jerrod said. "Sometimes whole weeks go by and I never think of her at all. If it weren't for her picture on my desk, I couldn't remember her face. I can't remember what she looked like when she laughed, or what she sounded like. When I try to, I don't know if the memories are real or something I've invented to fill the empty place where she used to be."

"Jerrod…"

"So that's what I think about every time I'm on a missing-kid case. I know what those families are feeling. I know what it's like to try to clutch at vapors, the last fading memories of someone who used to be as much a part of you as your left hand or your right leg. No one should have to feel that."

"Jerrod…"

"So I ended up in private security, working kidnap and recovery cases. The things people did to kids—*do* to kids—it's sick. It's sicker than you can believe. And then to find out the people I was working for didn't give a goddamn about the girl herself… They just didn't want to have to pay the ransom. Wanted me to get her back or get her killed trying. They went behind my back to make damn sure one or the other happened. And sure enough…"

"Jerrod!"

Her voice was sharp, piercing, cutting through the black, inky fog that had been building in his thoughts. She was fifteen yards behind him, and when he looked back, the toe of his right foot snagged on a tree root, sending him tumbling forward in a heap.

"Awww, fuck," he said, spitting bits of rotting leaves from his mouth.

"Are you okay?" Erin asked, quickly catching up and kneeling beside him.

"Yeah. I just feel stupid. I'm supposed to be training you, and instead I'm stumbling around as if I'm half-drunk."

"Everyone falls, Jerrod."

He shook his head. "You don't get it, Erin. You think I'm the white knight, and maybe I am. But being a white knight means you *can't* fall down. Every time I fall down, some innocent kid disappears. Every time I fall down, some other family ends up trying to remember if she was ever there at all, or if they just invented her. Every time I fall down, the world's just a little shittier than it was the day before."

Erin shook her head. "Jerrod, you can't take the whole world on your shoulders. You've done things, saved people, that nobody else could have. But there are still bad people in the world, and they're still going to do bad things, and you're not responsible for every shitty thing that happens anywhere. If you take that on, you're just going to kill yourself, and *then* who's going to save the people you would have saved?"

"Easy for you to say. You get a story either way."

She shoved him to the ground. "Fine! Go on thinking you're the only one doing good, the only one who *can* do good. Go on with your not-quite-almighty God complex. But I have news for you, Jerrod Westlake. The position of God is already taken, and you're not it."

Then she stunned him by taking off at a dead sprint, uphill through the final half mile of dense woods. For a moment, he sat and watched her, a sense of pride in how gracefully she ran mixed with total shame at what he'd revealed.

He'd been right. She didn't want to go to the dark places in his mind. Who would? He didn't want to go there himself. And he would damn sure never take her there again.

But neither was he going to let her beat him back to Pete's place. He was still the trainer. Respect must be maintained, even if he didn't deserve it.

He scrambled to his feet and sprinted off after her, feeling his body rise onto the balls of his feet, muscular legs reaching out to grab the ground ahead and kick it back behind him until his heels nearly touched his butt, arms pumping in a steady rhythm, breath huffing deep and smooth, mind clearing, the world suddenly rushing past as his body found its place in the universe.

In less than a quarter mile, he'd caught up with her, and with a final burst he shot past, everything in life reduced to reaching and contracting quadriceps and hamstrings and calves and diaphragm and heart muscle, body in motion for the sake of motion itself.

As the woods thinned and Pete's house came into view, he throttled down to an easy jog and finally to a walk, and Erin fell in beside him, their ragged breathing sounding as if…as if they'd just done something he shouldn't let himself think about.

"Wow," he said.

"Yeah." She smiled. "Wow."

"I'm glad you're back," Pete said, stepping out on the porch.

Jerrod took one look at Pete's face and knew something was horribly wrong. "What's going on, Pete?"

Pete drew a slow breath, as if trying to find words within the bulk of his torso. "Jesus, Jerrod, these people play for keeps. They've taken Georgie."

# 16

"What the hell happened?" Jerrod asked, pacing Pete's living room as he sucked down springwater.

Erin found it equally impossible to sit. The muscles of her hips, thighs and legs were alive with random tingling sensations. When she'd mentioned it three days ago after their first training run, Jerrod had explained that it was normal. Muscle fibers that had grown accustomed to steadily contracting and releasing as she ran were still receiving that increased blood flow, necessary to flush out the lactic acid that had built up as a normal by-product of activity. Her heart and lungs were still functioning at peak efficiency, but because she was no longer stressing her body with motion, her blood was hyperoxygenated. The combination produced random firings in her muscle fibers, leading to the twitchy tingles she was now experiencing.

After he'd explained, Erin had asked him if he'd

had some medical training. He'd simply given her one of his patented shrugs and said he'd learned his medicine in the school of oh-shit-that-hurts. She didn't believe him. His clear, thoughtful, reasoned explanations for the ways her body was tormenting her were too studied to be simply random. It was yet another part of himself that he was keeping behind a wall.

Now, as she drained her second half-liter bottle of water, she saw his walls starting to crumble. It was as if he'd found a role in the Bureau that was near enough to his core to make him feel productive but distant enough from his past to keep him from feeling haunted, but now the safety that role provided was eroding, and ghosts were rearing up from the dark corners of his mind.

"Nobody knows what happened," Pete said. "I called the Austin Field Office. Said I'm working on a memoir and wanted to double-check some facts on a case I'd worked there. Asked if Georgie was around. That's when whoever answered the phone put me through to the ASAC. Guy named Monfort. Like, in about two seconds."

"Uh-oh," Jerrod said.

"Uh-huh. I acted confused, wondered if I'd been transferred to the wrong desk. Gave him the same story and my Bureau I.D. code. That's when he told me that Georgie left work three days ago and nobody's seen her since. Not at home. No message. The Bureau is treating it as a missing-persons case."

"Shit," Jerrod said.

"Exactly," Pete agreed. "He didn't mention you by name, but he did say their thinking is that she might have gotten caught up in something another agent is working on. Said two of his best agents have dropped out of sight. He did *not* like that. At all."

"Maybe you should call this Monfort guy?" Erin asked.

Jerrod shook his head. "I don't trust him. Derek is a young buck who's old school."

Erin tried to make sense of that and finally gave him a blank stare. "Umm, could you translate that please?"

"The Bureau has something of a dark history in terms of politics," Jerrod said.

"A lot of guys believe the Bureau's primary mission is self-preservation, and the best way to do that is to protect the political structure," Pete said.

"The old school," Jerrod said, picking up. "Kiss up to the hands that feed you, and they'll keep feeding you. Some rationalize it away by saying it ensures the Bureau stays around to do the good things it does. Others don't even bother. For them, the politics *is* the rationale. And Derek's one of those. Young, ambitious and political."

"That's a dangerous combination," Erin said.

"Now add smart to the mix," Jerrod said.

"Worst of all breeds," Pete said. "So y'all need to relocate your stuff to the cellar. I have a hidey-hole down there you can use. Figure we have maybe two hours before we get a visit, and y'all can't be here."

Erin nodded and looked at Jerrod. Something in the set of his jaw, the sharpness of his eyes, conveyed a wellspring of rage that sent a chill down her spine. It was the same look she'd seen earlier, when he'd told her about his sister.

"C'mon, Jerrod," she said. "Let's get busy. Can't have Pete getting dragged into this mess. We need to go connect to the Net anyway, so I can check e-mail."

"Yeah," he said. "We do."

They hadn't brought much, a bag each, and re-packing took almost no time. Pete led them down to the basement, where a Peg-Board-backed work-bench stood against one wall. Although it was on casters, he nonetheless asked Jerrod for a hand, and the two of them hefted it and carried it away from the wall.

"Why not just roll it?" Erin asked.

"It would leave marks on the floor," Pete ex-plained. "Any agent worth his salt would wonder why it'd been moved and decide to check it out."

The basement walls were lined with flagstone, a neat but very masculine room with a score of wood-shop projects in various stages of completion. On the wall was a single photo, of Pete and Jerrod together, arms over each other's shoulders, each with one hand extended, thumbs up, standing in front of a riotous splash of tropical palms. In front of them was stretched the most massive fish Erin had ever seen.

"Grouper fishing in Florida," Pete explained, taking the photo from the wall. "Took us half an hour to fight that fish into the boat."

With surprisingly dexterous fingers, Pete slid two flagstones from the wall behind the workbench, revealing a two-foot square, perhaps three-foot deep, compartment. Erin saw something gleam dully in the light. He pulled out a Glock nine-millimeter.

"I keep a couple of spares, just in case."

"We shouldn't need them yet," Jerrod said. "And it's better if we don't, just in case some cop decides I changed lanes wrong."

"Understood," Pete said. He replaced the handgun, placing the photo in the compartment and taking out an old photo of himself in the military. The frame was exactly the same size as that of the photo he'd taken down, and he hung it on the wall, then shook his head. "I was an ugly cuss back then. But it fills the space."

They tucked their bags into the compartment, and Pete and Jerrod replaced the workbench. Pete then picked up a table leg he'd been working on and pointed to the lathe. "Time to make some sawdust.

Y'all get going. I'll see you after dark. You know the back way in, right?"

"I hope so," Erin said, nodding. "We've been running it for three days straight."

"I do," Jerrod said. "See you tonight, buddy."

Pete was putting in earplugs as they climbed the stairs, and moments later they heard the whining buzz of the lathe shaving wood. They left the cellar door open and headed for their stolen car.

"I hope this thing isn't on the watch list," Erin said as she climbed in.

"Probably only on the local list around Pueblo. Has different tags now, anyway," Jerrod said. "We'll be fine."

His voice was tense, precise, almost mechanical.

"Looked like you and Pete had fun fishing that day," Erin said as he drove toward the smallish downtown area of Woodland Park.

"Yup."

"Good times."

"That they were."

"Jerrod…" she began.

"Don't," he said. "Look, Erin, you're sweet, and I know you care. You're one of those bright souls who always wants the world to become better as you pass through it. And I admire that. I do. But that's not where I am. It's not where I need to be for this."

"We're in this together, Jerrod."

"We're in this together, sure," he said, then touched his forehead. "But in there, no. We're not there together. I don't want you there."

Erin shook her head. "You're the one who made me start looking at the terrain around me. Looking for threats. You're part of that terrain."

"I'm not a threat to you. We're on the same side."

"Are we?" she asked. "We can't be on the same side if you're off on your own side. You said you had to train me so you could trust me to hold up my end if things go south. *I* need to trust *you,* too."

"You won't have to worry about me."

"You can say that. Maybe it even convinces you. But it does *not* convince me. Not enough to walk into whatever it is we're headed into, when I *won't* know enough to know what to do next. I've walked away from my apartment, from my bank account, from my car, from my whole life, Jerrod Westlake! I've dumped it all to go off the grid with you, chasing this story. And you want me to trust you, to put my total faith in you, but you tell me you don't want me to know what's happening in your head. Put the shoe on the other foot, Special Agent. How trusting would *you* feel?"

Erin realized her hands were shaking and her voice had risen an octave. But this time she would not back down. "We're either in this together all the way, or I'm out. I'm not going after Mercator with one eye over my shoulder, wondering when that shit built up inside you is going to explode."

"I don't explode," he said.

"Everyone does," Erin shot back. "Turn up the pressure cooker enough, and everyone will explode. And you're on a high, fast boil. I see it. Pete sees it. I could see it in his eyes. You're the only one who doesn't seem to see it. And that's what worries me."

"Oh, I see it," Jerrod said. "I see it too damn well. But your pushing isn't going to change it. You're only turning the temperature up higher."

"Well, pardon me for living," Erin said. "Pardon me for giving a damn."

"That's the problem," Jerrod said. "That's what you can't do. *That's* when you explode."

"Really."

"Yeah, really."

"Sounds like a bunch of macho male bullshit," Erin said, folding her arms over her chest.

Jerrod spotted a parking space next to a coffee shop advertising Internet access and almost lurched the car to a halt. His eyes met hers. "What's the worst thing you've ever done? The absolute worst?"

"I put my kid brother in the hospital," Erin said, without a moment's hesitation. "He was riding my bike, and I wanted it back. He was six, and I was eight. So I picked up Mom's broom and threw it like

I'd seen people throw spears in some show we'd watched the night before about lion hunting in Africa. Damn if it didn't go right through the front wheel. It lodged in the spokes and snapped the bike over forward. Billy went flying and landed on the neighbor's gravel driveway. Two stitches in his forehead. He still has a scar right in the middle, above his eyebrows."

Jerrod nodded. "Well, imagine it's not a scar on his forehead. Imagine it's a slash right across his throat and his blood is smeared all over the wall, and he's lying in a heap."

She looked at him. "You did that?"

"I might as well have. I was leading the mission. I'd left a captain on security in the hallway while we went in to capture a couple of bad guys. The only thing that kid did was wake up in the middle of the night when he heard a door being kicked in across the hall from where he lived. So he came out to check. And my captain slit his throat."

"You didn't kill him," Erin said.

"Doesn't matter. With authority comes responsibility. That's a hard-and-fast rule of military life. It was my op. I was responsible for everything that happened on the mission whether I did it personally or not. So that dead kid was on my head. The rest of it was, too."

"What was the rest of it?"

Jerrod looked at her. "Once we were on the chopper, I took my KA-BAR and buried it to the hilt in the back of captain's leg, two inches above the knee, and pulled. Cut through his hamstring like I was cutting off a slice of roast beef. Fucker should've bled to death, but the rest of my team held me back while our medic treated him. But that wasn't the worst thing."

Erin nodded, listening.

"The worst thing is, I was fighting my guys there in the chopper, wanting to finish the bastard off. And not just because he'd killed a kid. Because he'd screwed our mission. We had to get out of the country after that. Fast. Lost some good leads. Let some assholes get away, guys we could have taken down if we'd been able to stay. The moment I saw that kid in the hall, I knew we were blown. And that son of a bitch actually smiled when he told me what he'd done. To this day, I wish my guys had let me kill him."

"Holding all that hate…" Erin said, shaking her head.

He nodded, rubbing his arm. "He's the guy who fucked over my last K-R-and-R mission. The army buried what happened in that hallway. Too many rocks they couldn't let get turned over. I got out. He went spook. Never saw him again until an op over in Indonesia. He set me up to get ambushed."

"That's where you got hurt," Erin said, nodding toward his arm. "The one that hurts in the cold."

Jerrod went silent for a moment, looking out at the street. "I was ready to die. Wanted to die. What the hell. It couldn't be any worse than the hell I was already in. Only reason I didn't is because the girl I was there to save, she decided to die a little for me. I was in and out of shock. She led us out. Led *me* out. She pointed, I shot. And every time she pointed, every time I shot, every time I saw some guy slump to the ground with a hole where his face had been, I saw another piece of her die. And yeah, she'd have died for good if I hadn't been there. But she'd have died with a clean soul. Instead…"

The silence hung between them, aching. Erin knew there was nothing she could say to change how he felt. She wished she could wave a magic wand to erase the pain. But there was no magic wand. She rested a hand on his arm, offering whatever silent comfort a touch could.

"When you're a kid," Jerrod said, staring out with unfocused eyes, "if you have good parents, they teach you right from wrong. Your mom or dad probably had your ass in a sling for what happened to your brother."

She nodded. "Oh, yeah. The one time Dad ever spanked me. Not that he needed to. I knew it from the moment I let go of the broom. Everything that happened in the next three seconds was my punishment."

"Yup. You learn what's right. You learn what's wrong. But what if then you grow up, and you want to be a hero and do what's right, so you join a bunch of people who teach you how to do what's *necessary?* They tell you if it's necessary for the mission, it's all right. So you do what's necessary, and they give you ribbons and tell you you're a good soldier, one of your country's finest. They tell you people ought to honor you. And you know what?"

Erin shook her head.

He continued. "That's all bullshit. Honor me? A guy on my team killed a ten-year-old kid in cold blood. I tried to kill him—in even colder blood. Then I go rescue some girl who never did a damn thing wrong in her life until I went to save her, and I watch the blood freezing in her little heart, like frostbite rotting away her innocence. Yeah, it was *necessary.* But it wasn't *right.* You can never make it right."

"No," Erin agreed, her chest tight. "You can't."

"I don't need to be honored," Jerrod said. "I need to be forgiven. Forgiven for the lives I've fucked up, doing what was *necessary.* Including yours. And now Georgie's."

"I'm not a priest," Erin said, "but you haven't fucked up my life. Mercator did that. You've kept me alive. I'm not going to forgive you when I ought to thank you."

He looked up as a flock of birds landed on the ledge of a building. "Yeah. That's what everyone always says. Whatever."

"Whatever?" Erin asked.

"Yeah. Whatever." He drew a breath. "Like I said, Erin, you can't get into my head. I wish *I* couldn't, but I have to. I don't want you to go where I've gone."

"Mercator isn't giving us many choices," Erin said. "That's what you're training me for, right?"

He looked at her. "No. I'm going to teach you just enough to keep you from slowing me down. But I'm not going to train you to be what I've been. What I am."

"You're not a monster," Erin said.

"Maybe I am. Maybe you have to be a monster to hunt monsters."

"If you were a monster, you wouldn't care."

"Which is worse?" he asked. "The monster who doesn't know he's a monster, or the one who does... and goes right on doing monstrous things anyway?"

"When I was sixteen," Erin said, "I had a boyfriend. No, not a boyfriend. A crush. It lasted right up to the point when he came over to my house one night and we were sitting on the back porch, kissing some, and he put his hand on my breast. I pushed him away, said no, I didn't want that. He didn't like that answer."

"Oh, no."

"Yeah. He pushed me down on the porch. I saw

the change happen in his eyes. This guy who'd seemed so sweet two minutes before was…someone else. He was over me, had his hand on my collarbone holding me down, on my neck, really, but not really." Even the memory still sickened her.

Jerrod nodded silently.

"He was unbuckling his belt when my dad came out," she said. "I don't know if Dad had been watching all along, or if he'd just seen us at that moment. I never asked, and Dad never said. But the man who came out that door was not the dad I'd always known. In the blink of an eye, he had Mike off me and up against a wall, his hand on Mike's neck and Mike's toes barely touching the porch, saying 'How does it feel? How do *you* like it?'"

"That's a dad," Jerrod said.

"I finally came to my senses enough to scream," Erin said. "That's when Dad let Mike down off the wall. I've always wondered if…if I hadn't screamed…would Dad have…?"

"Are you asking?" Jerrod asked.

She shook her head. "No. You couldn't know. Maybe he would have. Maybe not, since he'd dealt with the threat and made his point. But he wasn't a monster. He was the most *non*violent man I'd ever known—until he saw his daughter in trouble."

"I'm not your dad," Jerrod said.

"No, you're not. But you're not that captain,

either. You recognize the difference between what really is necessary and what's right. What Dad did— what he almost did, anyway—wasn't right. He never talked about it again. Didn't even tell Mom what happened. Like he knew he'd come close to crossing a line that night."

"I've done more than come close," Jerrod said.

Erin nodded. "Yes, you have. You've swum in the evil on the other side of that line. You'll probably be swimming in it again before this is over, and I'll be swimming with you. Not from choice, but because lifeguards have to go in, even when they don't want to, when the evil reaches up and grabs someone and starts dragging them under. That's what my dad was that day. That's what you've been most of your life. Being a lifeguard isn't the same as being a fish. You may swim in the water, but you don't sleep in it, you don't breathe it, you don't need it to live. The captain you stabbed, he was a fish. A monster. You're not. You're just…not."

Another silence filled the car; then a reluctant laugh escaped Jerrod. "You sure I'm not a fish, like the captain?"

"Absolutely. You're a lifeguard."

He snorted, but after a long pause he rolled the word around in his mouth. "Lifeguard," he repeated, drawing it out. Finally he half smiled. "Does that mean I get a TV show with a bunch of big-busted bikini babes on my arm?"

Erin laughed. "Sorry. You gotta make do with me." Jokingly, she pushed her arm beneath her breasts and lifted them, deliberately trying to distract him. "Think these would look good in a bikini?"

"I could do worse," he said, winking. "Much worse."

She swatted his arm. "Down, boy. Let's go get that e-mail. Then we'll see what else happens."

# 17

Georgie listened as Dawn crawled back into her cage, almost feeling Dawn's sigh as the cage door was closed and locked. Only when the lights went out and the door to the room closed did she dare to speak.

"Morning, Dawn."

"Is it?" Dawn asked quietly. "I can't tell."

"I think so," Georgie said. "They seem to have a routine. You in the morning, when they wake up. Me at night. I think."

"Now that you mention it," Dawn said, "I smelled bacon. I think you're right."

It was a tiny but significant victory, Georgie knew. Sensory deprivation worked, in part, by denying the victim any sense of the passage of time. Time was life's ultimate mistress, defining experience, delineating life itself. Without time, agony and despair seemed eternal. But if the victim could retain a sense of time, of its passage, its rhythm, then what was now might not always be. With time came hope.

"Are you okay?" Georgie asked.

"Yeah. It was…" She heard the pause in Dawn's voice, the almost silent sigh. "The usual. I just wish I could shower."

"I know," Georgie said. "I hate that feeling."

"When it trickles down the inside of your leg…"

Georgie's stomach sank. A girl as young as Dawn should not know about that sensation. A girl that young should not describe it with such casual, clinical precision. Worse, a girl that young should not be able to say it without adding "yuck." That Dawn did know about it and could describe it so coldly made Georgie want to retch.

"I'm sorry," Dawn said, into the silence.

"No, honey," Georgie said. "No. It's not you. And yes, that's the worst part."

"I just try to think about you."

Georgie's heart tore, the pieces going in opposite directions, pain for the girl's plight and an almost atavistic recoiling from what the girl seemed to be thinking. "Dawn, I'm not…"

"It's okay," Dawn said quietly. "I don't think I am, either. I don't even know if it's that. But I think about you…like…holding my hand. Stroking my hair. Kissing my cheek. My mouth. Sometimes you even…"

Dawn needed to talk, Georgie realized. Needed to say what she was thinking. Georgie had read about sexual abuse in her Bureau training. Fantasies were a common way for victims to cope with the involuntary physiological responses to abuse. Rather than attributing arousal to the abuse itself, the victim created a sexual fantasy to justify her arousal while still safeguarding her psyche.

Dawn had apparently made Georgie the object of her fantasies. And she needed Georgie to give her permission.

"Go ahead," Georgie said.

"No. Like you said. We're not…that."

"Please, Dawn. Go ahead."

"You're sure? I don't want to…do what they do, to you. I mean…"

"Dawn. It's okay."

Time seemed to stand still before Dawn spoke. "You lean over. Rest your nipple on my cheek. I take it in my mouth. Sometimes I turn my head for real…as if you're really there."

"Like a pacifier."

"Yeah. Kind of."

Georgie imagined a warmth only inches from her breast. A warmth she longed to embrace. At the same time she felt the stirrings of another warmth, lower. One she could not embrace. She knew Dawn's shattered heart was crying out for affirmation. It would not be enough for her to simply say, *That's okay, that's normal, I don't mind.* Dawn needed more than indulgence. But Georgie feared her own response if she went beyond that, what involuntary reactions she might set loose in herself. Especially since she was in as much need as Dawn for protective fantasies.

She had to reject those stirrings. Had to. Because Dawn needed her. Then…and now, to permit the then.

"I would do that for you," she heard herself say. Like a mother, because a mother was what Dawn really needed.

She heard Dawn's breath catch.

"And kiss my forehead?" Dawn asked.

"Yes."

"My head cradled in your arms."

"Yes."

"Your breath tickling my bangs."

Georgie giggled. "Yes."

"My arms around you."

"Yes, Dawn."

"Feeling your heartbeat."

"Steady and strong for you."

"Not afraid to cry anymore."

"I'd kiss your tears away."

There was a long pause. Georgie couldn't tell if the quick, quiet breaths were sobs or…something else. And in that moment, she realized that it didn't matter. Dawn needed to cleanse herself in whatever way would most soothe her tortured soul.

Finally Dawn spoke. "Thank you, Georgie."

Georgie could not find words to respond. Anything she considered—"you're welcome," or "it's all right"—seemed so out of place as to be ludicrous, or worse.

"That's how I get through it," Dawn said.

"It's a perfectly normal defense mechanism." The words were out before Georgie could block them, born of her battle with her own thoughts, but no less cutting.

"Yeah."

She heard the disappointment in the girl's voice, and knew she'd taken the one beautiful thing Dawn had found to hold on to and broken it.

"I'm sorry, Dawn."

"No, you're right."

"No," Georgie whispered firmly. "I'm not. I *am* there with you, Dawn. When you bring me there, I *am* there. With you. Cradling you. Nursing you. Kissing away your tears. Humming a lullaby, telling you that…I love you."

"I love you, too," Dawn said.

Georgie bit her lower lip, grateful that the cotton pads taped over her eyes were absorbing her tears. Her lips quivered. For a moment, she let herself wish that they were not locked apart, that she could take that tender, beautiful child into her arms and cradle her to her breast and do exactly what they'd just described. That she could do it and not care how her body, or Dawn's, responded. That she could just hold Dawn and, for a few moments, feel as if their world were a safe, secure, warm little nest where love was not an epithet.

Tentatively, her heart hammering, Georgie extended trembling fingers to the bottom corner of the cage. Her fingertips clawed back the blankets, slowly, trying to visualize them in her mind so that she could replace them exactly the same way later. Then she felt the metal bars of Dawn's cage and reached through.

"Dawn?" she whispered, tapping her fingertips against the cold metal. "I'm here."

Moments later, she felt warmth. Fingertips finding hers. Holding.

"Thank you, Georgie."

"Thank you, sweetie."

"Sweetie," Dawn repeated. "My mom called me that a lot. When we weren't fighting."

"She was right," Georgie whispered. "You are."

"I miss her."

"I know."

"But at least I have you."

"Yes."

"I'm…sorry…that I… I couldn't take it without you there. I'm sorry."

"Shhhhhhh."

"Will you?"

"Will I what?" Georgie asked.

"Will you take me there, too? When they…?"

Georgie tried to blink back tears and felt the sting of cotton on her corneas, her lips compressing as if caught in the same vise that was squeezing the breath from her. In any other world, in any other time, her thoughts would repulse her. In this world, in this time…

"Yes, Dawn. You'll hold my hand."

She felt soft lips on the tip of her index finger. Just for an instant.

"Thank you, Georgie. I want to help you, too."

The sob finally burst out of Georgie's chest, anger and pain and sorrow and guilt and the shimmering beauty of a sparkling soul reaching for the last tendril of hope and finding it in her. In the thought of her.

"Are you okay?" Dawn asked.

"No. Yes. I…"

"I know," Dawn whispered. Then, after a long moment, she spoke again. "Georgie? Can I…?"

"What, sweetie?"

Dawn's lips touched her fingertip again, quivering, as if too terrified to speak the words. Georgie's heart thudded. *Don't feel it,* she told herself. *It's not for you. It's for her. Don't feel it.*

Easy to think. But would she hear her own thoughts? Or would her body betray her and leave her no different from the monsters in the other room? How many stains could a soul bear before it gave up on ever being clean again?

*It's not for you. It's for her.*

In the end, it was as simple as that.

"Yes, sweetie. Of course."

The lips closed on her fingertip again, the girl's smaller fingers slipping though the bars to hold Georgie's hand still. To hold her hand still, as Dawn drew in her fingertip and began to suckle.

The darkness did not rise up. Whatever had lain in her loins…slept. What pulsed through her instead was a dam-bursting flood of warmth and peace that she had heard described but had never before felt. Because she had never borne a child. Until that moment.

"Yes, sweetie," Georgie whispered softly, her voice finding a timbre she had never before spoken, only heard. "It will be okay. I promise."

The girl, her girl, did not speak. She felt her finger wiggle as Dawn nodded. They would get out of this. Together.

"Try to sleep, little sweetie," Georgie whispered.

The girl half nodded, the rhythm of her suckling already slowing as she lapsed into the world of dreams. Perhaps, Georgie prayed, she would be in those dreams. Right where Dawn needed her.

Being the only good thing she still had the ability to be.

# 18

Jerrod looked at the image a second time, and then a third. The temptation to feel stupid was buffered only by his certainty that Erin was as befuddled as he was.

"Hmm."

"Exactly," she said.

"Green shield-looking thing with thirty brown blotches that look like beans."

"Yeah."

Jerrod frowned. "Y'know, your source is a real pain in the ass."

Erin nodded. "I'm starting to agree. On the other hand, it obviously means *something*. He says to meet him there. Maybe he's afraid he's being watched?"

"That would be the logical conclusion," Jerrod agreed.

Mercator would certainly be tightening its internal security against a leak it knew existed but which it had not yet found. That kind of tightening was usually done in the form of increased document monitoring, bag searches as employees left the building and the like. Erin's source would no doubt think all of it was directed at him and him alone. In the end, of course, it was.

On the other hand, his cryptic message was exactly that: cryptic. So much so that Jerrod had no idea where to even begin looking for an answer. Neither, apparently, did Erin. And now that Georgie had gone missing, patience had become an act of will.

"Maybe it's the logo for a restaurant," she offered. "Or a coffee shop or…something."

"Would you eat somewhere with a logo like that?"

"Probably not."

"That green is putrescent, even if the brown blotches are beans and not turds."

"Jerrod!" But she laughed anyway. Despite the tension and frustration, she hadn't entirely lost her sense of humor. Just mostly.

"The thing is," he said, pulling his chair closer, "he obviously thinks we're going to figure it out. So what do we know about this guy that might help us?"

"Well, I'm pretty sure he's male. And his choice of contact methods, through cybercafés and anonymous servers, leads me to think he's more computer savvy than most people."

"Right. Which might mean he's younger."

"My age, maybe. Or younger still."

"But he's apparently in a position of some consequence, to get the info he sent you."

"True." She nodded. "Okay. Late twenties, early thirties. And he's obviously aware of how network security works, or he wouldn't have been so busy covering his tracks."

"Also true," he agreed. "Only one phone call, and that one brief, you said."

"Yeah, basically he just told me to stay on the lookout for important mail. He didn't even say whether it would be e-mail or snail mail."

"How many e-mails did you get at work?"

"None. I got one at my personal address before I set up my anonymous account. He was already using one. Then, after we linked up, he changed his account again."

Jerrod nodded, rubbing his chin thoughtfully. "So he was able to find your private e-mail and made repeated efforts to cover his electronic tracks. Are you sensing geek?"

"To some extent."

"Cybercafés and geeks." Jerrod looked at the shield. "It would be nice if I were ten years younger and more versed in this crap. 'Cuz I'm utterly clueless."

"That's a guild logo."

Their heads snapped around simultaneously to look at the young woman, perhaps twenty-four, who had spoken. She was a portrait in contrasts, wearing a conservative pantsuit, yet with a metal beaded ring through her left eyebrow.

"What?" Jerrod and Erin asked in unison.

The woman shrugged. Her voice carried a hint of *why can't you understand the obvious?* "It's a guild logo, from an M-M-O-R-P-G."

"A what?" Jerrod asked.

"A massive, multiplayer, online role-playing game. People become characters in virtual online worlds. Some are pseudomedieval, like Dungeons & Dragons in the old days. Some are set in space. Some in ancient China. You do use the Internet, right?"

"Not for that," Jerrod said. That she'd so casually referred to Dungeons & Dragons, a game he'd played in his youth, as "the old days" reminded him yet again that he was fast becoming an old man, disconnected from a society that would soon overtake him. "But I get the idea. So what do you mean by *guild logo?*"

"Players usually form groups, called guilds, to go on bigger adventures," the woman explained. "Quests that no single character could do on their own. They invite friends they've met online or friends from school or whatever. Most people design logos for their guilds. The game displays the guild logo next to the character, and a logo also makes it easier to find a guild in the list. If you click on a guild logo, the game zooms you to that guild's meeting place. You can chat with the other guild members, plan adventures, have cybersex...."

Jerrod put up a hand. "I get it. So okay, where do I find this guild? What game?"

She shrugged. "How would I know? There are dozens of games out there. You should look up the guild's site on Google and find it that way."

"In English?" Erin asked.

"Most guild founders start Web sites," she explained. "On MySpace or wherever they can find free hosting. Some keep a history of the guild's adventures, have chat forums to post ideas, argue about officers and rules, who's going to get kicked out and who should be let back in."

"Right," Jerrod said. "Sounds like junior high school all over again. So how do we find this one?"

The woman sighed. "Here, let me."

Jerrod was half-worried that she would perform some kind of mind-meld, communicating through cyberspace by the mere power of her concentrated thoughts. He was somewhat relieved when she actually had to touch the keyboard.

"What are these things?" she asked. "Turds?"

"I think they're supposed to be beans," Erin offered with more hope than certainty in her voice.

"Any idea what age your gamer is?" the woman asked.

"I'm thinking midtwenties," Jerrod said. "But that's just a guess."

"Probably beans, then," the woman decided. "If you were looking for a high school kid, they'd be turds." She spoke as if it were self-evident to any sentient being. "So okay, we go to Google and type in *guild, beans* and *thirty,* and we see what pops up. If that doesn't work, we'll look for the Guild of the Thirty Turds, which actually sounds like a club I hung out in when I was in college, but let's not go there."

"No," Jerrod said. "Let's not."

"Ahh, that's better," the woman said, looking at the list of search-engine replies. "Geezey Peasey, Miss Louisey, who'd have thought there'd be so many bean guilds? Don't these people have lives?"

Jerrod considered pointing out the irony in that question but held his tongue. She was being nice, helping them out of the kindness of her heart. Well, that and the chance to feel superior to her elders. Regardless, there was no good reason to antagonize her.

He tried to keep up as she clicked from site to site with almost dizzying speed. The faster she clicked, the older he felt. Finally he simply let himself be mesmerized by the flickering images, waiting patiently for this young spirit guide to lead them through the cybernetherworld to enlightenment, or what passed for it in the twenty-first century.

"There ya go," she said, her mouse finger hovering as if in anticipation of further exercise, though her eyes had already come to rest. "The Bean Counters."

"That makes sense," Jerrod said.

"Yeah," Erin agreed. He heard the disappointment in her voice and gave her a quizzical look. She shrugged. "I was kinda hoping for the Guild of the Thirty Turds."

"No you weren't," the woman said. "Trust me on that."

Jerrod and Erin exchanged nods. She seemed to be almost as at sea as he was. The unspoken worry over their entry into terra incognita was short-lived.

"*O-M-G*," the woman said.

"That much I do know," Erin replied. "Oh, my God."

The woman nodded. "Right."

Jerrod looked at her for a moment. When he could bear it no longer, he spoke. "So?"

"So?" the woman asked, looking at him.

"So…what? What *oh, my God?*"

"Oh, yeah. That." She pointed to a name on the guild's Web site. *Shadygrene.*

"Umm…?" Jerrod asked.

"I know that guy," she said. "Shadygrene. He was

a senior when I was a freshman. Had the cutest little stud with a gold dolphin on it, right at the bottom of his…you know. I guess he was going to have it taken out when he got married. I liked it."

Jerrod shook his head. "Ohhhh-kayyyyy."

"I know," she said, blushing. "*T-M-I.*"

"Too much information," Erin translated.

"Got that," Jerrod said.

"All…something," the woman mused aloud. "Alton! That's it. Alton Castle. Cute guy. *Loved* the dolphin."

"That was…surreal," Erin said, after swallowing a bite of her cheeseburger.

They'd left the cybercafé after doing a bit more research on Alton Castle. He was, according to his on-line résumé, a junior accountant with Mercator. That fit with the information he'd given Erin over the past months. He was a hometown boy, born and raised in the area. He'd attended the University of Colorado at Colorado Springs, where he'd earned his bachelor's degree in accounting, magna cum laude. Unlike the stereotype of the boring accountant, he'd had quite an active social life, not only active in a campus role-playing game group, but also president of his fraternity and a member of several campus honor societies.

That also explained how he'd secured a choice job in the accounting department of Mercator's

Colorado Springs headquarters. Hometown boy made good, then drawn into an evil he'd probably never imagined, still trying to play the sword-wielding, dragon-slaying hero he imagined himself to be in a virtual world.

"Yes," Jerrod agreed, as if reading her thoughts. "It all fits. It kinda makes you wonder."

"What?" she asked.

"Well," he said, "so many kids are playing these online games now. Our generation grew up with television. Alton's grew up with the Internet. To you and me, their world seems bizarre. *Is* bizarre. And yet, maybe in its own way, it's better."

"How so?" Erin sipped the surprisingly rich, smooth coffee that was the headline offering of the restaurant he had chosen. "Wow. This coffee is amazing."

"It's Durango coffee," Jerrod said. "A Colorado specialty. According to their Web site, the company was founded by a train robber who came to the sensible conclusion that he wasn't getting any younger and trains weren't going to get any slower, so he'd better find another way to make a living. He went into the coffee-roasting business."

"Another local boy makes good," Erin said.

"Yeah. Interesting that he started as a train robber, though. A man of action, a renegade, turned businessman. Like Alton Castle. Except Alton's action happened in a role-playing game."

"Ahh," Erin said, making the connection she'd missed earlier. "You're suggesting that the younger generation will be more activist than we were because they grew up with heroic computer quests, not sitting in front of the boob tube."

He nodded. "One can hope."

Erin smiled. "On the other hand, look at you. You grew up in the boob-tube generation, yet you went into the army and special ops and then the FBI."

"And you became a crusading journalist," he said. "Let me guess. Your favorite movie was *All the President's Men,* right?"

Erin shook her head. "You would not believe how often I'm asked that. Watergate was one of the high points of American journalism, if you believe the media were meant to be the public watchdogs over government."

"You don't?"

"Oh, I do," she said. "Let's be honest. The moment people stop babysitting power, power becomes unremittingly corruptive. Someone has to be watching, saying, 'No, you can't get away with that.'"

"But?"

"That's not why I went into journalism," Erin said.

"Why, then?"

"I like to write, Jerrod. Simple as that. I knew it was a lot easier to make a living writing news stories than writing fiction. And I like people. They're… strange, usually in good ways, sometimes in bad ways, almost always in *interesting* ways."

"And then there's the adrenaline rush," he said, chuckling.

"Yeah, there's that, too," she conceded. "But writing for a daily paper, that rush is an everyday thing. There's always a deadline staring you in the face. Always the scramble to fit together what will matter the next morning in time to get it to the compositors and printers, and off on the trucks to the newsstands and people's front porches. By the time they're reading it, we're already moving on to what will matter the next day. And the day after that."

She took another sip of coffee. "If you can't get jazzed on adrenaline, you can't make it as a journalist. Because you're always under a gun of some kind."

"This time it's just a more literal one."

"Yeah." She nibbled at a French fry. "I hope they're not giving Pete a hard time."

Jerrod laughed. "I suspect it would be more the reverse. Pete's an old salt. He's seen it all and done most of it. He doesn't rattle easily."

"Unlike this Alton guy," Erin said. "Now, there's a man who's in way over his head. You may be right that the Internet generation will spawn more wannabe heroes. But there's a hell of a difference between wading into a band of trolls in a video game and taking on Mercator in the real world."

"You got that right," he agreed. "You don't get extra lives here. And if we can find Alton Castle, they can, too. If they're diligent. And they will be."

"Which means we need to get to him first," Erin said.

Jerrod nodded. "Because if we don't, he'll be one dead bean counter."

He didn't mention Georgie. He couldn't bring himself to say her name. But in the back of his mind a clock was ticking, and with each wasted moment, it seemed to tick faster.

"These kids…" he said into a silence that seemed to be thickening. "We've got to stop this ring."

"I know."

"But they have more time than…" He still couldn't say her name.

"More time than your friend." Erin nodded. "I know."

"They've got no reason to keep her alive except to get information out of her. And she has almost no information, Erin."

She reached out at once and squeezed his hand. "Then let's get a move on. Time's wasting."

He rose, throwing some bills on the table. He just hoped to God that Georgie's time hadn't run out.

\* \* \*

Alton Castle went to the men's room every day at four-thirty. His wife liked to tease him about the regularity of his habits, but this was one he'd developed after a couple of unpleasant experiences in traffic jams on the way home. Simple expedience.

Of course, being that regular also made him predictable. When he entered the men's room he saw a familiar face at one of the sinks. They exchanged brief nods as Alton went into a stall, rather than using the urinal. He preferred not to use urinals when someone else was around.

But this afternoon he felt something more than mere shyness. His heart started to hammer, because the guy outside had no business in this part of the building. In fact, he was part of a whole different section of the company. A section that oversaw Mercator's security, among other things.

Latching the door behind him, he found he couldn't move, not even to pretend to use the facilities. He stood and waited, mentally counting the seconds, but there was no sound of a door opening and closing.

The man wasn't leaving. Alton's heart nearly stopped as he realized he was trapped. If that guy wanted him for any reason, there was no way out of here.

But why would anyone want him? Had they

somehow managed to find out about his e-mails from the computer café?

"Alton." The man's voice was deep, firm.

Alton's mouth turned as dry as the Sahara. "Y-yes?"

"We need to talk."

There it was. Alton's knees turned rubbery, and he was sure he was about to crumple to the floor. So he'd wanted to be a hero? Yeah, except that he would have liked a magic sword, protective armor and all the spells he had online. Never had he felt so naked.

"Alton," the voice said again, "I'm not after you. But we need to talk. It's the only way I can help you."

Alton didn't believe him, but from somewhere he found some strength. They couldn't prove a thing, he told himself. They could suspect, and they could fire him, but they couldn't prove a thing.

He emerged slowly from the stall and saw the other man holding out a hand for a cordial shake. Reluctantly, he extended his own and felt the power in the other man's grip.

"I'm Chuck Besom," the man said. His eyes were as hard as flint. "I know you discovered something… wrong with the records."

"How…?" Alton cut himself off.

"Never mind how. I just found out myself. We don't have a lot of time. Nobody else knows you're involved, not yet, and I want to keep it that way."

Alton nodded jerkily.

Besom handed him a card. "Call me when you make contact with the reporter. Set up a meeting. Just tell me where it is so I can provide protection."

"Why should I trust you?"

Chuck Besom leaned toward him. "Because I just found out what they're shipping on those corporate jets, and it *has* to stop. When you've set up the meet, I'll tell you where the…packages are being held before shipment."

"Why not now?"

"Because once you know this, you can never set foot near Mercator again. Once you know this, if they know you know it, you're a dead man. I can give you everything. *Everything*. But I'm not going to do that until I'm sure you have a way to disappear. The reporter you're trying to meet, she has resources to help you do that. Once I know you've set up a meet, I'll tell you everything you need to know. Just give me a couple of hours' warning, so I can set up protection."

Alton looked into those hard eyes and believed. He absolutely believed when Besom walked out, leaving him unmolested. Any remaining smidgen of doubt vanished when he passed through security a half hour later without so much as a glance from the guards.

Someone else was on the side of right with him. All the strength flowed back into his limbs, and he began to think ahead. He would meet the reporter after all. He would give her all the information he had. He would give her the card and let her call Besom, too.

But first, he thought with a shiver of paranoia, he had to get his family out of town.

Just in case.

# *19*

Jerrod and Erin quieted as they jogged through the aspen forest behind Pete's house. The day had been both busy and strangely, tediously slow.

Earlier, they'd found out as much as they could about Alton Castle from public sources, because Jerrod knew he couldn't risk calling in Bureau help on this yet. They'd discussed several ways of meeting the man and finally decided to meet him on his terms, in his virtual reality. But not before they'd done a bit of loose, firsthand observation.

Picking out Alton as he emerged from Mercator was easy enough. He hadn't changed that much since his high school yearbook photo. They'd followed him from the office to his home, a small but well-kept ranch in the Tri-Lakes area. If Mercator had him under surveillance, Jerrod had seen no sign of it. Alton's daughter had burst out the front door and run into his arms as Jerrod drove past.

It was a brief moment, but to Jerrod it spoke volumes. Alton Castle wasn't offering bait to lure them into a trap. He really was what he'd portrayed himself to be in his past contacts with Erin: an ordinary man who'd stumbled over an extraordinary evil and wanted to fix it. Jerrod knew that feeling all too well.

Erin's voice called him back to the present. "I don't see any cars around Pete's place," she said quietly as they knelt in the tree line.

Jerrod nodded. "No, but that doesn't mean much. If the Bureau has put a stakeout on him, you wouldn't see it."

"But *you* would, right?" she asked.

He shrugged. "Let's hope so."

It was unlikely that the FBI would have moved a team into one of the neighboring homes, Jerrod thought. Neighbors tended to notice things like that, and ordinary encounters could quickly compromise operational security. Still, he took a few minutes to scan the windows of the houses next door, looking for the subtle cues of surveillance: curtains opened just a few inches or a blind slightly askew.

Seeing nothing there, he turned his attention to the woods around them. In the distance, Pikes Peak loomed over them like the shoulders of the earth itself. Between that distant mountain and Pete's house lay dozens of lesser hills that offered a view of that part of the valley. Few of them were useful sites for a stakeout. An operation of that kind required ready ingress and egress, so that teams could change shifts without attracting attention. Hiking through miles of rugged forest would be exhausting for the agents involved, leaving them too worn-out to stay alert.

If the topographic map Jerrod had bought in town was accurate, that left only a couple of hills that had both a view of Pete's house and good access roads on their reverse slopes. It was on those that he focused his attention.

"What are you looking for?" Erin asked.

"Anything that seems out of place," he explained. "Reflections from glasses or watch crystals. Straight lines. Anything too regular or too evenly *ir*regular. Nature has its own shapes. We humans break those up, even when we try to imitate them."

"And do you see anything?"

He scanned the hills carefully, his tactical training picking out the places he would have chosen if he were the one watching Pete's house. If anyone was out there, they were good. Good enough that he couldn't see any sign of their presence. And that was damn unlikely.

"I think we're okay," he said.

"You don't sound certain."

He looked at her. "If I ever sound certain, you'll know I'm about to make a big mistake."

"That's a lot of self-doubt to carry around," she

said, her eyes seeming to search his, as if hoping he were speaking in metaphor.

He wondered that himself, for a moment, and quickly realized he was not. Not anymore. There had been a time when he would have embraced Churchill's dictum of "Action This Day." But that was a long time ago. Action, fully committed and unhindered by doubt, was a luxury he could no longer afford. Life had taught him to measure twice, or even thrice, and hope to be cut only once.

"When we started training, I told you that uncertainty will get you killed," he said. "Well, the lack of it will get you killed even faster."

"That's rather a Hobson's choice, huh?" Erin asked.

"Or a Zen riddle."

"Ommmmm."

Jerrod stifled a laugh. "Shh. You're going to make me break cover."

"Umm, we're not under the covers, dear," she said. "We're in the trees."

His heart stopped for a beat. "Yes, we are."

"I'm sorry," Erin said. "I didn't mean that like it sounded."

"Oh, yes," he said, smiling. "You did."

Their eyes met for a long moment. "You're right."

He looked up at the waning late-evening light. "We should wait until dark to go down to Pete's."

She nodded. "Another hour or so."

"Something like that."

"Long enough," she said.

"Yeah, it would be."

He knew this wasn't love, or even something like it. It was fear, as much as anything. They were deep into a mess that was dragging him back to places he'd hoped he'd left far in his past. Places that could get them both killed. Some part of him recognized that what he felt in that moment was not much different than the urges that had driven soldiers into the arms of women from New York to Pearl Harbor to London to Paris. There was a reason the Subic Bay U.S. Naval base in the Philippines had been nicknamed Pubic Bay.

It wasn't love. It was a basic animal urge. Try to preserve the species before heading into battle. And yet, when he looked into her eyes…

"You're not certain of this, either," she said.

"Not even close."

"Neither am I."

"Maybe we shouldn't?" he offered.

"Probably not," Erin said, leaning closer. "But we have an hour to kill. And I don't want to do another of your training runs."

"Neither do I," he admitted.

"And if we just sit here, we're gonna freeze."

"That we will."

"So we've gotta keep warm somehow."

"Yeah. We do."

Her lips tasted slightly of coffee. He almost laughed at the irony, a sweetly bitter kiss. What was that saying? Take the bitter with the sweet? God, she was sweet.

He couldn't remember the last time lips had touched his this way. Had they ever? Probably not. Certainly not. Sipping. The lightest of brushes, yet lingering for just that extra moment each time. He realized his arms had found their way around her, fingertips trailing up and down her spine as his lips parted with hers to deepen the kiss.

"Definitely warmer this way," she murmured.

"Hush," he whispered, before stifling her voice with another kiss.

She fitted her body over his, her hips straddling his as he knelt, melding, her curves fitting into his hollows, his firmness to her softness. It was a dance as old as the human species, one they fell into with hardly a lost beat, as if they had been sharing this for years.

She was an experienced lover, and more assertive than the women he'd known before. Her hips arched, grinding her pelvis against his through their pants, a wordless invitation that could not be mistaken for anything short of pure, hot lust. And that was fine, because pure, hot lust was also what had overtaken him.

She shrugged her wool sweater up over her head, and he quickly, deftly opened each button of her blouse. She let her shoulders roll back, not taking the blouse off but simply letting it slide down, caught where her hands rested at the back of her hips, her breasts swelling the cups of her bra, rising and falling with every breath.

But when he reached around to unclasp her bra, she shook her head, a playful smile on her face. "Not yet, soldier. You're not desperate enough yet."

"Wanna bet?" he asked.

"Oh, yeah," she said. "Trust me."

She shimmied back and, with her forearms still trapped in her blouse, began to use her lips and teeth to open his belt, then to unbutton his jeans. Then, impossibly, for he could never have imagined this woman in this way, she took his zipper between her front teeth and began to pull.

She'd made it halfway down when need overtook him and he pushed the zipper down the rest of the way, sliding his jeans and Jockey shorts down to his knees. She gave him a brief, playful smile and lowered her head, trailing more of those soft kisses along the length of his erect shaft, soft moans rising in his throat to match the low growls in hers. Finally she let her tongue join in the dance, laving him slowly, then swirling, then slowly, then flicking, then slowly, until his entire being screamed with the need she had promised.

"Ohhhhhhhhhhhhhhhhh."

She looked up and winked, her tongue still dancing, then paused for a moment. "Told you."

"Don't...talk...."

She giggled. "Why? Is there something else you wish my mouth were doing?"

"Yesssssssssss."

"What do you say, soldier?"

"Pleeeeaaaasseee."

"That's better."

She was amazing. No, she was more than that. She was a dream he'd never permitted himself to imagine. Her every kiss, every soft suckle, seemed to reach through his entire body, pushing him and holding him back all at once, making him want, need, long, ache, squirm.

He only realized that he'd closed his eyes when he opened them to watch as she finally slipped off her blouse and unbuttoned her own jeans. Moments later her hips were poised over him, hovering just out of reach, his belly muscles making his cock twitch. The whispers of cold air between their bodies propelled him with an urgency that he could not resist, and he lifted himself to her warmth.

In less time than it took to complete the thought, they were joined fully, her mons pressed to him, her eyes locked on his, her thighs squeezing tight against his sides, her hands beneath his shoulders, fingers curling, nails digging through his shirt.

"Fuckkkkkkk yessssssssssss," he said.

She giggled. "Well, you talk like a soldier."

"Would you *please*—"

The words were cut off by an incredible pressure on his shaft as her muscles clamped down tight.

"You were saying?" she asked, brushing his nose with her lips.

"Sooooo good."

"Much better," she said, relaxing the pressure and beginning to ride him in a slow, steady rhythm, just enough stimulation to keep him fully engaged, never quite enough to push him over the edge. "Much, much better."

"You're…wow," he whispered.

"Why, thank you, soldier," Erin said, smiling broadly. Her eyes softened, eyelids dragging as if weighted. "You're pretty fucking incredible your-self."

There was a raw intensity in their joining, words he'd rarely spoken offered now without shame or re-morse, driven forth by every grunting thrust, every clenching embrace, every trembling breath.

Maybe it wasn't love. But in that moment, he didn't give a damn. It was life. And life mattered.

When he exploded, his hips arching up hard to hers, he heard her own gasping grunts echo his. Her hair whipped his face as she shook her head back and forth, her neck finally arching until she looked almost like a wolf ready to howl at the moon.

She held back the howl, but the moon didn't mind. Its blue-white light bathed their climax, chilling their backs and arms as they lay together after, clinging tight, as his shaft remained buried in her warmth.

"Wow," he finally said.

"I'll second that."

"It's going to get cold now."

"Yeah. The sun's gone down," she agreed.

"I still…"

She pressed herself impossibly tighter to him, her face pressed to his neck. "Yeah. Me, too."

"Just for a little while."

"Yes. Just for a little while."

But in her mind, too, the clock had begun to tick, insistent and full of threat. Stolen moments and stolen time. She feared how they might add up.

# 20

"Not yet," Chuck Besom said. He knew they were not words Kendall was accustomed to hearing in response to an order, but that was too damn bad. "We can't do it until we have Westlake out of the equation."

"Bullshit." Kendall's face darkened. "He's one man. He doesn't even have Bureau support now. I just got off the phone with my source. Westlake has been classified a 'person of interest' in a missing-persons case."

"Good for them," Besom said. "The day the Bureau can tell the difference between chicken soup and chicken shit, hell will freeze over and aspen leaves will be real gold. I've read Westlake's personnel files. Plural. Not just his Bureau jacket, but also his special-ops work. He's not someone we can ignore."

Kendall shook his head. "You and Westlake and

this Tatum guy are living in the dark ages. The days of single combat, knights jousting mano a mano, are ancient history. The Westlakes and Tatums of the world are a dime a dozen, still clinging to notions of individual heroism in a world where institutions dwarf anything one man can do. Maybe you're right and the FBI can't tell chicken soup from chicken shit. But it has power, the power of the U.S. government. It could shut us down. Without them, Jerrod Westlake is just another pissed-off combat vet who probably ought to be in a psych ward."

Chuck sighed. It was like talking to a wall. Kendall wanted to close a deal with a client in Colombia, and that apparently meant shipping a "package" from the training camp with a planeload of NetWare camo gear, as if having a command post full of computer-generated and sifted "situational awareness" would make him any less subject to the fog of war. Now that Chuck knew what those "packages" were, he wanted to delay this shipment as long as possible, until he could bring this house of cards down on someone else's head.

"Ninety-six hours," he said finally. "It'll take that long to line up the plane."

"See that it doesn't take any longer."

Fighting the urge to laugh or spit, Chuck instead drew a slow breath. The Colombian client and Kendall both lived in a fantasy world. They thought their databases and spreadsheets and Bluetooth BlackBerrys put them on another plane, above lesser beings who dealt with mud and rust and blood and fear. Getting ahead was all they cared about, and for Kendall, getting ahead meant making huge foreign-arms deals.

The real world, the world Chuck had once lived in, the world Bill Tatum and Jerrod Westlake still lived in, was a different place. In *that* world, one man did matter. In *that* world, it took only one finger squeezing a trigger to spatter your information-laden brain all over a wall and make your fortune someone else's.

Chuck had no doubt that, even as he and Kendall stood here arguing, Jerrod Westlake was putting together bits and pieces of a plan that would culminate with Chuck's face in his sights and his finger on the trigger.

"Ninety-six hours," Chuck said again, and walked out. Tatum was on the way in, but Chuck didn't even give him a nod.

He *did* pause in the anteroom to listen at the closed door, though. That was the biggest advantage of these meetings taking place after everyone else had left for the day: there was no one to see him standing there eavesdropping.

"Don't worry about Chuck," Tatum was saying. "I know we can ship the girl. But the FBI woman is a no-go. She's not an anonymous runaway picked up off the streets. There are a lot of eyes looking for her. Even if there weren't, she's not going to be a compliant sex toy for some banana *generalissimo*. She'll keep thinking, keep looking for that one mistake that will give her a chance to escape. And she's going to remember every face she saw along the way."

"The client wants her," Kendall said. "He was very specific. He liked the video."

*"Video?"* Tatum asked, sounding dumbfounded. Even Besom, with his ear to the door, almost jerked back at the stupidity of that.

"Oh, please!" Kendall shot back. "You helped start this enterprise, Tatum. You were the one with all the brilliant ideas. If Chuck hadn't introduced us, none of this would be happening. And how the hell do you think I sell these items? Like pigs in a poke?"

In that moment, Chuck realized he'd been mouse-trapped. He'd introduced Kendall to Tatum. Tatum was now ready and apparently willing, to judge by what he was hearing, to squeeze Chuck out of the middle. And Kendall wasn't nearly as worried about deniability as he'd claimed.

The two men were a dangerous combination, and not only because they would blithely push Chuck Besom out of the way and into a six-foot cell—or a six-foot hole. It was worse than that. They were a perfect storm of arrogance mated to ignorance. So

far, Mercator—meaning Kendall, as the board would
never have approved kidnapping homeless people
to use as training subjects—had gotten away with
this plan because Chuck was a careful, cautious man
who weighed every risk before taking any action.
Neither Kendall nor Tatum would do that. In fact,
they hadn't. They weren't just grabbing training
subjects. They were shipping young girls…living,
breathing loose ends.

Kendall dismissed Westlake as an irrelevant
jackal, while Tatum believed himself to be the better
predator. And if Kendall had made any progress in
locating the leak inside Mercator, he hadn't told
Chuck about it. They were headed to sea on a boat
made of Swiss cheese.

Chuck had already decided to jump ship. He'd
made that clear to Alton Castle earlier. The only issue now was how to make sure he didn't land in
shark-infested waters.

Tatum finally spoke. "Okay, whatever. You're going to do what you want to do."

"Perks of being the boss," Kendall replied. "So
when can we have them ready for shipment?"

"They'll go as soon as Chuck gets the plane."

Kendall nodded. "Four days, then. Make sure the
woman's broken by then."

And there it was, Chuck thought. He might be out
of the loop, but he could turn the loop on itself.

Quickly, before he could be caught listening, he hurried away down the carpeted corridors.

Pete had the good grace to nod silently and bury his nose in a book when Jerrod and Erin crept in an hour after sunset. A blind man would have known something had changed between them in the past twelve hours. Well, provided that blind man had an even remotely competent sense of smell.

Good for them, Pete thought. Jerrod had been alone for too long, and Erin seemed like a helluva woman for him.

Still, he had to suppress a smile as they swept in and through the living room, reeking of sweat and fallen leaves and the musk of sex. He said nothing as they made lame and unnecessary excuses for needing to shower. As if they had done anything to be ashamed of.

A half hour later, they emerged freshly scrubbed and wearing a passable pretense of simply being investigative partners on a case. And that, too, was fine by Pete. He was content to celebrate in silence for them.

It wasn't as if they had no work to do.

"Bean Counters," Pete said, repeating the name of Alton Castle's online guild, after Jerrod and Erin had laid out what they'd learned. "Gotta like a guy with a sense of humor. Even if it's the only sense he has."

Erin tipped her head to the side. "I don't know about that. He's young. He's smart. Living the American dream. Go to college, study hard, get good grades, get a good job, get a good wife, have a good kid and a good hobby. Rake in the dough for forty placid years, then retire to Arizona, buy some plaid Bermuda shorts and take up golf."

Pete laughed and held up his hands. "I surrender."

"What?" Erin asked.

Pete looked to Jerrod. "Is she always like this?"

"Like what?" Erin insisted.

"Yeah," Jerrod said, smiling.

*"What?"* Erin finally shouted.

"You were born to be a journalist," Pete said. "You can take sixty years of living and condense it to a single paragraph that's eighty percent cool observation and one hundred percent biting commentary."

"Thanks. I think," she said.

"No, it *was* a compliment," Pete said, leaning forward and meeting her eyes. "You see things. See people. See a story in everything around you. It's a gift."

"It's not so different from what you and Jerrod do," she said. "Y'all are supposed to see everything, too."

"Jerrod?" Pete asked, knowing there was a difference but not knowing how to put it into words.

"It's simple," Jerrod said to her. "You can see happy endings. Maybe not all the time, but at least sometimes. We can't."

"You do catch the bad guys," Erin said.

"Yeah," Pete said, nodding. "We do. But we can't take back what they did. All we can do is try to stop them from doing it again. But the evil…well, that's already been done. We can pull out the nail, but we can't pull out the hole."

"Neither can I," she said.

"Maybe not," Jerrod said. "But you get to see stories that don't have nails in them."

She shrugged. "Not lately."

"Well, there is that," Pete agreed. He drew a breath. "So this Castle guy, you think he's stand-up?"

"Yes," Erin said immediately. "I don't see any reason not to trust him. And we need him."

There was the real difference, Pete recognized. Erin could look at someone and, finding no reason to distrust him, take him at his word. For law-enforcement types, it just didn't work that way. Everyone was lying until you could prove otherwise.

"So, okay," Pete said. "You're supposed to meet him in this game?"

"That's what he asked for," Jerrod said. "He probably doesn't know we know his real identity. If it weren't for him having used the same screen name since college and us tumbling over someone who'd known him then, he'd still be as anonymous as he thinks he is."

"But you're going to need a face-to-face."

"Yes," Jerrod said. "But let's do it his way first. If we show up at his door, he'll clam up. He's a family man. I'll bet his wife doesn't know anything about any of this. He'll have kept her out of this."

Pete shook his head. "He'll have to testify sooner or later. He can't stay anonymous forever. And if y'all could find him…"

"We thought of that, too," Erin said. "Pete has a point, Jerrod. Yes, we have to meet Alton his way, but we can't leave him dangling in the breeze much longer."

"What are our options?" Jerrod asked. "Pete says the Bureau's after me now. How, exactly, are we supposed to protect Castle?"

"And there's also Georgie," Pete said. "The guys who came here today, they're sure she's been abducted. And probably killed."

"They said that?" Erin asked.

Pete shook his head. "They didn't have to. I've worked with guys like them my whole career. I know how to read between the lines."

"Shit," Jerrod said. "If they've killed Georgie…" His eyes reflected anguish and anger.

"That's what they think," Pete qualified. "*I* don't think they've killed her. Call it a hunch. Call it a wish. But I think she's still alive."

Jerrod's eyes were stony. "You'd better be right. For their sakes."

Pete knew that look. Not much scared him. Not much ever had. But Jerrod could. And had. And was now.

"When will this Castle guy be online?" Pete asked.

Erin looked at her watch. "If he follows his usual schedule, he might be there now."

Pete rose from his chair. "Let's go to my office. My laptop's there."

"Are you sure the Bureau isn't monitoring your ISP?" Jerrod asked.

"No," Pete said. "But when you get that look in your eyes, buddy, I'm not going to wait around. So unless you want to go back out to a cybercafé tonight, I'm willing to take the risk."

"Let's do it," Jerrod agreed.

*Thank God,* Pete thought. Jerrod was on the edge. If they couldn't find a gap in Mercator's walls soon, Jerrod was going to blow one open.

And that could get very ugly, very fast.

# *21*

Alton studied the skimpy map of the Undertaker's Estate. It was, as he'd expected, short on detail, most especially the significant details of where monsters lived, where they hunted and where the Sarcophagus of Emil lay. Yet even with what little information he had, he knew his guild would need at least two dozen characters to survive. But if they found the sarcophagus and got it back to town, they could sell it for enough to build a master guildhall. It would be a major accomplishment.

<InkyWretch: Hello, Shadygrene>

The message popped up in a private chat window. Who was InkyWretch? He clicked on the screen name and found it was an entry-level Scribe, a brand-new character. Could it be Erin McKenna?

\<Shadygrene: EM?\>

There was a long pause.

\<InkyWretch: Yes.\>

Alton forced himself to take a breath. Okay, so he was talking to the reporter in real time. That did not mean the world was crashing down around him any more than it had been when he'd left work. Except it was, and he knew it. And she was his only way out.

\<Shadygrene: This maze is too big.\>

\<InkyWretch: *nods* It looks like it. Have the monsters attacked?\>

\<Shadygrene: Not yet. But they will soon. I can feel it.\>

\<InkyWretch: How much time?\>

\<Shadygrene: Not long I think. Another shipment soon.\>

At that there was another long pause. Alton wasn't supposed to know that Chuck Besom had put through another shipping order. But Alton kept an eye on that account in the Mercator system, checking it every time he had reason to scan shipment orders. Chuck had scheduled another executive jet in four days, and Alton had no doubt that the flight would have another young girl on it. In fact, as it rarely took that long to get a jet, Alton suspected Besom had delayed it on purpose.

<InkyWretch: *brushes off your green eyeshade*>

Alton flinched as he saw the words. On the one hand, it was no surprise that a smart woman like Erin McKenna would discern the wordplay behind his screen name. She had probably also already figured out why he'd called his guild the Bean Counters. That narrowed her search considerably. Did she already know who he was? Besom had figured it out, but Besom claimed to be on his side. But if Erin and Besom knew, how many others might have figured it out? His hands started to sweat and shake.

<Shadygrene: How much do you know?>

<InkyWretch: I heard the dolphin was cute. *lol*>

Alton blushed, despite his fear. She knew who he was. She'd obviously even talked to someone he'd known back in college, back when he'd thought a

body piercing might make him seem as adventurous
as he'd wished he were.

<Shadygrene: Hi Erin>

<InkyWretch: Hi Alton>

So okay. She knew. And time was short.

<Shadygrene: Four days.>

<InkyWretch: The next plane?>

<Shadygrene: Yes.>

<InkyWretch: Do you know where?>

<Shadygrene: Yes. R/L?>

He hoped she'd know that he was asking for a real-
life meeting. He hoped he had the courage to meet her.
He had to trust her. And Erin, being accustomed to
meeting background sources, would know more
about how to set up a secure real-life meeting than he
did. His heart felt as if it would burst out of his chest.

<InkyWretch: I have a friend. He knows stuff. I'll
put him on, k?>

A friend. That could be anyone. He trusted Erin. Did he trust her taste in friends? Did he have a choice?

<Shadygrene: k>

<InkyWretch: hi shady>

<Shadygrene: Hi…umm?>

<InkyWretch: call me g>

<Shadygrene: k. We need to R/L.>

<InkyWretch: we do. suggest your old playroom>

<Shadygrene: @U?>

<InkyWretch: yes…2hrs?>

So they knew the student hall where he'd hung out during his university days. That ought to have surprised him, but given that she'd known about the dolphin… God, this was creeping him out.

Still, meeting in just two hours? He would need to get back home first, tell his wife to take the kid and leave. And call Besom. It would be tight. He stared at his online character, an armored warrior with all kinds of weapons. He wondered if he had even a tenth of the guts he pretended to have when he was in character.

Did it matter? He'd committed to this quest back when he sent the first e-mail to Erin. He had to follow through.

\<Shadygrene: k. 2hrs\>

\<InkyWretch: E again. Thank you. g says so too.\>

*Thank you?* Shouldn't he be thanking them? Or maybe not. Not yet. Too much could still go wrong.

\<Shadygrene: cu l8r\>

\<InkyWretch: Huh? Oh, yeah. See you later.\>

Before logging off, Alton did as instructed. He pulled Besom's card out and called his office number. To his surprise, the man was there.

"Two hours," he said. "I'm meeting Erin and a friend of hers at the student center at the university."

Besom's voice was flat. "Thanks. You'll find a package by the swing set. I'll have you covered."

When Besom hung up, it was only by chance that he noticed the "line open" light remained lit for another four seconds. In the busy daytime hours he never would have seen it, not with phone lights blinking constantly. But he noticed it now.

His line was tapped.

"Christ." Jumping up, he grabbed his jacket.

Chuck Besom's father had been an electrician by trade and temperament. He'd been a lifelong union man, a proud member of IBEW Local Twenty-five on Long Island. Chuck had watched his dad resist offers from men with more brawn than brains, men who thought ancestry and a gang of goombahs entitled them to a thumb on the scales of every union in New York. Chuck's dad had not only refused for himself, he had convinced his union buddies not to pay protection money.

"The only protection they're offering," his dad had said in a raucous union hall as young Chuck watched from the back, "is protection from themselves! We got that already. We got the freakin' cops. And if the cops won't help us, well, I don't see a man here who won't stand up for his own."

Chuck had never been prouder of his dad than he was that night. Never before, and not for the next month while his dad still walked this earth, before the goombahs put six rounds in his broad chest as he walked home from Paddy's. Chuck had heard the shots and known immediately, somewhere in his heart, long before the cops knocked at the door and

Father Flannery uttered the words that left Chuck's mom a hollow shell.

But the goombahs hadn't reckoned on the raw guts of Irish workingmen who spent six months a year barking their knuckles bloody in eighty-hour workweeks, salting away enough to get through the lean winters when work was sparse. A dozen men had been involved in the murder of Chuck's dad. And over the next five months, a dozen news clippings were slipped through the mail slot of Chuck's home. Most looked a lot like routine accidents. The few that didn't were written off to other goombahs.

That sort of thing happened when the cops and the union men shared ancestors who had fought together since the days of Cromwell. There were only a few hard-and-fast rules in Chuck's childhood. Never laugh in Mass. Never back talk Mom. Never squeal. And, no matter how many scraps you had with your cousins, never let an outsider come between you.

Betrayal and squealing did not come easy to Chuck Besom.

But neither did getting fucked by management.

This whole deal had been a cock-up. Kendall Warrick hadn't been satisfied to make a fortune selling overpriced toys to his own and other countries' militaries. The wave of privatization that had swept over Washington in the past twenty years had offered boardroom warriors an opportunity to dabble with the real thing, to go beyond simply imagining they were armchair generals to commanding private armies. The government found reasons to let them, and Warrick had leaped at the opportunity.

Chuck suspected that Warrick's boyhood fantasies had been shaped more by James Bond than George Patton, because Warrick had been less interested in the burgeoning private security market than in private intelligence work. In the post-9/11 climate, interrogators who were willing to work outside the box, shielded by veils of corporate privilege, had become high-value assets.

Besom had suggested using homeless people as interrogation subjects as a solution to the supply issue. He was, after all, no angel. But he had no doubt it was Tatum who had provided the idea of using Besom's tactics to nab runaway kids and use them as sex slaves to sweeten a deal.

So while betrayal went against his every grain, being betrayed, as he had been by Warrick, was even worse.

It was, Warrick would doubtless argue, a win-win game for Mercator. Customers would be glad to pay for anything Mercator wanted to sell so long as his "sweeteners" came with the shipments. And shipping the girls to South America meant there would be no bodies or evidence trails that led back to Mercator.

Oh, Chuck could see it all so clearly now. How he had been used and lied to. Before he was done, he was going to rub Kendall Warrick's face in the mud and blow out his brains.

The student center at the university was a modern complex set on a low hill, offering a sweeping view of the parklike expanse of the central quadrangle. At this time of night, foot traffic on the quad remained heavy enough to give Jerrod pause. While most of those milling around were too young to be anything but college students, the night classes were obviously popular with adults. That meant dozens of passersby to be scanned, studied and ruled out as possible Mercator surveillance.

The exercise was made all the more difficult by three complicating factors. First, a cloud front had moved in since sunset, obscuring the moon and stars, blanketing the quad in a thin mist that made everything and everyone seem to exist as impressionist forms. Second, as on any college campus, people-watching was a popular pastime. The density of attractive, young, single men and women melded with deep biological imperatives to yield an unconscious urge to look a bit closer at those passing. Separating the routine, harmless, hormone-driven glances and stares from those of an experienced surveillance operative was difficult at the best of times. In the current weather conditions, it was all but impossible.

The third complication was the woman sitting next to him. Erin was stunningly attractive and drew more than her share of long looks. The memory of their encounter in the woods earlier had left Jerrod feeling mildly protective of her in the face of so much young male scrutiny. No, that wasn't true. Not if he were honest. His feelings weren't protective. They were possessive. And that meant the kind of entanglement he'd avoided for most of his adult life. The exceptions to that avoidance had been universally bad in their outcomes. There was no reason to think this one would be any better.

And that train of thought made it all the more difficult to casually but dispassionately study each and every passerby, looking for telltale behaviors that were evidence of more than ordinary interest.

"Doesn't it get painful to be so keyed up all the time?" Erin asked quietly.

He realized that, in fact, she was right. While he was trying to present himself as comfortably slouched on the cool, metal bench, in fact, his body was on high alert. His feet were tucked back under the bench, not because he was relaxed but because that kept them almost directly beneath him, so he could get up in an instant if he had to. His hands seemed to be resting in his lap, but in fact, his arms were poised to propel him upright and into action. And yes, the muscles in his shoulders and neck were already beginning to burn with the tension.

"Yeah," he said. "I'm sorry."

"No reason to apologize," she said. "I understand why. It's just…until I met you, I'd never thought much about what it's like for…well, people like you."

"People like me?"

"Soldiers. Spies. Undercover agents. It's not just the way you think about the world or how you have to feel about yourself. It's the way you sit, the way you stand, the way your eyes are never quite still. It's exhausting just to watch. I can't imagine feeling that way all day, every day, day in, day out."

"I don't think about it," he said.

"Of course not," Erin said. "How could you? That would make it even more impossible."

"So why bring it up?"

She looked down. "Okay, now *I'm* sorry."

He glanced over at her, feeling as if he'd just stepped on a child's toy. "That was a shitty thing for me to say. I'm not good at this."

"At what?"

"This," he said, looking at her. "Having a casual conversation with someone I'm starting to…like."

She smiled. "The reporter in me wants to ask why you're only just now starting to like me, but only because the reporter in me likes to ask questions that make people squirm. So putting that aside, I'll say this. First, my timing sucks. This isn't the time or the place for us to have this conversation."

He shrugged. "That's easy to say when you're sure to get another time and place."

Her eyes studied his for a moment. "Yes. Exactly."

"And we're not."

"No."

"But we still can't have this discussion now."

"No, we can't," she agreed.

"I'm sorry," he said.

"So am I."

He couldn't say what exactly had drawn his attention. It might have been an oddness of posture, an exaggerated slouch blended with a firmness of bearing, or a glance lingering that half instant too long.

"Put your head on my shoulder," he said quietly. "Don't look around. Just do it."

As Erin leaned against him, he slipped an arm around her, not resting it on her shoulders but instead positioning his hand on her lower back, ready to push her forward when the moment came. He felt her muscles tense, but to her credit, she didn't shift or move away.

"They're here?" she whispered.

"Yup. Ten o'clock, next to the trash can between

the streetlamps. He's alone, but there will be others. I just haven't made them yet."

"How many others?"

"If I'd planned this op, I'd have at least a five-man team. There will be two others around us somewhere, to cut off the lines of escape. Plus two in a van nearby. I'd also want a spotter-sniper team up high, but I doubt they could set that up on a college campus."

"That would be risky," Erin said. "Too likely to be noticed, after what happened in Virginia."

"Right," he said. "So figure three on the ground, plus the driver and a guy at the van door. The three ground men are armed for sure. Probably the door guy, too."

"And you left your gun back at Pete's."

"Uh-huh."

"So what's the plan?" she asked.

"The rule," he said, "is outnumbered plus out-gunned equals get out. But we can't."

"Why not?"

"They're not here for us," he said. "Or not just for us. They want Castle, too. Even if we could get out, he can't. Untrained and alone, he won't stand a chance."

"Don't be so sure of that, G."

Jerrod tried not to flinch but knew he had. He hoped it hadn't been visible. The voice had come from behind and to his left. He dared not turn his head. "Where are you?"

"Basement window, behind the bushes."

"You're inside already?"

"I just got here."

"I see him," Erin whispered, looking over Jerrod's shoulder while kissing his neck. "It's Castle."

That was at least one variable out of the equation, but there were still too many others.

"Did you come in the back door?" Jerrod asked.

"No. They have another guy there. I came in through the tunnel from Bateman Hall."

"There are tunnels here?" Jerrod asked.

"Sure. Blizzards get ugly, even if they don't happen often. The whole campus is connected underground. They were steam tunnels at first, but students always used them to avoid the weather. The university decided college students weren't idiots, or at least weren't going to stop being idiots, so they fixed them up."

"And that's our way out," Jerrod said.

"Down the stairs to your left, after you get inside," Alton replied. "I'll be waiting in the stairwell."

"Be ready to move," Jerrod said. "Once Erin and I get up, they're going to know. And they'll be moving, too."

"Then we'll have to move faster," Alton said.

He sounded awfully sure of himself, Jerrod

thought. Either he really was as sure as he sounded or he had no idea what they were up against. Jerrod hoped it was the former—and feared it was the latter.

# 22

Erin felt the push at her back and rose with Jerrod, trying to make the motion as casual as she could. But as they rose, Jerrod let out a low curse.

"Go," he snapped. "Go fast."

They were perhaps thirty yards to the right of the front door. Ten seconds. Ten seconds that seemed to last forever.

Her heel hit a patch of compressed snow, the foot shooting from beneath her. She winced at the burning pain in her groin as her hamstring overextended for an instant, before she caught her balance. The impossible sound of a bumblebee flying overhead was so incongruous that, for just an instant, she looked up for it. But the spark and *spang* from the wall behind her immediately made the connection that experience had not. It hadn't been a bumblebee.

It had been a bullet.

"Go! Go! Go!" Jerrod said, an urgency in his quiet tone that left no doubt that he also knew they were being shot at. His fist had clenched into the back of her coat, half pushing and half carrying her as he bellowed, "Shooter!"

Pandemonium broke out in an instant, as students primed by endless hours of media coverage and countless silent nightmares began to scream and scatter. It was, Erin realized, exactly the response he'd wanted. With so many people moving, the two of them wouldn't be such easy targets.

The glass door of the student center almost hit her in the face as it was pushed open by a uniformed campus cop, one hand moving to his sidearm, the other arm reaching out to drag people into the building. She lost her balance for a second time as he yanked at her shoulder, sliding facedown over the tile floor, feeling weight on her legs for an instant before she was shoved forward.

"Stay down," Jerrod said, pushing at her thighs.

To the mixed sounds of a boxer smacking a heavy bag and the crack of snapping wood, she saw the campus cop's leg spurt red and then collapse beneath him. A second later, spiderweb cracks radiated from three holes in the glass door.

The floor seemed too slippery, as if someone had spilled water over the smooth tile. When Erin looked down, she realized the fluid was not clear but bright red. A young girl fell into Erin's path, her eyes wide with shock and pain.

Erin flashed back to the attack in her apartment and for a moment, felt as if she were looking through a window into the past. But the girl seemed far younger than Erin could ever remember being. Her eyes met Erin's in a silent plea, and the decision was made before conscious thought intervened.

Rolling onto her side, Erin pulled the girl next to her and crawled through the writhing mass that had only a minute before been immersed in the casual, carefree passage of student life. She glanced back and saw that Jerrod was dragging the cop in exactly the same way, his eyes urging her forward.

The stairwell door was open, but Erin could see there was no way she could drag the girl through it. The space behind was packed with panicked students, some running up, some down, others frozen in place or caught in the crush of bodies.

"She's hurt!" Erin screamed. "Help us!"

Her voice seemed to cut through the panic on two faces, and four strong arms reached down, two grasping the collar of Erin's coat, the other two clutching the girl's. Erin felt a moment of weightlessness as she was hauled through the opening, only a moment later registering the pain as her hip bone smacked against the metal door frame.

The world seemed to spin and tumble as she was

passed down the stairs like a bizarre combination of a musician in a mosh pit and a skier in an avalanche. She landed against a man's chest with a shoulder-wrenching thud and looked up into the face of Alton Castle.

"Erin McKenna," she heard herself say, her voice impossibly casual. "Pleased to meet you."

"Where's your friend?" Alton asked.

"Up there somewhere," she said.

Alton helped her to her feet, and she looked up the stairs. Between the shuffle of bodies and arms and heads, she saw Jerrod's broad back. He was on one knee, one hand clamped over the cop's leg, the other arm reaching past the door frame. The cop's holster was empty, and she didn't have to imagine what his other hand was doing.

Two earsplitting cracks echoing off painted cinderblock walls made it clear he was returning fire.

"Jerrod!" she yelled. "Get us out of here!"

"Negative," he yelled back over his shoulder. "These kids are sitting ducks, and we've got wounded."

"Who is this guy?" Alton asked in disbelief.

"Our best friend and their worst nightmare," Erin replied. "But we can't stay here. Jerrod!"

"The cops are on their way!" a girl yelled, holding up her cell phone.

Jerrod glanced back at her. "Tell them it's a Red Two event. One officer and four students down inside. I say again, officer and four students down. Maybe more outside. Multiple perps. I say again, multiple perps. Send SWAT and have a medevac on standby."

The girl nodded, a finger pressed to her ear as she repeated his words into the phone. "First responders…five minutes…something else…hold on…here."

She held out the phone to Jerrod.

"Put the phone down and press both hands on the wound," Jerrod said, nodding down to the injured cop. As soon as her hands replaced his, he took the phone. As he brought it to his face, he spoke to the girl, "Push as hard as you can. Just like that."

The cop's face was already pale, but Erin could see his chest rising and falling. She looked around for the girl she'd dragged in and saw her propped against a wall with a blood-soaked hand over her ear.

"Yes," Jerrod said into the phone. "You heard right. Red Two. Multiple wounded. Multiple shooters." He paused for a moment. "At least one critical. Right. In five."

"Jerrod!" Erin yelled again. "We can't stay here!" She didn't care if it sounded cowardly. If they were still here when the cops arrived, the next shipment would be long gone by the time the three of them broke through the mountains of red tape Mercator would throw their way.

His eyes met hers, and, after an instant, he nodded.

She knew his impulse was to stay and protect the wounded, to keep the attackers at bay until help arrived. She also knew he'd realized why they couldn't.

"I don't know who you are or what she means," the cop said to Jerrod. "But from what I saw outside, she's right. They're going to know the cops are coming. I can make sure these kids are okay. Get the hell out of here, and none of us ever saw you."

"Okay," Jerrod said.

One of the students had removed his belt and was wrapping it around the cop's leg. Erin could hear the man's teeth grinding through his groans, but he caught his breath after the tourniquet was in place and held out his hand. Jerrod gave the cop back his pistol, and made his way down the stairs to Erin and Alton.

"You lead the way," he said to Alton. "Get us out of here."

For the first few minutes they simply followed the flow of students who had also realized the tunnels were the safest escape route. But at each junction students peeled off to head for their own destinations. The university had obviously planned for this possibility and instructed the students to return to their dorm rooms or other designated assembly areas, and to stay there until released. The foot traffic thinned until the three of them were alone.

"Where, exactly, are we going?" Erin asked, having long since lost her sense of direction.

"Bateman Hall," Alton said. "It's on the far side of campus. We're almost there."

"Why did you choose it?" Jerrod asked.

Alton tipped his head questioningly to one side.

"I'm asking," Jerrod explained, "because if there's an obvious reason, they might have thought of it, too."

"Ahh," Alton said. "Well, that's where my wife lived until her junior year. I drove to her place so often when I was in school here that I kind of went there on autopilot tonight."

Erin nodded. That didn't seem like the kind of reason the Mercator people could predict. She felt her shoulder muscles begin to relax.

"Sounds good," she said. "So, Alton, meet Special Agent Jerrod Westlake. He's been helping me."

"I gathered that last part," Alton said, extending a hand. "Alton Castle. Miscellaneous bean counter."

"You're hardly that anymore," Jerrod said.

"No," Alton agreed. "Okay, Bateman's the next left."

"How are we going to get our car?" Erin asked Jerrod.

They'd parked back at the student center. By now, the parking lot would be swarming with police, and both their jackets were smeared with blood.

"We don't," Jerrod said. "We didn't leave anything in it, so no loss."

"Until you have to buy another car," Alton said, one eyebrow arched.

"We didn't buy that one," Jerrod said.

The look in Jerrod's eyes showed no inclination for further explanation, and Alton didn't pursue it. Instead, he guided them down the passage in silence, as if he were wondering exactly whom he'd hooked up with.

And well he might wonder, Erin thought. In the ten minutes they'd been together, he'd seen a gunfight and learned that the people he'd expected to protect him had been driving a stolen car.

"We've been on the run," Erin said. "They broke into my apartment in Houston. Jerrod had been working the Mercator case and had come down to check on me that day. As it turned out, he showed up in the nick of time. We've been off the grid for a couple of weeks."

"And that's why you couldn't wait around for the cops," Alton said. "I thought you were trying to get me out of sight."

"We were," Jerrod said. "But yeah, it wasn't just you. There's an FBI agent, a friend of mine, who's missing and presumed abducted. I'm assuming Mercator has contacts in the Bureau."

"They do," Alton said. "All through government."

Jerrod nodded. "I'm a person of interest in Georgie's disappearance. And I'm not ready to let them know why they should be interested in me."

"Georgie is the missing agent?" Alton asked.

"Yeah. I'm guessing Mercator snatched her because they thought she might know what I'm working on. As it turns out, she doesn't. And once they know that…"

"I think I know where she is," Alton said, as they climbed a flight of stairs and emerged in the lobby of a dormitory. "I got some inside info, but I haven't reviewed it yet."

"Wait," Erin said. "We've got to do something about Alton's family. If Mercator figures out he's involved, they won't hesitate to go after his wife and kids."

"Going there now would only confirm it," Jerrod said.

"It's okay," Alton interrupted. "I sent them away a couple of hours ago."

Erin bit her lip nervously. "Are you sure they went?"

Alton nodded. "I told her I was in trouble, and the trouble might come after her and our daughter. She left."

Erin resisted the urge to ask where they'd gone, instead settling for a touch on Alton's shoulder. "You're a good man."

"I guess," he said, guiding them out into the parking lot. "That wasn't my wife's opinion when I called her. I hope she'll come back when this is over."

"She will," Erin said. "She'd be a fool not to, and you look too smart to have married a fool."

The campus was eerily quiet as they crossed the vast expanse of the parking lot. The police had arrived, that much was obvious from the flashing blue-and-red lights that reflected off the low-hanging clouds.

"Damn it," Erin said. "They're going to shut this place down. Nobody in or out. It won't matter if we get to Alton's car or not."

Jerrod nodded. "But you're forgetting something."

"What's that?" Erin asked.

"I have my creds. Once they see those, they're not going to be stopping us. Not yet. They're still busy trying to sort out what happened."

Alton's car was a small four-wheel drive that looked to Erin like the bastard son of a Volkswagen Beetle and an SUV. The thought made her laugh.

"What?" Alton asked.

Erin shook her head. "Nothing. Adrenaline."

"I'll drive," Jerrod said.

Alton offered no argument. Erin could see that he was shaking a little and looked way too pale. He'd been cool in the crisis. Now he looked ready to come apart.

As Jerrod had predicted, they had no trouble at all leaving campus. They passed through the road-block with little more than a glance at Jerrod's badge and a wave.

"Do you suppose those shooters are still there?" Alton asked, turning his head to look around.

"They were gone before we were," Jerrod answered. "Those guys were pros."

They crossed through the center of town at a reasonable speed, yet with the kind of purpose that suggested they knew exactly where they were going. No meandering in a way that might draw someone's attention.

"Pete's house?" Erin asked as they crossed the bridge on the west side of town and headed toward the mountain pass.

Jerrod nodded and glanced in the rearview. "We're working with a buddy of mine, Alton. But we're going to take a bit of a hike."

"Okay," Alton answered. "But this car can get us through pretty much anything."

"The Bureau may be watching my buddy's house. So we'll have to walk in the back way."

Alton nodded slowly. "This is all a whole lot more fun when it's only a game."

"Yeah," Jerrod said. "It is."

Erin couldn't disagree.

# 23

It was night. But what day was today?

Georgie and Dawn had worked out their own pattern of time. Though it was keyed to and driven by forces beyond their control, Georgie had encouraged Dawn to seize what knowledge they could. Their first moments after one of them was returned to her cage were focused on comforting each other. After that came the detailed debriefings with which Georgie had built a mental picture of their situation. Each of them used her time outside her cage to listen for specific voices and sounds, to count steps taken and turns made, to think outside her own body, and the practice had also allowed them to distance themselves from what was happening.

What Georgie hoped her captors would take for quiet compliance was something else entirely: careful attention to the tiny details that might, if sifted together and then prised apart, offer opportunity for escape.

That concentration meant she was only peripherally aware of the man between her legs. What he was doing was, to her, utterly irrelevant. What mattered were the voices she heard from the next room.

*Saturday night...plane will be here.*

Someone was going somewhere Saturday night. She tried to hear more, but much of the conversation was muffled by the walls or drowned out by the grunts of the man above her. Grunts that, Georgie knew, would only end when his desire was sated. So she let her body focus on the task at hand, ignoring his words of approval. It wasn't for his sake. She needed him to shut up, and this was her only way to do it.

Sure enough, her efforts quickly pushed him over the edge. As his ragged breathing slowed, she tried to visualize herself in the next room, to put faces to each voice. That she hadn't seen any of their faces was irrelevant. The act of visualizing the different speakers allowed words to begin to come through.

*Mess at the university...missed Westlake and the reporter...cover story won't hold.*

Jerrod was nearby! Georgie knew her disappearance would not have gone unreported. The Bureau would be out in force, looking for her. Even if Jerrod hadn't resurfaced, he would have found out. He always did. And he would be coming for her. For her and for Dawn.

For the first time in what seemed like an eternity, Georgie allowed herself to hope.

*Get them out…yes, he wants both.*

Get Jerrod and the reporter out? No, that didn't make sense. Then it struck her. And she knew who the plane was coming for on Saturday.

As quickly as her hope had risen, it sank. Saturday.

What day was today?

Maybe Dawn would know. Georgie made a mental note to ask Dawn if she knew what day it was. Another man replaced the one who had just finished. This was the mean one. A few days ago he'd said something about not liking sloppy seconds and had decided he needed a different receptacle. Georgie just grimaced as he pressed himself in and made her mental note into a mantra to carry her through what came next.

What day? What day? What day?

Wednesday, Bill Tatum thought. Four days. Why was it taking four days? They'd never had to wait this long for a plane before. And having missed Westlake and the reporter at the university, he didn't like having to wait now.

Fact was, he knew why it was taking four days to get a damned plane. Chuck Besom had turned. He'd delayed the plane on purpose, to buy time to get his ass out of a sling. Well, that wasn't going to work. Besom was a dead man, probably even this very moment, assuming Tatum's other team hadn't fucked things as badly as the one at the university.

But killing Besom wouldn't solve all Tatum's problems. There was still a four-day wait, in a location that—by now—Tatum had to assume was compromised. Besom had undoubtedly told the leak the location of this base. And Tatum had to assume the leak had then made contact with Westlake. That meant Westlake would be coming—soon.

Another man might have quailed at that thought. Bill Tatum did not. Indeed, he welcomed the idea. It would be one more box checked off on his life's to-do list. A box he'd been waiting to check off for a long time.


"So exactly what information do you have?" Jerrod asked as they drove up through the winding gorge toward Woodland Park in the dark.

Alton, still keyed up, was sitting in the center of the backseat, one elbow on each of the front headrests. He looked, Jerrod thought, like a schoolkid who didn't want to be left out of his parents' conversation. More likely the truth was that Alton simply didn't want to be alone with his own thoughts.

"You've heard of RoughRider Protection, right? It's the main Mercator PMC."

"Yeah, I've heard plenty about them," Jerrod said. He decided not to tell Alton that he'd worked with RoughRider guys on a couple of jobs. Trust was a commodity in short supply just now.

"Okay. Well, Chuck Besom heads up that division. He cornered me in the men's room over in my building yesterday and told me he knew what was going on, that I was passing information, and that he wanted to help me. So he told me to set up a meeting with you, told me to let him know, and then he'd stash some information for me to pass on."

"No wonder," Jerrod said heavily.

"No wonder what?"

Erin answered. "No wonder we just went through the shoot-out at the OK Corral."

"Wait," Alton said. "Just wait a second."

"Okay," Jerrod agreed, his voice like steel.

"He did leave the packet of information at my house, just like he said. I didn't use my name when I called him, and I called from a cybercafé, so I don't think they could've known who I was."

"You called him at his office?" Jerrod asked.

"Yeah," Alton said.

Jerrod looked over at Erin, and she nodded. After a moment, Alton spoke again. "So?"

Erin craned her neck. "Did you say when and where you were meeting us?"

"Yeah."

"They'd tapped Besom's phone," she said. "They didn't pick you up when you went home to get the package because they didn't know who you were. They were waiting for us at the university because they knew where you'd be, and when. And they know who Jerrod and I are. Once they spotted us, we would lead them to you and—"

"Their problems would go away," Jerrod said.

"Maybe Besom's a good guy after all," Alton said.

"Actually," Jerrod remarked grimly, "I think Chuck's playing his own game. I used to be in special ops, and I know him by reputation. Word is he's the kind of guy who's always thinking five, even ten, moves ahead. But he also has a rep as a stickler for loyalty. If he's turned on Mercator, he has a reason. Most likely one involving his own ass and the proverbial sling."

Alton was silent for a few minutes. When he spoke, his voice was tentative. "I know you guys have a lot more experience at this stuff than I do. But…I don't think Besom was lying to me. He seemed really pissed at Tatum when he told me—"

"Tatum?" Jerrod interrupted. "Bill Tatum?"

"I don't know. He just said Tatum."

It had to be, Jerrod thought. Tatum wasn't a common name. There couldn't be more than one in that kind of position at a place like Mercator. "That explains a lot. A whole lot."

"Who's Bill Tatum?" Erin asked.

Jerrod looked at her. "An asshole with a limp."

"Oh, my God," said Erin in a sagging voice. "Him?"

Jerrod nodded silently.

"What's going on?" Alton demanded from the backseat.

"Old scores," Erin said. "Old, old scores."

Alton had thought he was in decent shape. He had a stair-climber at home and used it once or twice a week for a half hour or so. Okay, not true, he finally conceded to himself. Maybe once a week, for ten minutes. Because his legs were telling him these people were mountain goats.

"Can we take a break?" he asked.

"We could," Jerrod said, "but we'll be there in ten minutes. Why not take the break then?"

"Because I might pass out first?" Alton asked.

Erin laughed. "You'll get used to that. I did."

When Jerrod had talked about hiking the last bit, Alton had imagined an easy stroll along a well-worn path. Instead, he found himself jogging to keep up as Jerrod and Erin navigated through the rock-strewn forest in the dark as easily as if it were broad daylight. And they moved with a confidence that left him wondering if he'd ever felt that sure in his own body.

"You guys do this a lot?" Alton asked.

"Yeah," Erin said. "He's been dragging me all over this mountain for a couple of weeks now."

Alton nodded, then cried out in searing pain as his foot rolled over the edge of a tree root. When he felt able to breathe again, he cursed beneath his breath. "Damn, I should have seen that."

"Trust your feet," Erin said. "They know what they're stepping on before your brain does."

"That makes no sense at all," Alton said.

"Nothing makes sense right now," Jerrod replied.

"No, that's not true," Alton said, defiantly. "We're the good guys. Those Mercator goons are the bad guys."

"You think it's that simple?" Jerrod asked.

"I do," Alton said.

Jerrod shook his head and seemed to pick up the pace. Alton tried to keep up as he looked over at Erin. "Is he always this way?"

"Yeah, usually."

"How do you put up with him?"

Erin smiled. "Because I know he's one of the good guys, even if he doesn't."

"How reassuring."

"It's complicated," Erin said.

Alton nodded. "Tell me something I don't know."

Erin looked at him. "Jerrod saved my life when Mercator came after me in Houston. Then again in Austin and again tonight. That's what I know."

"Quite the white knight," Alton said.

"The current metaphor of choice is lifeguard," Jerrod offered. "I'm officially not a fish."

"Umm…" Alton said.

"Don't ask," Erin said. "Self-analysis isn't his strong suit."

Impossibly, Alton found himself wanting to laugh. At least he wasn't having to carry the backpack of documents that Besom had left for him. Jerrod had it slung over his shoulders. It was a schoolkid's backpack, Alton realized, not much different from the one his daughter carried every day. On Jerrod's broad back, it looked like a toy. If the weight was a problem for him, Jerrod gave no sign of it.

Maybe that was what he should focus on. It was, quite literally, a weight off Alton's own shoulders.

"What are we going to do once we've read that stuff?" Alton asked.

"You're not going to do anything except go deep into hiding," Jerrod said. "You've already done enough."

Alton shook his head. "I want to be there when you take them down. I want to see it firsthand."

Jerrod slowed and then halted at the edge of the tree line. Erin stopped beside him, and Alton took his cue to drop to his knees. When he did, the ankle he'd turned minutes earlier decided to remind him of its presence.

"Shit," he said, rubbing it.

"We'll ice and tape it when we get to Pete's house," Jerrod said, without looking back, leaving Alton to wonder if the man had eyes in the back of his head. "As for being there at the takedown, that's not gonna happen."

"Why not?" Alton asked.

Jerrod finally looked back. "I don't want you to have those memories."

# 24

"Holy shit," Pete said, shaking his head. "If there's a hell, these people deserve front-row seats."

They'd spent the past three hours guzzling coffee and reading the files Besom had passed to Alton, who translated the corporate jargon when necessary and otherwise kept his ankle propped on an ice pack. The documents laid bare a story that made Pete want to vomit.

"I grew up thinking we wore the white hats," Erin said. "Americans didn't torture. Americans didn't hire out torturers. Americans sure as hell didn't snatch our own people off the streets for torturers to use as practice dummies, or sell girls overseas as sex toys."

"*Americans* still don't," Pete said. "These people are criminals. Nothing more. Don't paint the entire country with that brush."

Erin shook her head. "They're criminals working

for our government. They're not lone wolves, Pete. You know that."

"What Mercator's doing is way over any line you could possibly draw," Pete insisted. "And a lot of these contracts are with foreign governments. I'm not saying our people are lily-white. They're not. But I don't think many of them would okay *this*. This whole damn privatization move has removed oversight from the picture."

"Does it matter?" Jerrod asked.

Erin looked at him. "Of course it matters whether my country would sanction this kind of thing."

"Right *now*," Jerrod said, "whether they know the whole scope of what Mercator is doing is irrelevant. We know they have Georgie and this other girl. And we know they're planning to ship them off to hell in seventy-two hours. If we take this to the Bureau, Mercator will stall and stonewall until Georgie and the girl are gone, or just put bullets in their brains. Their lives are ticking away, while we're discussing civics."

"It's not that simple," Erin said.

"No," Jerrod said, rising to his feet. "It's exactly that simple. In the end, you have to look past the flags and the flowery words and big principles and focus on the human lives. Georgie's life. This other girl's life. The others they've already taken. The others they will take. Yeah, maybe if we stop this school of sharks, there's just another school of sharks somewhere else. But if we stop *these* sharks, we stop *their* killing. We save the lives *they'd* take. In the end, you can only save the ones you know about. But you *have* to do that."

"You *are* a lifeguard," Alton said quietly.

Pete watched as Jerrod looked down at his trembling hands in silence, obviously realizing that he'd just been shouting. Pete's voice was barely above a whisper. "Too much coffee, amigo?"

Jerrod's eyes met his. Pete tried to wipe his mind clean, to keep his face calm. He watched Jerrod mirror his slow, deep breaths. Finally the cutting edges in Jerrod's eyes seemed to soften.

"Yeah, sorry," Jerrod said. "Too much coffee."

Pete took out the sketch of the training compound that Besom had provided and laid it next to a topographic map Pete had printed from a CD-ROM meant for hikers. He'd tried to put the coordinates for a satellite photo into Google, but there were no detailed images for the area.

"So what can we expect to run into?" he asked.

Jerrod nodded and looked at the map. He traced the closely spaced brown lines around the camp. "The compound is on this plateau. Good sight lines into the valley where this stream runs. Looks as if it was probably a hunting lodge before Mercator bought it. One road in, and we can bet that will be guarded."

"You're assuming they know we're coming," Pete said.

"Tatum knows Besom passed a package to someone else in Mercator, someone who was meeting us. He knows his guys didn't get us at the university. He'll assume the package got through, and that his location and operation are compromised. If he's still there, it's because he still wants to sell his hostages, and because he knows I'll try to get them out before I take anything to the Bureau. He's greedy enough to still want to sell them. And vindictive enough to hope I'll try to rescue them. Yeah, he's still there, and he's waiting for me."

"You're walking into an ambush," Alton said.

"I am," Jerrod agreed. "But I have no choice."

Pete studied the layout for a few moments. "This isn't one you can do alone, amigo. Georgie and the girl won't be in any shape to walk out, so we'll need a vehicle. That means a driver. It also means someone to secure the main gate at the road while you're getting the hostages. At least a three-person operation."

"Exactly," Jerrod agreed. "Tatum will know that. He will also have the gate blocked, so we can't storm it in any vehicle smaller than a tank. We'll have to go in on foot and secure the main gate from inside before Erin gets there with the car."

"Wait a minute," Erin said. "You've had me running up and down mountains for two weeks. Pete's got a lot more miles on him." She shot Pete an apologetic look but kept talking. "I should go in with you on foot and let Pete drive."

"No," Jerrod said. "You may be right that you're in better condition, but Pete's had the tactical training and experience. I'm not going to put you in the line of fire."

"I know how to shoot a gun," Erin said. "My dad took me skeet-shooting when I was a teenager. I was pretty good at it."

"These won't be clay pigeons," Pete said. "It's a different thing, shooting another human being. And clay pigeons don't shoot back. These guys will."

"I *know* that," Erin said, pointing to the map. "Look, here's the closest cover we're going to have for a vehicle. It's at least four miles to the compound from there, and it's all uphill. Whoever goes in will have to be moving fast. We both know you're not up to that anymore."

Much as it pained him to admit it, Pete knew she was right. Thirty years of service to his country had left him with a larger-than-average collection of lingering nicks, dings and dents. And while he'd kept himself in shape as best he could, he simply couldn't press his body as far or for as long as he'd once done. Not enough for a four-mile uphill run, anyway.

"She's right," Pete finally said, looking at Jerrod. "I'd probably be sucking wind by the time I got up there. You're going to need someone who can still function."

"I can go," Alton offered.

"No way," Erin said. "Even if you were in shape, you sprained your ankle today."

"I can't do it," Jerrod said, looking at her. "I can't put you there."

Erin returned his stare. "We don't have a choice, Jerrod. Pete's right. You can't do this alone, and this is what you've been training me for. Just don't give me a pistol. I'm terrible with a pistol. But with a shotgun, I'll hit what I aim at."

Jerrod looked at the map in silence. Pete could feel his friend's pain. He knew what bringing that girl out of Indonesia had done to Jerrod's psyche. He knew his friend did not want a repeat experience. But in practical terms, they had no better options.

"We need a mock-up," Pete said. "Up the hill behind my house. Somewhere to do a run-through or two."

"Or three," Jerrod said, nodding. "You still have your riot gun?"

"The Mossberg?" Pete asked. "Yeah, I do."

Jerrod looked at Erin. "That'll be yours."

Pete saw neither fear nor excitement in Erin's eyes. She simply nodded, as if they had decided on a Chinese take-out order. That she was so matter-of-fact about it said a lot about her, and about Jerrod's training methods. She would do fine.

Or he would never forgive himself.

Jerrod looked back at the map. "Okay, we'll go in like this."

Chuck Besom knew he was hovering in that netherworld of exhaustion and anxiety. He knew he couldn't go back to the office, and he couldn't go home. He had no doubt that, at this very moment, there was a hit team with his photo on the op-plan clipboard. All he could do was drive around the city, keeping to the main streets, while he thought about his exit strategy.

Getting out of the city by air was a nonstarter. Mercator had the kind of access that allowed them to put him on watch lists. Simply buying a ticket would mean they were waiting when he stepped off the plane, and Mercator's reach was global. That left ground transport: bus, train or car. Trains were few in number, limited in destination, and thus off the menu. Buses offered a wider range of destinations but would leave him helpless and exposed for hours, hours that Warrick and Tatum would be using to find him.

So driving was his only option.

The problem was, where to go? How far could he get on the money he had in his wallet? And how long could he drive before exhaustion landed him in a roadside ditch?

The only answers he could think of so far were

"I don't know," "Not far," and "Not long." Which added up to "Not promising" in terms of his own life expectancy.

He needed quick energy, and the drive-through window of an all-night coffee shop seemed the best and fastest alternative. With a quick glance in his rearview mirror, he prepared to change into the right lane.

And that was when he spotted them.

Three men—he assumed they were men—in a beige, late-model SUV. He'd no sooner begun to change lanes than they had tracked behind him, four or five car lengths back. Old training in countersurveillance techniques flooded his mind. The school solution would have been to do exactly as he'd planned: drive to the coffee shop and see whether they followed. Of course, that solution assumed relatively incompetent trackers who would either follow him or give some other visible response. Professionals would simply drive on past, with no reaction other than a few words whispered into a headset microphone, telling the next tail vehicle where he was and to take over the active post.

Given a choice, Bill Tatum would be using trained surveillance operatives. But even Mercator had finite resources, and the botched operation at the university had doubtless occupied some of Tatum's best assets. There was a chance Besom was being followed by relative amateurs. It was a chance he had to take.

He flicked on his turn signal and slowed, not wanting to make it obvious that he suspected he was being followed, and pulled into the coffee shop parking lot.

The SUV seemed to slow a bit, though perhaps that was only because Besom himself had slowed. Regardless, it did not follow him into the parking lot. Chiding himself for his paranoia, he pulled into the drive-through lane and ordered an extra large iced mocha cappuccino with a double-add-shot. The combination of sugar and the caffeine of four shots of espresso ought to wake up his system and give him enough energy to think.

The girl at the window couldn't have been more than sixteen. Blond ponytails shimmered over each shoulder, and she had that mountain-fresh, freckled face that Besom found so attractive and so common in this part of the country. Girls here didn't spend all day inhaling chemical sludge like the girls in most cities. It showed in that youthful glow that no make-up artist could mimic.

"Six fifty-seven," she said, with a tired but still-cheerful smile.

He handed her a ten-dollar bill and returned the smile. She was far too young to be really attractive—he did not share the loathsome tastes of

Bill Tatum and his operatives—but she was obviously doing her best to fulfill her company's dicta regarding customer service.

"Chilly night," he offered.

"And you're drinking something cold," she replied blandly as she counted out his change. "That doesn't make much sense."

"I guess not," Besom said.

"What the…?" she began.

The look on her face said all he needed to know. He barely had time to turn his head as the two men who had climbed out of the SUV raised their hands and the darkness erupted with trails of white-orange light.

The first volley missed him, though his windshield and passenger windows shattered. Stomping on the gas pedal, he couldn't resist a glance up at the service window. Four neat holes had been punched through the glass, and the girl was nowhere to be seen.

Besom hoped, prayed, that she'd had time to duck.

It was the last prayer he offered. A split second later, the back window of his car exploded and the world went eternally black.

# 25

"Okay," Pete said as he pulled an all-black shotgun out of a hard carrying case on the ground. "This is the Mossberg 590, pump action, iron sight. Range about forty yards. Short barrel, twenty inches. This is for maximum knock-down power at close quarters. Not the kind of thing you would have used in skeet-shooting."

"No, my dad's gun was definitely longer."

"Most hunting shotguns are, to reduce the pellet spread and get better accuracy at longer range. With this, you don't have to be a marksman to give your target, or even a group of targets, a problem. Most civilians use the two-and-three-quarter-inch shell. With those, she'll hold nine rounds. We'll go with the three-inch tactical shell once you get the feel of the weapon. Only eight rounds and you'll get more kick, but you *will* knock the target down."

Erin hefted the shotgun, surprised that it wasn't heavier. She remembered her dad's gun as weighing a lot more. Maybe because she'd been younger then. Or maybe Jerrod's training had made her stronger than she knew.

Standing beside her, Pete showed her how to work the pump. "This is how you load another cartridge into the chamber. Since she only holds eight tactical rounds, you need to use them wisely. Reloading is quick, but not the kind of thing you want to do with people shooting at you."

Her dad's gun had been double-barreled. Two shots before a reload. She expected the pump to be difficult, but it proved to be easier than she anticipated. The action was smooth and easy to operate. After a couple of tries she pulled a TV pose as she worked the pump, and Pete grinned. "That's the way."

He pulled a box of ammo out of a bag and motioned her to squat beside him. "The Mossberg is a brilliant piece of engineering," he said. "Cops call it a riot gun, because they can use it in close quarters. Remember, this isn't about marksmanship. You're not shooting clay pigeons or pheasants. Hit the target and put him down."

Erin nodded, watching intently as he loaded the shells into the gun. Then he ejected them and had her do it.

"Good," he said. "Mossberg makes one with an autoloader, but I haven't felt the least need to upgrade. This is efficient, faster than you would think once you get used to it, and it does the job."

320 *Rachel Lee*

"Got it," Erin agreed. To her way of thinking, eight shots was a big upgrade from a double-barreled skeet gun.

"You can shoot from the hip if necessary," Pete explained. "But for now, let's do some straightforward target practice."

The paper bull's-eye targets, four of them, were pinned against the side of a hill. The pellets could go no farther than the dirt behind them.

Pete stood behind her, reminding her to hold the butt snugly against her shoulder and explaining how to sight along the barrel, speaking quietly as he did. "You gotta understand. It's going to be different when you see a man out there. You gotta be ready for that, Erin. You're probably not going to kill him unless it's a head shot, and you don't aim for the head, because it's too small a target. Assume your targets will have body armor. Aim for bottom center mass, belly button to crotch."

She nodded, breathing rapidly as she pressed her cheek to the stock of the gun and sighted. Real people. She *had* to be able to pull the trigger or she would be of no earthly use to anyone. Jerrod's life might depend on her. Or Georgie's. Or the other girl's.

"Don't jerk the trigger," Pete said. "Take a breath, hold it, release it, then squeeze." He pulled ear protectors into place, covering her ears. "Okay, have at it," he said loudly enough to be heard.

For a few seconds she closed her eyes, gathering herself. Then she aimed at the first target and squeezed.

Ear protectors muffled the sound, the recoil wasn't anything like she had expected, and in an eyeblink the target shredded, riddled with holes.

"Wow," she whispered, astonished by the sheer power of this weapon. With the ear protectors on, her whisper sounded loud in her own ears. Shattering skeet hadn't really given her any idea of what a shotgun could do. The sight of that target did.

Pete was behind her and he tapped her shoulder, reminding her that she wasn't supposed to take a break. She pumped another round into the chamber and pulled the trigger again.

It was easy. Maybe too easy, some puritan part of her conscience noted. Another part—the dominant part—felt sheer exhilaration at the power of the gun. Shooting, she suddenly remembered, was *fun*.

At least at targets. When she'd emptied the chamber, she stood down the way Pete had taught her, barrel pointed to the ground away from her feet. He slapped her on the back, handed her more shells and went to put up fresh targets.

She ejected her spent shells and reloaded, looking forward to the next round. Skeet-shooting had been fun, but she was a bit shocked to find she enjoyed seeing the shredded targets to mark her accuracy. For the first time in her life she understood why there were so many target ranges around. There was nothing quite like this.

Then she looked up and saw that Pete had replaced the bull's-eye targets with human silhouettes.

In an instant, it didn't feel fun anymore.

Aiming between the belly button and crotch, as Pete had instructed, she sighted, squeezed and pumped in quick succession, noting that most of the pellets spread over the lower torso and legs. Someone, she thought, wouldn't be having many kids.

Her accuracy was sufficient that he backed her up and made it harder. By morning's end, she was at maximum range and hitting her targets eight shots out of ten. It wasn't perfect, but life rarely was.

Then he loaded her with the longer-range tactical rounds.

There was definitely more kick, but she found it easy enough to control after the first couple of nervous shots.

"You got it," he told her when he took the Mossberg back and she removed her ear protectors.

He smiled, but it wasn't his usual grin. This one held something like sadness.

It was a sadness she felt, too. Her weapon had always been the pen. Now she would be carrying a deadly weapon with every intention of using it. She had to force herself to remember that she would be doing it to save innocent lives.

Pete seemed to read her mind. He gripped her shoulder and looked deep into her eyes. "Erin, just remember why you're doing this. There's a little girl out there who you need to save."

"And Georgie."

"Yes, and Georgie."

Erin nodded. Her head knew he was right. Her heart was taking a little longer.

After lunch, they went to another hilltop to look over the mock compound Jerrod and Alton had laid out. Given the time they had to work with, it was nothing fancy, with building and gate outlines sketched out with dead tree branches and rocks. But it worked as a full-scale map and gave them a good sense of the camp layout.

"There is no doubt," Jerrod said, "that Tatum will be expecting us. No matter what I think of him personally, it remains that he knows his job, and he's damn good at it."

"You mean," Erin remarked, "this isn't going to be a walk in the park?"

Pete snorted, Alton barked a laugh, and Jerrod scowled at her. "You're getting your attitude back," he said.

"Yeah. It's kinda nice, actually."

"Don't let that attitude get us killed."

"Hey, that attitude got me where I am today," she replied. "Which, now that I think about it, might not be such a good thing."

Even Jerrod couldn't contain his smile. "Depends on how you look at it."

"Absolutely. So I'll look at it as being Sigourney

Weaver in *Alien*. More reassuring than being a reporter who knows squat about what I'm doing."

It was cold out there on the hilltop, and not even the higher hills around them seemed to cut the wind. Snow lay in every shadowed patch beneath the trees, and bare ground showed only where wind had blown the snow away. They'd chosen this site because it was a small plateau, like the one they would be assaulting, and at roughly the same altitude.

"There isn't a lot of snow here," Jerrod offered. "I don't know what we'll find there, though. And you can't tell how deep it is just by looking at it. One step you're in six inches, and the next you're in six feet. We're going to need skis or snowshoes. Which would you prefer?"

"I've skied a bit. I've never used snowshoes."

"I've got cross-country skis," Pete said. "For both of you."

"Skis it is, then," Jerrod agreed. "We may need to use them on the approach, but we don't have time to practice that. So I hope you can remember how to do it fast, because we'll be moving uphill. What we need to do now is go through the assault itself. Alton?"

"Yeah?"

"You look like a blue Popsicle. Why don't you go back to Pete's place?"

"Because this is as close as I'll ever get to being a hero. I don't want to miss it."

Erin's face softened. "You're already a hero."

Alton shook his head. "Not like you guys."

Jerrod stepped toward him and gripped his shoulder. "Yes, like us guys. You did the really hard, scary stuff and you had no way to protect yourself. Don't ever, ever think you're not a hero."

After a moment, Alton nodded. "But I'm not leaving anyway. I want to watch."

"Fair enough," Jerrod said. "You'll be the hostage, over in the lodge there. Between shivering and your ankle, getting you out will be something like what we'll face with Georgie and the kid. Pete, you're driving."

"Love my SUV," Pete said with a grin, holding an imaginary steering wheel.

"It'll have to do, unless you have a Hummer up here that I'm not seeing," Jerrod said. He turned to Erin. "We run it like I showed you on the map. We come up from the south and take the lodge first. That makes the gate guards react to us, makes them look in two directions. When they break position, Pete roars up."

They began the practice drills, first walking through their maneuvers, then picking up the pace to a fast jog. Erin's assignment was to stay behind Jerrod's left shoulder, to shepherd the hostages, cover their rear and be ready to provide support fire if needed. It seemed easy enough, but Jerrod changed their exact route every time. At one point, expecting him to bolt around a corner, she moved to follow and charged right into his back. It was the moment he'd been waiting for.

"That's exactly what you *can't* do," he snapped. "We have to be a single unit. A single mind. If I move, you move. If I stop, you stop."

"That would be a hell of a lot easier if you'd do the same thing every time," she snapped back.

"And I would," he said, "if I knew exactly where the bad guys were going to be and what they're going to do. But we don't know that. I'm imagining different positions and different reactions every time. That changes what I do. That has to change what you do, too."

"I can't see what you're imagining," Erin pointed out. "I feel as if I'm stumbling around blind."

Jerrod nodded. "Good. That's what you ought to feel like, because that's exactly what you're going to be doing. You won't see what's around the corner until you get there, and I'll be going first. That means you react off me. You can't think about it. You have to just do it. Every time. Or we get killed. Got it?"

She made as if to reply, then bit it off. "Fine."

Jerrod sighed. He knew she was angry. But this was no time for histrionics. He forced himself to take a slow, deep breath before he spoke.

"Look, I know you're tired. I know this is intense, and it's not something you're accustomed to. I'm sorry I'm snapping at you. And I wish there were an easier way to say things."

To his surprise, Erin smiled. "You're right. I'm being a bitch."

"Stop," Jerrod said. "You're being a rookie. I'd never call you a bitch, and I won't let you call yourself one, either. This isn't about testicles or ovaries. It's about experience."

Erin took a step back and looked down. "Wow."

"What?" Jerrod asked.

"That lit your fuse. I'm sorry."

"Yeah, it did," he said. "It was a cheap way out. I watched you shoot this morning. I've watched you on our runs. You're not the best soldier I've ever worked with, but you're far from the worst. Don't ever slur yourself like that. All that does is keep you from getting better."

"Aye, aye, sir," she said.

"We say hooah."

"Hooah," she repeated.

"Good, let's run through it again. And you'd damn well better be on my left shoulder, no matter if I do backflips and sing 'Yankee Doodle Dandy.'"

He hoped she caught both the seriousness and the humor. Her smile said she did. "Hooah, sir."

The sun vanished behind the mountains early, leaving a long, lingering twilight. They used the time to run three more drills, and each time, Jerrod varied his route and pace. Each time, Erin stuck to his left shoulder as if bonded by an invisible chain. Forcing her to make that mistake, and confronting her with its implications, had drilled her role into her mind. In fact, he realized, she'd learned faster than most of the rookie special-ops guys he'd worked with.

As the sun set fully, the air chilled to the point that Alton could barely stand on his injured ankle. Jerrod wanted to make one more run-through, figuring Alton's condition at this point was probably closest to what they would face with the real hostages. But there was also the issue of Alton making the injury worse as they dragged him back and forth across the makeshift training site.

Military sense said to run the operation again. Compassion said otherwise.

"Let's stop here," Jerrod said. "Before our hostage ends up tearing some ligaments."

"I'm still good to go," Alton sputtered bravely through shuddering lips. "Honest."

"I know you are," Jerrod said. "That's why we're going to go down the hill while you can still walk. We need to pack up the car tonight and be on the road before dawn. We've got a long drive tomorrow."

A drive into hell.

# 26

*Hungry.*

She'd never been this hungry before, Dawn thought. When she'd been on the street, sometimes she'd gone two or three days between meals. But this was different. The men had simply stopped feeding her, even the scant diet that she'd grown used to over the past few weeks. This wasn't just hunger. It was malicious hunger, and it seemed to gnaw at her belly more than anything she'd known before.

But, Georgie had told her, it was also information. Every change in their routine, no matter how seemingly insignificant, was a puzzle piece. It was up to Dawn and Georgie to put those pieces together. She had to think. But she couldn't think. Because she was…

*Hungry.*

What did it mean, that she couldn't think? That was the question, if only she could hold on to it long enough for her brain to work through it. Why? Why weren't they letting her eat? Why was she so…?

*Hungry.*

She heard Georgie groan. The sound came out somewhere between the one Dawn remembered making when her dad woke her for school and the one their dog Pepper had made that last day as he lay on the kitchen floor. It was the day Dad took Pepper to the vet and came home alone and crying. It was the day Pepper died. It was that groan.

"Georgie?" she whispered. "Are you okay?"

But Georgie just moaned again, more quietly this time, and more slowly. The way Pepper had done.

Dawn shoved down the aching, gnawing pain in her belly and worked at the blankets between their cages until she found a place wide enough to slip her fingers through. She felt around, hoping for the smooth skin of Georgie's back or that downy place just above her buttocks, the soft but tousseled strands of her hair or the prickly firmness of her unshaven calves.

Anything that was Georgie.

Anything that was still alive.

"Georgie?" she whispered again. "I'm here, honey. Touch me. Please."

Another quiet, slow groan.

Dawn felt her eyes prickle. No, this couldn't be. She couldn't have held on this long just to lose

Georgie. Georgie was life. Georgie was hope. Georgie was strength. Georgie was goodness.

Georgie was all she had.

Georgie couldn't die.

Then all she would be was…

*Lips.*

Lips on her fingers. Slow breaths. In, then out. In, then out. Dawn felt a cheek, but it was too warm. Puffy. And when she touched the jaw, another impossible moan.

They'd beaten Georgie, Dawn realized. Those men had hit Georgie on her face and kept on hitting her until Georgie stopped whatever she'd been doing, if she'd even been doing anything at all. They'd beaten her until they made her moan.

The fuckers.

Her mom wouldn't have let her use that word. She'd used it on the streets, but she hadn't meant it. Not the way she meant it now.

The *fuckers.*

If they'd killed her Georgie, Dawn was going to kill them back. Maybe she would kill them anyway. They deserved it. And no, Mom and Dad wouldn't want her to do that, and yes, Father Peter would say it was wrong. But Mom and Dad and Father Peter weren't here with these *fuckers.*

"I'll get them, Georgie. I promise I will."

"N-nooo."

"I will, Georgie. They hurt you, and I'll hurt them right back. I'll hurt them until they don't remember what not hurting was. And then I'll kill those fuckers."

"N-noo. J-Jerrod."

Jerrod?

"Who is Jerrod?"

"S-soon."

"Jerrod is coming soon?"

"Mmm-hmm."

They'd made her crazy. Georgie had never mentioned anyone named Jerrod coming for them. If she knew someone was coming, she would have said so. So that was it. They'd made Georgie crazy.

"I'll get them," Dawn said. "I'll find a way."

"N-noo. J-Jerrod."

"There's no Jerrod, honey," Dawn said, her words slow and even, as if she were speaking to an infant. "There's just us. You and me. Georgie and Dawn. They hurt you. I'm going to hurt them back. I promise."

She would just wait until they took her out of her cage in the morning. Wait until one of them stuffed his cock in her mouth. Oh, would she get them good. She could almost taste the blood, but it wouldn't be her own this time.

Yes, she would get them. Because they'd hurt Georgie. And that made her…

*Hungry.*

* * *

As the miles rolled past, Erin found it more and more difficult to stay awake. But every time her chin dropped to her chest, Jerrod nudged her.

"Why can't I sleep?" she finally asked.

"We're going to have to be one hundred percent fresh in the morning," Jerrod explained. "But you're going to be keyed up tonight. If you sleep now, you'll be up all night thinking about what's going to happen tomorrow, what might go wrong, what you might have to do. I want you so tired you'll drop when we stop."

"I'm there already," she said.

"Good. Stay there."

It made a kind of sense, she realized. She was already running over tomorrow in her mind. Or she was until the images began to twist and contort and she realized she was dreaming, and then her head snapped back up, or Jerrod nudged her in the ribs.

"Is this why they keep you awake for days on end in boot camp?" she asked.

"Exactly," Jerrod said.

"I thought the idea was to grab sleep whenever you can. Every ex-military type I've ever known could sleep standing up if he had to."

He nodded. "That's usually true. But not always. Sometimes you have to shift your sleep schedule to the op schedule. To make sure you're at your peak when the op calls for it."

"I see. So why is Pete snoring?"

"Probably because he's asleep," Jerrod said with a wry smile. "He's used to this stuff. And he doesn't have to ski four miles up a mountainside at dawn tomorrow."

Erin shrugged. "He doesn't snore as loud as I thought he would."

"I hadn't thought about it."

"Well, I mean, he's a big guy. Big guy equals big snore, right?"

"I guess."

"But he makes little snores. Almost like a low, slow whistle. It's kind of cute."

"If you say so."

This time it was Erin who gave the nudge. "I'm bored, okay? And if I try to think about tomorrow I fall asleep. So I'm talking about how Pete snores. Deal with it."

"I am," he said with a wink.

"You made me screw up on purpose yesterday, didn't you? When we were doing the run-throughs."

"Yup."

"Then you jumped down my throat about it."

"That I did."

"You know you're a bastard, right?"

He nodded. "But not a fish."

"Nope. A bastard lifeguard."

"Bastard lifeguards are good guys?"

"Yup."

"Even the ones that snore."

"Of course," she said. "I snore, too."

"Do not."

"Do so. My ex-insignificant other made a point of telling me so."

"He was a jerk."

"Of course," she agreed. "All ex-insignificant others are jerks."

"Just like all D.I.'s are bastards."

"Exactly. It's in the job description."

"Got it," he said.

"Y'know," Pete offered sleepily from the backseat, "the two of you act like an old married couple."

"Go back to snoring," Erin said.

"Was I snoring?"

*"Yes,"* Erin and Jerrod answered in unison.

"Well, shit. I'm sorry about that."

"Don't worry," Jerrod said. "Erin says you have a cute little snore."

"Thanks," Pete said. "I think. So where are we? How long was I out?"

"A couple of hours," Jerrod said. "A couple of hours to there, and you were out a couple of hours."

"Synchronicity," Erin offered.

"If you say so," Jerrod replied.

And again with that wink.

They had, she realized, reached the point where they could have complete conversations in just one or two words. Like an old married couple, just as Pete had said. She didn't know how to feel about that.

"You know we're going to do this, right?" she asked.

"Uh-huh."

"Do you think I'm going to screw up?"

He looked at her. "Yeah, probably. Everyone does on their first op. The lucky ones screw up and live to tell about it."

"That's reassuring," she said.

He reached over to pat her hand. "You're going to do fine. Yeah, you're going to screw up. Part of being a good soldier is knowing that ahead of time. Not putting yourself in places where a single screw-up will get you dead or compromise the mission."

"I never wanted to be a soldier," she said.

"That ship already sailed."

"I know. It's just…going into a forest fire, fine. Suiting up and going through the smoke chamber, fine. Even being at an accident site. Grisly, yes. Sad, undoubtedly. But I wasn't setting out to *hurt* anyone."

"You can't look at it that way," Jerrod said.

"But it *is* that way."

"Yeah," he said, glancing over. "It is. And if you want to change seats with Pete, that's fine by me. I don't want to make you do this. Believe me."

"Pete hasn't drilled for it."

"He'd pick it up," Jerrod said. "He watched us."

"And you know that's not the same," she insisted.

"No, it's not."

"So I have to do it."

"And you'll do fine," he said.

"And '*fine*' might mean I kill someone."

"Yeah, it might."

"So, what's it…?"

"What's it like to kill someone?"

"Yeah."

He took a long breath. "It sucks. Every damn time. But only later."

"How do you mean?"

"At the time, they'll look just like those targets you shot up yesterday. Because that's what you'll make them look like, in your mind. A guy pops around a corner with a gun, and you sight and breathe and squeeze, and he goes down. Then you look for the next target. And the next. And you keep doing that until we have the hostages and we're in the car and gone. And then it hits you. You killed someone."

Erin nodded slowly. "Yeah. That makes sense."

"Then the really shitty part starts," Jerrod continued. "The part where you remember his face, because you didn't notice it at the time, but when you remember, it comes back. You remember the details. How his eyes looked in that last moment. How he fell. You start wondering if he had a wife or kids, or a mom and dad back home waiting for him. You wonder if it was worth it. You wonder if it would have been better if it was you dead and not him."

"I get it," she said, not wanting to chase the thought any further, and not wanting Jerrod to chase it, either. But she'd started it, and he didn't stop.

"If you're the praying type," he said, "and I am, you start talking to God. Asking questions that God isn't going to answer, not in this lifetime. You try to pretend you hear the answers, but in your heart you know it's just your own imagination, trying to convince you that you did what was necessary, that if you hadn't done it you'd be dead and the mission would've gone to hell. Eventually you decide that's a bunch of shit.

"And then you change your mind. And back and forth until you finally just get bored thinking about it and decide that whatever's done is done, and whatever redemption there is will only come once you're cold in the same ground they're in. And you go on with life and tell yourself you're working for the right and the greater good for the greater number, or at least the greatest good for your side. Then a reporter comes up and asks you how it feels. And you want to say 'Fuck off. Go do it yourself and find out how it feels.'"

"Which brings us to the present," Erin said.

"So it seems."

"I'm sorry, Jerrod."

He shook his head. "Don't be. That made more sense than most of what I've thought for the past ten years or so. You're right about fish and lifeguards. It sounds trite, but there it is. Tomorrow, you gotta go in the water. And maybe you'll have to kill some fish. But you'll be doing it as a lifeguard. And that's the only comfort you're ever going to have."

It was indeed cold comfort, Erin realized. But cold comfort was better than none at all.

# 27

Besom was gone. And the packages were almost ready for transport. Tatum had double-checked the arrangements. The plane would be here tomorrow night. By then the packages would be too weakened by hunger to offer much resistance, and sedatives would take care of what little was left. But that was for tomorrow night.

For tonight, he had a different op to plan.

Westlake would hit them tomorrow, so tonight Tatum had to plan an ambush.

Tactically, the key question was what help Westlake would have. Tatum had learned that the reporter's source was Alton Castle, but the geek accountant would be useless. Westlake had a friend in the Colorado Springs area, a retired FBI agent, but Tatum's contacts said Westlake hadn't contacted the man. That might mean Westlake really hadn't contacted his friend, or it might mean Tatum's contacts had been lied to and hadn't done the eyes-on surveillance to verify it one way or the other.

Most likely, Tatum thought, it was the latter.

So okay, Westlake probably had an ex-agent for help. And the reporter, but she wouldn't be worth anything in a firefight. So, two of them.

One would have to drive. The old guy. That left Westlake on foot. If he came on foot. But he would be a fool to do that alone. Even Westlake was just one man. So they would rush the gate in a car. Probably an SUV, if Westlake's buddy had one, or they could steal one.

That left Tatum fat with options. An improvised explosive device—an IED—or two would be the first line of defense. God knew those worked well enough against civilian vehicles. Tatum had even seen them take out an armored Hummer more than once in Iraq. He didn't have time to make a shaped charge, but he wouldn't need one. A couple of coffee cans full of C-4 plastic explosive, buried in the road, one with a detonator connected to a cell phone, the other daisy-chained with det-cord. That ought to make a lovely howdy-do as Westlake and his buddy drove up.

But of course, an IED was nothing more than a remote-controlled land mine. And as every military officer knew, a minefield was useless unless it was covered by direct fire. And that, Tatum could supply.

Two teams of two with M-5 carbines each side of the road, sited for enfilading fire, cutting loose as soon as the blast wave from the IED cleared them. If Westlake or his buddy survived the blast, they would be cut down in the cross fire for sure.

But just in case "for sure" surrendered to the vagaries of reality—as it was wont to do in combat—Tatum would have a third line of defense. A mobile team, two men with M-5s in a Hummer, ready to sweep the road if either of the targets cleared the first ambush. Classic elastic defense with a mobile counterattack team, straight out of the training manuals.

A scout to set off the IED, two two-man teams for the ambush and a two-man mobile team. Seven guys, plus Tatum and his deputy to guard the packages. It was a good plan.

Of course the guys would be pissed at missing their last chances with the packages. But war, as they say, is hell. Tatum would take care of the packages for them. He hadn't taken a turn in a while anyway.

Yeah. It was a good plan.

Once Jerrod, Erin and Pete left the interstate and headed into the Sangre de Cristo Mountains toward Durango, travel became questionable. One pass remained open and maintained in this area of the state. Most other roads were closed to traffic beyond a certain elevation. A beautiful, scenic summer route vanished in the winter snows, often several hundred inches deep.

But alongside the paved roads that had been plowed during the winter, they discovered one of Colorado's little surprises: roadside camping turnouts. In the height of winter they were virtually unusable, but the signs of them were easy to detect, a circular break in the trees surrounding an auto turnout.

Pete and Jerrod had picked a point on the map that didn't lead directly to the compound where the hostages were being held, a road that was unlikely to be patrolled. There they pulled Pete's car over into the snow-buried turnout and started to put their plan in motion.

Erin soon found herself working so hard that she wanted to take her jacket off to let the body heat escape. Stupid, of course. At this altitude she would be sucked dry by the lack of humidity and would chill too fast from her own sweat.

So she helped set up a tent Pete had brought beneath the shielding branches of Colorado pines and spruce, dense enough to block out the twilit sky. The tent was big enough for four men, and she was given the job of spreading out three mummy bags, sleeping bags with insulated drawstring hoods for the head. When she emerged, she was surprised to find the men covering the top of the car with snow.

Protection against being spotted from the air, she realized. Then she was handed a branch, and along with Pete and Jerrod, she helped smooth away their tracks as much as possible. Since the road had been recently plowed, that wasn't going to be a problem, but why leave an obvious marker to where they had pitched their tent?

"This is mostly ranch land and state forest up here," Pete told them. "We're not likely to see another soul."

"I hope not," Jerrod remarked. "I don't want any more problems than we've already got."

He helped Pete string a tarp over the top of the tent.

"Why do we need that?" Erin asked.

"Two reasons," Jerrod answered. "First, we can camouflage it. Second, if we get a heavy snowfall tonight, this will protect the tent. But most important, when we light a lantern or flashlight tonight, you won't be able to see us from above."

"That's three reasons."

He glanced at her from beneath lowered brows.

She shrugged. "If you'd ever taken a course in public speaking, you'd know not to enumerate your points in advance, because it's going to disturb everyone if the tally comes out wrong."

"So?"

She flashed a grin she had a hard time feeling. "I

figured since you're teaching me so much, I could reciprocate."

A chuckle escaped Pete as Jerrod rolled his eyes.

They threw some relatively light pine branches up on the tarp, and a few shovelfuls of snow. Erin, reaching down to pick up a handful of the white powder, remarked, "If the wind blows, this stuff is going everywhere. I've never seen snow this light and dry."

"Altitude," Pete answered. "Low humidity. Until the weight of new snowfall packs it down, it'll be like talc."

"It fell like this?"

"It's been drying out since the blizzard. No packing."

She nodded, comparing it to her footprints, and saw what he meant. Big difference. Why did she think that was going to make skiing a bit of a challenge?

Once inside the tent, Pete turned on a battery-operated lantern, then brought out a two-burner propane camp stove.

"We can't use that in here," Erin said.

"Sure we can."

Without a word, Jerrod stood and unzipped a flap at the top of the tent. It wasn't a big hole, but it was clear what it was for. As soon as he opened it, she could feel air coming in from beneath the front door flaps.

"Okay," she said. "I didn't know you could do that."

"We're gonna eat hot tonight," Pete said. "Lots of food and hot drinks. It'll be the last we get until the op is over."

Jerrod nodded, sitting cross-legged between Pete and Erin. Little conversation passed at first. Only a few hours remained between them and the operation tomorrow, and they were supposed to sleep through most of those hours. Erin, feeling keyed up now instead of sleepy, wondered if she would be able to sleep at all.

After a really large meal of basic freeze-dried foods and boiled rice, they took their turns using the outdoor facilities. Jerrod insisted on accompanying Erin, and she thought that if he didn't trust her any more than this, he ought to leave her behind.

But that wasn't it at all. As soon as they were far enough from the tent to be showered in starlight, he grabbed her arm and pulled her tight against him beneath the sheltering boughs of a spruce. In an instant he wrapped her in a bear hug, and she could feel the heat of his breath against her cheek as he spoke softly in her ear.

"You don't have to do this," he said. "I'm trained. I can handle it alone."

Part of her wanted to agree. The chicken in her. But another part was offended. "I can do this," she argued, struggling against his hold.

"I know you can. I know. I know."

He repeated the words almost like a mantra. Something about the way he said them stilled her. "Jerrod..."

"Shh," he said, settling her more comfortably against him and leaning his back against the tree. "Shh."

She leaned against him, wishing her cheek could feel more than the frigid outer lining of his parka. But she could hear the beat of his heart. Strong and steady. All of a sudden she wondered if she could live if she never heard that sound again.

One of his hands cupped the back of her head, pulling her even closer.

"You need a wingman," she said finally. "Somebody has to watch your back."

"I'm worried about who's going to be watching yours."

She didn't want to think about that. If she started thinking about that, she would probably run all the way to Texas. "I'll be fine," she said instead, lying through her teeth.

"You better be. I've only got a few things I really care about in life anymore, and somehow you turned out to be one of them."

"Wow," she murmured, and turned her face up to look at him. With the reflection of starlight off the snow, his face wasn't a blank to her. She could read it, and what she read there awed her.

He leaned in and kissed her, slowly, deeply,

tasting her mouth as if he owned it. Dizzily she responded to his kiss, using it to push back the enormous shadow that loomed steadily closer with the passage of time. Clinging to it for the life and hope it seemed to offer. If this was all there ever was, she was suddenly fiercely glad she hadn't missed it.

When they broke apart, both of them were breathing heavily. Their eyes locked. Erin heard the hammering of her heart in her ears, a rapid thudding that masked any other sound.

When Jerrod finally spoke, he said none of the things she had both hoped and feared to hear.

"Hurry up," he said. "We need to get some sleep."

Then he released her and walked a dozen paces away, giving her some privacy.

For the longest time, it seemed, she couldn't collect herself. But finally she did, thinking life had a strange sense of humor, forcing a woman to squat in the snow.

There had to be a better way.

"Y'know," Pete said when they returned, "it strikes me that Tatum will probably have the road mined for us."

Neither of them replied for a moment as they slipped into their mummy bags. Pete had already crawled into his while they were taking care of nature's urges, however many they had chosen to indulge. Part of him wanted to offer to stand watch outside. This might, after all, be their last night on earth. Another part of him knew he, too, would need to be alert and ready to go tomorrow, and that meant he needed to sleep.

Maybe they could take care of things after he dozed off.

"You're right," Jerrod finally said. "And he'll have put them in today, so the overnight snow and winds will hide them pretty well."

"Mines?" Erin asked. "These guys have land mines?"

"Not official ones," Pete said. "But that's not a challenge for someone with Tatum's training. Who do you think developed the original planning and tactics for the IEDs we've seen in Iraq?"

"I hadn't thought about it," she answered.

"We did," Pete said. "Well, along with the British, back during World War Two. We trained resistance movements all over Europe to harass the Nazi occupiers. Then, after the war, we trained anticommunist insurgents. The Special Forces training manual has an entire chapter on how to make improvised booby traps. Shouldn't be much of a surprise that the same technology and tactics came home to roost."

"I guess not," Erin said.

"Point is," Pete continued, "Tatum will know how to make those. And if he's as good as Jerrod says—"

"He is," Jerrod interrupted.

"Then he'll have placed some out there."

"Yup, he will," Jerrod agreed. "But we'll have the edge on him."

"How's that?" Pete asked.

"Tatum's thinking we'll rush the main gate. He'll have teams there to intercept. But they'll have to break their posts when Erin and I come in the back way. They won't be there to set off the IEDs."

"Unless they have trip wires," Pete offered.

Jerrod shook his head. "They won't. Remember, he's planning to get those hostages out tomorrow. He doesn't want to be wading through trip wires."

"True," Pete said. He hoped his buddy was right. Truth was, while he had been Jerrod's mentor at the FBI, their roles were now reversed. Jerrod knew far more about this kind of op than Pete did. But as the nightly news showed month after month, even experts could be surprised.

"You're not driving up until you see us at the front door with the hostages," Jerrod said.

"Right," Pete agreed.

"We'll have secured the compound by then. Don't worry, pal. I'm not going to get you blown up."

"You'd better not," Pete said. "I still want to finish that armoire I'm making in the basement."

"You'll get to," Jerrod said. "I promise."

Pete winced in the darkness. It was a fool's promise. Jerrod could no more guarantee Pete's survival than he could guarantee his own. That he felt a need to try said he'd read Pete's anxiety to a tee. Pete fought down his sense of shame.

To his surprise, Erin reached over and patted his mummy bag. "I feel the same way, Pete."

"We all do," Jerrod said. "Every damn time. You just have to go through it in your mind, planning out what you intend to do, what you think will happen. You block out the negative. Every time you see the op in your mind, you see a way out. You see yourself doing something that keeps you alive and makes the mission work. When you think about the other part, the part that makes your bowels go loose, you turn that into a chance to react and make things come out right. And you keep doing that until you convince yourself you're invincible."

"Even if you're not," Erin said.

"That's right," Jerrod said. "It's a lie, and at some level you know it's a lie. But it's a lie you have to make yourself believe. Every damn time."

That was fine, Pete thought, for Erin and Jerrod. They would be moving, active. He would be sitting and watching, waiting. Then he would drive up, knowing he might be passing over live explosives, with a live human being ready to trigger them. And if that happened, there wouldn't be a damn thing Pete could do about it.

He wouldn't know what hit him. That, at least, was some comfort. A very small, very cold comfort, but it was enough to help him sleep.

# 28

"Why are we here?" Erin asked, looking up from the tree line toward the plateau.

"Well," Jerrod said, "that depends on whether you believe in intelligent design or a randomly mutating and self-balancing universe."

He'd been doing this for the past hour. She knew he was trying to keep her loose and relaxed, but it wasn't working.

"No, I meant why are we *here?*" she asked again. "We were going to move up from those trees over there. This is at least a half mile longer in the open."

"Because there's nothing like a Mark One Eyeball," he said calmly.

"Translation?"

"On the map, the best dead ground would've been from those trees," Jerrod said. "But the map didn't include snow. And as I'm sure you've noticed, we have quite a bit of that snow stuff."

"Right."

"So," he continued, "places that I thought would be dead ground are level from snow accumulation, and places I thought would be open have dead ground behind snowdrifts. That's why they teach that there's nothing like a Mark One Eyeball on the actual ground. The map is not the terrain."

"Okay," she said as she watched him unsling his skis. She followed his lead, laying hers out and stepping into the binders. "The map is not the terrain. You could've said that way back there."

"And miss the opportunity for scintillating conversation?" he asked. "Perish the thought."

"I know you're doing this to keep me relaxed," Erin said. "But I'm not going to laugh my way up that hill."

"Ahh," he said, pausing to look into her eyes. "Well, that's where you're wrong. I'm not doing this to keep *you* relaxed. I'm doing it to keep me relaxed."

"Headline: Superman Senses Kryptonite, Tells Jokes To Relax," she said, winking.

He laughed. "Yeah, exactly. Well, we're out of phone booths, so let's get on with it. Stay in my tracks as best you can, just in case."

"In case what?"

"In case Tatum's put any surprises out this way. I'll be on the lookout for signs of digging, trip wires and the like. I doubt he'll have gone to the trouble of wiring this side of the compound, but he might have. You wouldn't know what to look for, so...just stay in my tracks and keep an eye up the hill."

Erin nodded. *This is it.* "Got it."

The first two hundred yards were fairly level, and she found the going easy enough. She'd skied before, on a trip with friends in college. Years and years ago. Yet her body fell into the rhythm almost as if it had been only yesterday. Press and push back with one ski, while lifting the other slightly and moving it forward, then repeat. She pushed some with her poles, but only enough to balance the movement of her legs.

All the while, she kept her mind off the shotgun slung over her shoulder, the end of the barrel covered with plastic wrap to keep out the snow. That was for later.

Jerrod had learned the newer style of cross-country skiing, turning one ski outward and digging in the inside edge as he pushed, looking more like a speed-skater. Erin had never liked that kind of skiing but was willing to concede that it was probably more efficient. If Olympic skiers used it, it was probably because it worked. But when she tried it, her inner thighs quickly told her to go back to what she knew. She chose to herringbone only when her skis couldn't find purchase. Not often, thank God.

All the while, her eyes kept sweeping the horizon

line of the plateau. They couldn't see the lodge from here, and that was good, because it meant no one in the lodge could see them, either. But if someone were out walking the perimeter of the plateau, well, they were like cockroaches crawling over a white tile floor.

She didn't see Jerrod stop so much as sense that he had, and she brought herself to a stop just before the tips of her skis reached the backs of his.

"What is it?" she asked.

"Something's been digging here," he said quietly, pointing his pole to a spot ten yards ahead. "It's way too far from the lodge to be part of his perimeter, but I'm going to check it out anyway. You stay here."

"Staying here, aye," she said.

Fact was, the last thing she wanted to do was stay where she was, exposed, helpless and useless. But she knew there was nothing she could do to help him, so she stayed and watched the skyline. Moments later she heard a muffled chuckle and glanced down in time to see a rabbit bound out of the hole and toward the trees.

"You disturbed his sleep," Erin said.

"Poor li'l guy," he agreed. "Water break."

She nodded and took her canteen from under her coat. By that time she needed no encouragement to take in water whenever she could. She took a sip and let it sit in her mouth, rewetting the tissue that had dried out from the high mountain air, then finally swallowed and took another small sip.

"Ready," she said, replacing the canteen next to her belly. "Find another rabbit, Superman."

He smiled. "Superman. Lifeguard. Let me know when you've accumulated enough metaphors."

"I'm a writer," she said. "It'd take me years to run out of metaphors."

"Okay, then," he replied. "Guess I'll need to start keeping a list."

That was as much as they could afford to say about what might happen after today, she realized. Her heart squeezed with the thought that they might not have a tomorrow. But if they did…

It wasn't a thought she could indulge in right now. From here on, the ground sloped up increasingly steeply, and the going would get harder.

Just focus on the skyline, she told herself as the sun began to pale. Focus on the skyline and let tomorrow take care of itself.

Dawn had thought about whether to fuss as they took her out. They often got angry when she did. But it might look suspicious if she didn't. So she twisted her weak limbs as best she could, knowing it was useless. Even so, she didn't feel helpless today.

"Still some fight in you," he said.

It was the boss. She'd learned his voice, though

she'd never spoken to him. Since Georgie had been brought here, the only words she'd spoken to her captors had been *food* and *water.* If they thought that she'd regressed, so much the better.

"Food?" she asked.

"Oh, yeah," he replied. "I'll feed you in a minute. Your favorite meal of all."

What he had in mind, she knew, was not her favorite meal. Her favorite meal was angel-hair pasta with Italian sausage pesto. Her mother made it often, using homemade basil and pine-nut pesto. When she got out of here, she would ask her mother to teach her how to cook. And if she didn't get out of here, well, she hoped her mother would remember her when she made angel-hair pasta with Italian sausage pesto. Maybe, Dawn thought, her soul would be in the food, and her Mom and Dad wouldn't miss her so much.

No, she wouldn't think that way, because she *was* going to get out of here.

She felt his hands lifting her onto the table. A part of her wondered what the table looked like. It was smooth on her back and bottom, like polished wood. She tried to imagine the grain of the wood, to distract herself, but she couldn't make the image come clear in her mind.

"Yes," he said, pulling her shoulders to the edge of the table. "Your favorite meal."

She heard the zipper. Part of her wanted to open her mouth, to be ready, but she'd never done that before. So she let his fingers dig into her cheeks, right in front of her ears, forcing herself to clench her jaw at first, so he had to work to pry her mouth open.

"Oh, yeah, he's going to like you," the man said. "Still a lot of spunk left. You'll be fun."

Her mouth finally opened.

She smelled it before she felt it. It didn't matter if the men had just showered that morning. It smelled different from their other odors. Pungent.

And then it was in her mouth.

*Not yet.* Something in her head told her this wasn't the right moment.

Instead, she let her mind go away to Georgie. Georgie hadn't made a sound last night, but Dawn had been able to hear her quiet breathing. Once Dawn had reached through the cage and touched Georgie's cheek, and Georgie's lips had closed softly around Dawn's fingertip. Her lips had been crusty with cuts starting to scab over.

They had hurt her Georgie.

Dawn let the anger build, a warmth spreading through her mind and body, invigorating her exhausted limbs and thoughts. Letting it build up in her until she could feel the muscles in her cheeks trembling with anticipation.

*Now.*
She bit down and began to thrash.

*"You fucking bitch!"*
Jerrod heard the scream just as they reached the top of the plateau. In an instant he'd kicked off his skis. He didn't even glance back at Erin. She would have heard it, too. "Go! Go! Go!"

Unlike downhill ski boots, cross-country boots had flexible soles. They weren't ideal for running, but there was no time to change. The extension at the end of the toes, where they attached to the skis, forced him into a longer, loping stride.

*"God-fucking-damn-you-eeeeiiiiiiiiiiiiii!"*
The curse rose into a scream of impossible agony as Jerrod reached the back wall of the lodge. Now he took a quick glance back over his left shoulder and found himself almost staring down the barrel of the Mossberg. He pushed it to the side.

"Careful with that."

"Fuck careful," Erin said, with fire in her eyes. "Let's get in there before he kills her."

Whatever reservations Jerrod had held vanished in that instant. This was not Erin McKenna, reporter, swept up into a maelstrom beyond her understanding or capacity. This woman was a soldier.

"Stay at my eight," he said, referring to the eight-o'clock position.

"Got it. Go!"

He didn't remember having drawn his pistol as he took a moment to flick off the safety. Then he moved quickly to the corner of the lodge, raising a fist by instinct, the standard military "Halt" signal.

There wasn't time to look back now, but he didn't need to. Erin's hand squeezed his shoulder to let him know she was in position, squatting behind him.

He took a quick peek around the corner.

They weren't going to get in unseen.

*Crocodile,* Dawn thought as she spun and thrashed, her fists punching out blindly, blocking some of his blows but not all of them. *Crocodile death roll.*

It might be her own death roll, but his inhuman squeals spurred her on. Finally her head ripped free, and she spat the flesh from her mouth.

"You fucker-fucker-fucker-fucker-*fucker!*" she yelled, her mind turning red like the taste in her mouth. "You fucker-fucker-fucker-fucker-*fucker!*"

The girl's voice was like a trigger in Erin's psyche. She didn't know if she began moving before Jerrod, and she didn't care. That girl needed her. *Now.*

She realized she was still at Jerrod's left shoulder as they rounded the corner. She was already raising the Mossberg, having flicked off the safety in the instant she heard the girl's voice.

Two targets. Fifty yards and closing.

The range was too great for accuracy, but she didn't need accuracy. She needed superior firepower. The flat *pop-pop-pop* of Jerrod's pistol vanished beneath the *boom-schlick-click-boom* as she fired and worked the pump in a smooth, steady rhythm.

The targets flopped to the ground, thrashing. Erin held her fire as Jerrod took aim and loosed two head shots. The targets were still. Good.

They ran together up to the front corner of the lodge, Jerrod sweeping their front with his pistol, Erin looking to their exposed flank over the iron sights.

*Stop.*

She'd already halted by the time she heard the little voice in her head. Glancing over, she realized they'd reached the front of the lodge and Jerrod had halted. A tiny part of her took pride that she was still exactly thirty-six inches from his left shoulder, at precisely an eight-o'clock orientation.

It was as if they shared a single mind.

*Go.*

The organism that was Jerrod-Erin moved around the corner, and its four eyes immediately spotted the man climbing out of the Hummer in the driveway. The organism fired. *Pop-boom-pop-pop-boom.* Another target down.

Four legs clomped across the redwood deck in front of the lodge, one set of eyes looking forward, the other to the side, ducking beneath the windows like an amoeba deforming and reforming around a grain of sand. A quick pause at the door, then one of the forelegs shot out to send it splintering open with a crash.

The girl's face was covered with blood. She was kicking and clawing at the man whose hand was clamped at his crotch, trying to stem the red spurting between his fingers, his face contorted and his eyes squeezed shut in pain and rage.

To the left, in Erin's field of fire, another man was pulling his pants up while reaching for a rifle. He never finished.

*Boom-schlick-click-boom.*

"Bill Tatum," Jerrod said.

The man clutching his crotch heard the words and opened one eye. His face froze.

*Pop-pop.*

His face exploded. Another target down.

"Back rooms," Jerrod said.

Erin already had the thought before the words reached her. They were one. A deadly human virus scrubbing this place clean.

They moved door by door, kick-lunge-sweep-withdraw, simultaneous shouts of "Clear!" the only communication needed, until they reached the fourth door.

*Kick-lunge-sweep-oh-my-fucking-God.*

Two dog cages. The smell of sweat and blood and fear and urine. One empty. In the other, a form that seemed not quite human. A woman. One eye swollen shut, one cheek swollen as if it held a baseball.

"Georgie!" Jerrod yelled, crossing the room in two loping, thudding strides. He wrenched the cage door open, not bothering with the lock, pulling until the wire hinges gave way and the door clattered free. "Georgie!"

The girl from the other room raced in, and Erin had gathered her against her side, ignoring the fight she put up, wanting to be sure she was out of the line of fire. She glanced over and saw that Georgie wasn't moving. Instead, Jerrod was hefting her battered form over one huge shoulder like a sack of grain.

"Time to go," he said. "You keep the girl. I've got Georgie."

"Got it," Erin said.

At the sound of Erin's voice, the girl's blindfolded face snapped up. "Mommy?"

"No, sweetie. But we're going to get you back to your mommy. Just stick close to me."

"My Georgie?"

"I've got her," Jerrod said soothingly.

"Is she…?"

"She's still breathing," Jerrod said. "Let's go, sweetie."

"Dawn," the girl said.

"Dawn," Erin repeated. "Let's go, Dawn."

"Kill the fuckers," Dawn said.

"I will," Erin said. "I will."


Pete had been watching the front of the lodge with binoculars since he'd seen them enter. Now he saw them emerge, Erin holding a naked girl to her side, Jerrod with a woman over his shoulder. The woman wasn't moving.

Pete's heart pounded and sank in the same instant as he pushed the dial button on his cell phone.

"FBI, Pueblo."

"This is retired Special Agent Pete Thomassen. Jerrod Westlake and I have located Special Agent Georgie Dickson." He gave and then repeated the GPS coordinates. "Bring EMT and CSI. I say again, bring EMT and CSI. Come fast."

He hung up without waiting for an answer and released the brake. His back wheels spun for only an instant before they found traction. The car fishtailed for a moment, but Pete steered into each skid with practiced ease and righted it. He lost sight of Jerrod and Erin as he dropped into the valley before climbing the plateau.

His heart climbed into his throat as he crested the summit. If there was an IED, it would be there.

*Just drive.*

The *whoomp* erupted a hundred yards ahead, the road disappearing, the shock wave bouncing the car for a moment, forcing him to fight to maintain control.

*Just drive.*

Every fiber in his being said to stop, not to drive into the blast zone. But his army training had come back and already taken over. Keep going. Don't stop in a prepared kill zone.

*Just drive.*

The rattle of automatic fire split the air, and he waited for the whine and thud of rounds hitting his car. As he entered the smoke column from the IED, he saw two gaping holes, each four feet deep and twice as wide. He zigzagged.

*Crack-tinkle.*

Passenger-side window. Pete turned his face to the left to avoid the flying splinters of glass and felt a hot sting behind his right ear. Not a bullet. If it had been a bullet, he would be dead. And he wouldn't be wondering.

*Boom-pop-pop-boom-pop-boom.*

He cleared the smoke and saw Erin and Jerrod laying a hail of fire to the sides of the road as they ran toward him. He now realized why only one round had hit his car. The men had turned to return fire.

And they had Jerrod and Erin outgunned.

Pete swerved off the road and aimed for two men who were standing in a shallow fighting hole. He rolled down his window and reached out with a pistol in his left hand, thinking in a passing instant that he was grateful the Bureau insisted every agent learn to fire with either hand.

He knew he was unlikely to hit anything as he bounced across the patchy ground. But he could distract them.

Even as that thought reached his awareness, he saw one of the men turn, leveling an automatic carbine. But a car moving at sixty miles per hour covered eighty-eight feet per second. The man simply didn't have time.

Pete's front bumper dipped as he reached the hole, catching the man squarely across the knees. Pete felt the teeth-jarring jolt as the four-wheel-drive Jeep bounced up the other side of the hole and lurched another ten yards before slowing.

He didn't need to look to know what he'd left in his wake. One of the men was scrambling on all fours, flailing for the rifle he'd thrown as he'd dived out of the way. The other man was reaching for his buddy, helplessly, his legs gone, his face already turning as white as the distant snow, until his arm dropped limp.

*Boom.*

The other man never reached the black carbine a

few feet away. His head erupted in pink mist. As Pete looked over, he saw Erin shoving more shells into the Mossberg, her cold eyes surveying the wreckage she'd left before turning to level the shotgun on the other two men.

Pete spun the car back across the road and saw both men dive out of their position as he approached, dropping to their knees, arms overhead. Pete brought the car to a stop and climbed out.

"You guys okay?" he called to Jerrod and Erin.

"Yeah," Erin said.

"Seven down plus these two," Jerrod said, nodding at the two men. "We're clear."

"Good," Pete said. Only then did he feel the rising, burning pain at the back of his neck, the wet flow down his shoulder blades. "Oh, Christ."

The snow-covered ground rose up to meet him, wet and cold, shocking his brain back into gear.

"Pete?" Erin asked, her voice closer than he remembered her having been just a moment before. "Pete? Are you okay?"

"I think I'm hit," Pete heard himself say. "But I'm not dead yet."

He laughed at his own pathetic joke. If he could laugh, he was still alive.

"I'm not dead yet."

# Epilogue

"Hey, gorgeous," Jerrod said.

Georgie Dickson lifted an eyelid. "Hey, yourself. Don't lie. I look awful."

"No, you don't," he said. "You're as beautiful as you ever were. Even more. You're a hero."

"I don't even remember getting out of there," Georgie mumbled. Her jaw still wasn't working well. "I didn't do anything."

"I have someone here who disagrees," Jerrod said.

Something in his voice. In his eyes. Georgie knew, even before the honey-blond head dipped out from behind him. "Dawn."

"My Georgie," Dawn said. She paused for only an instant before crawling up into the bed and gently tucking herself in beside Georgie. Her blue eyes looked up. "You woke up."

"I did," Georgie said.

Something about the girl curled in beside her felt

familiar. Almost by instinct, Georgie's hand drifted over the girl's hair and shoulder.

"Mmmhhh," Dawn said. "You did that in your sleep a lot. The doctors said you knew I was here, that me hugging you…something about stimulation keeping you fighting or something."

Georgie looked up at Jerrod. "Was I…?"

"Severe concussion," he said quietly. "Fractured jaw. It's good that you were out for a few days. They had to do some repair work."

"Oh."

"But you're awake now," Dawn said, nestling closer.

"Yes," Georgie said. "I am."

Three other people were waiting in the doorway. A man and two women. The younger woman entered first. The way she glanced at Jerrod, the way she smiled, was the only introduction Georgie needed. This had to be his reporter source. "You must be Erin McKenna."

"Guilty as charged," Erin said. "And you're Georgie. I've heard a ton about you."

"Most of it good, I hope," Georgie said.

"Oh, yeah. Almost made me jealous." Erin winked. She had a cute wink, Georgie thought. Yeah, Jerrod would like this girl. "Lucky Jerrod."

"I am that," Jerrod agreed. He turned to the door. "And these are the Jettises. Kathy and Ken."

The two seemed to hesitate, until Jerrod and Erin

stepped back to the foot of the bed. Then they approached, as if afraid.

"My mom and dad," Dawn said.

"Don't squeeze her too hard," Kathy said. "She's still hurting, I'm sure."

"Mommmmmm!" Dawn said. "I knowwwwww."

Georgie tried to laugh, but her jaw quickly turned it to a wince. "It's okay. I think."

"We haven't been able to keep her out of your room," Ken Jettis said. His face seemed to reflect a half-dozen conflicting thoughts at once. "She said she wanted to be here when you woke up. The doctors said the contact was good for you, while you were…"

"Out," Georgie said.

"Yeah," Ken said, nodding.

Kathy reached down and put a hand on Georgie's hand, careful not to touch the IV catheter, fingertips fitting between Georgie's to caress Dawn's hair. "Thank you. She says you…well…she has two moms now, I think."

Georgie searched the woman's face for any hint of distress. She wasn't sure what she saw. Or what she felt.

"Dawn kept me going as much as I did her."

"Maybe," Kathy said. She blinked back tears and tried to smile. "What matters is that you both made it out. You kept our girl alive. Thank you."

"Yes," Ken said, softly touching Georgie's hair. "Thank you. You gave us our daughter back."

"We should let you all talk," Jerrod said to Georgie. "I'll update you on the case later."

Georgie nodded and winced at the pain in her neck. She wasn't at all sure she could stay awake long enough to follow the details. And the details didn't matter. She'd made it out.

And so had Dawn.

"Okay," she said. "Thanks for coming to get me."

Jerrod stepped to the other side of the bed and leaned down to place a gentle kiss on her cheek. "Thank you for hanging in there for me. Now, get to know these good folks, before you fall asleep."

"'Kay."

Erin took Jerrod's hand as they stepped into the corridor. "She's going to be okay."

He nodded. The smile he'd worn in the room had faded. "Yeah. In time."

"She's strong, Jerrod."

"She is that," he agreed, biting his lip. "Damn. What they did to those two…"

Erin shook her head. She wasn't going to let him go there. He'd wrought all the vengeance he could, and so had she. Even now, a week later, she still jerked awake at night, feeling the kick of the Mossberg and seeing the men falling. She'd killed two, the coroner said. Another was still in intensive care and might not make it. The others she'd hit had been patched up and were in jail.

"They held it together," Erin said, squeezing his hand. "They got through it together."

He didn't answer for a moment. Then his eyes met hers. "Like us, I guess."

"Exactly," Erin said. "Like us."

"You okay?"

She smiled and shook her head. "As okay as I was fifteen minutes ago, before we went into Georgie's room? As okay as I was ten minutes before that? Or the last time you asked, ten minutes before that?"

He blushed. "Um, yeah."

She leaned up to kiss his cheek. "Yes, Jerrod Westlake. I'm okay. Not proud. Not great, but grateful. Grateful to be alive. Grateful you're alive. Grateful we got the two of them out. And I'll settle for not great but grateful. That's…okay."

"I guess so," he said.

"You're okay, too," Erin said.

"Am I?" he asked.

She took his face in her hands. "Go in there and ask Georgie and Dawn if they're glad you're on this planet. Ask Ken and Kathy Jettis if they're glad you exist. Yes, Jerrod. You're okay."

He smiled. It wasn't much of a smile, but it was

something. "If I haven't said so since this morning, let me say it again. I love you."

She kissed him gently and longingly. "I love you, too."

For long seconds they stood lost in a private world where nothing bad could happen and every rainbow seemed to shine just for them.

Reluctantly, at last, as a loudspeaker blared a doctor's name overhead, he stepped back. "Let's go."

"Yup," she said. "I've got your back."

"Not this time. Let's go in together."

"Aye, aye," she said.

They walked through the door two rooms down.

"Holy hell on toast," Pete said as they walked in. He held up a stack of newspapers. "I'm looking at the next Pulitzer Prize winner."

Erin blushed. "Oh, please."

"'Oh, please' nothing," Pete said. "It's not every day that a story like this splashes across the front page of every major newspaper in the country. And most of them are running it with your byline."

"It couldn't have happened without you two."

"Whatever," Pete said, waving a hand. His right eye closed for an instant, and his lips tightened. "Damn! I hate having to keep still."

"That's what happens when you get yourself shot up," Jerrod said, picking up one of the newspapers and sitting beside Pete's bed. "You get a medal, sure, but it's still gonna hurt."

"Thank you, Captain Obvious," Pete said, tossing another paper at Jerrod.

"Yet another metaphor," Erin said, laughing.

She sat in a chair beside Jerrod and glanced over her work in print. Alton Castle's testimony, coupled with the documents he'd received from Chuck Besom and the evidence from the lodge in the mountains, had made an airtight case. A horrified nation was demanding an accounting of its lost. Multiple charges of kidnapping and murder were piling up on Kendall Warrick.

The top Mercator executives were, of course, denying all knowledge of the sordid affair. And neither Erin, nor the FBI had found anything to prove the scheme had gone any higher than Warrick. Mercator would clean house, not that it would be difficult, with both Bill Tatum and Chuck Besom dead. The survivors from the lodge faced charges of rape and torture, and Warrick would be thrown under the bus as the Judas goat to keep the company alive.

And there it would end, Erin thought. Oh, there would be Congressional hearings and lots of public breast-beating and name-calling, but in the end, Mercator would survive.

And get more contracts.

"You can't look at it that way," Jerrod said, breaking her reverie.

"Huh?"

"Even I could see it on your face," Pete offered. "That look of sheer disgust that says 'They'll get away with it.' Jerrod's right. Don't think about that. You did good, Erin McKenna."

"Yeah," Jerrod said, taking her hand. "You did."

"Yeah," she agreed, squeezing his hand. "We did."

Pete laughed. "Oh, you two! Get a room."

"We have," Jerrod said. "Got a nice hotel room here in town, about four blocks away. Amazing view of the mountains. When we look out the window."

"Which we *do*," Erin said, blushing.

"Of course," Jerrod said. "Once in a while."

Erin smirked at him. "We look out the window a lot."

He just smiled. "Not all that much."

Pete shook his head and laughed. "Like an old married couple."

Erin leaned her head on Jerrod's shoulder.

"Yeah. We will be soon."

# *Afterword*

$W$hile *The Hunted* is a work of fiction, the white slave trade is not. Girls as young as five are bought and sold, and training is often brutal. Runaways haunting our streets and the streets of other countries are often beaten, tortured and turned into addicts to make money for someone else. Some of this is highly organized. Some is at a street-corner level. All of it is intolerable.

Likewise, the use of private military contractors—mercenaries—in what our government euphemistically terms "high-stress interrogations" has been well-documented. The link between that horror and the horror of white slavery is, so far as we are aware, purely fictitious.

This is a work of fiction. But it is not a myth.

*Rachel Lee, 2008*

# nocturne™

### *The Bloodrunners*
### trilogy continues with book #2.

The hunt meant more to Jeremy Burns than dominance—
it meant facing the woman he left behind. Once
Jillian Murphy had belonged to Jeremy, but now she was
the Spirit Walker to the Silvercrest wolves. It would take
more than the rights of nature for Jeremy to renew his
claim on her—and she would not go easily once he had.

# LAST WOLF
# HUNTING

## by RHYANNON BYRD

Available in April wherever books are sold.

Be sure to watch out for the last book,
*Last Wolf Watching*, available in May.

SN61785

# REQUEST YOUR FREE BOOKS!

## 2 FREE NOVELS FROM THE ROMANCE/SUSPENSE COLLECTION PLUS 2 FREE GIFTS!

# RACHEL LEE

---

32416 THE JERICHO PACT     \_\_\_ $6.99 U.S. \_\_\_ $8.50 CAN.
32271 THE CRIMSON CODE    \_\_\_ $6.99 U.S. \_\_\_ $8.50 CAN.
32129 WILDCARD               \_\_\_ $6.99 U.S. \_\_\_ $8.50 CAN.
*(limited quantities available)*

TOTAL AMOUNT                                      $ _____
POSTAGE & HANDLING                     $ _____
($1.00 FOR 1 BOOK, 50¢ for each additional)
APPLICABLE TAXES*                       $ _____
TOTAL PAYABLE                                 $ _____
*(check or money order—please do not send cash)*

---

To order, complete this form and send it, along with a check or money order for the total above, payable to MIRA Books, to: **In the U.S.:** 3010 Walden Avenue, P.O. Box 9077, Buffalo, NY 14269-9077; **In Canada:** P.O. Box 636, Fort Erie, Ontario, L2A 5X3.

Name: _____
Address: _____ City: _____
State/Prov.: _____ Zip/Postal Code: _____
Account Number (if applicable): _____

075 CSAS

\*New York residents remit applicable sales taxes.
\*Canadian residents remit applicable GST and provincial taxes.

**MIRA**®

**www.MIRABooks.com**             MRL0408BL